ECHOES

Of

THE GHETTOS

TIERRE FORD

1

Disclaimer

This is a work of fiction Name, characters, places and incidents either are the product of the author imagination or are used fictitiously. Any resemblance to actual persons, living, or dead, event or locales are entirely coincidental

DEDICATION

Rih Son Devonta Ford
4/21/92 6/25/11
YOU FOREVER IN MY HEART AND THOUGHTS WILD MONEY

My Other Three Boys
Tierre Gresham
Chancellor Ford
Jackson Ford
DADDY LOVE Y'ALL. KEEP PUSHING FOR GREATNESS

My Wife
Emmaundia J Ford "Duchess"

THANKS FOR ALWAYS SUPPORTING AND HAVING OUR BACK
AND FRONT

My Mother
Brenda Barthell

My RIH
Joseph "Slow Joe" Ford

ABOUT THE AUTHOR

At just 12 years old, I started selling drugs in the 6th grade—following the blueprint I saw in my own home. My father was both a dealer and a user, and by the 7th grade, I had bought my first car, was paying my mama rent, and buying my own school clothes.

That same year, the school system labeled me as "slow." They placed me in a remedial reading class—embarrassed me, honestly. I was ashamed. But I still kept my swag, my gold chains, my Starter jackets, and my game face. I was one of the most popular kids in school, but truth be told, I had stopped learning. I was only there to show off.

Then one day, my reading teacher—who I'll never forget—looked me in my eyes and said, "You don't belong in this class. You're smart. Don't let them label you." Her words stuck with me, even though my CRT test scores said otherwise.

At age 12 years old I became my neighborhood's youngest drug supplier. I started with 10 dollars, and I flipped that all the way to over $500,000. Me and my Dad link up dealing together supplying the market. I dropped out of high school in the 10th grade. I bought my mother a house with a pool in the backyard, purchased luxury cars, before I was locked up at 19.

At that point in my life, I had never read a full book. Not one. But my father always told me, **"The mind is the most powerful tool in the universe. Street sense and book sense together? That's unstoppable."**

So I gave books a chance.

It started with street fiction. Then history. Then business. Then biographies about powerful and wealthy people. I started seeing myself in those pages—not always in their polish, but in their ambition, their boldness. Then I read **Think and Grow Rich and As a Man Thinketh.** Those two books changed my entire mindset.

That's when I met my friend Cool Harris. I saw some of his writing on a notepad, and it rocked my world. I realized I had something to say, too. From that moment on, I picked up the pencil—and I've never looked back.

I earned my GED, took business and college courses, and started studying resilience. I discovered that, back in the day, Black people were once forbidden to read. There's even a saying: **"If you want to hide something from a Black person, put it in a book."** That became my fuel.

Now, I write both fiction and self-help books, covering everything from mindset and mental toughness to financial strategy and spiritual growth. I pour my soul into every page with one mission: to light a fire inside someone who's ready for change.

To everyone who's followed my journey—thank you. Let's set the world on fire with truth, with courage, with knowledge. Let's break every chain and every myth that says we don't read.

Peace—And Keep The Faith.

TIERRE FORD

<u>SYNOPSIS</u>

In the heart of Atlanta's unforgiving streets, *Echoes of the Ghettos* weaves together the lives of hustlers, mothers, sons, and survivors—each navigating a city gripped by money, loyalty, betrayal, and the haunting legacy of the past. At the center stands Brian, a man trying to rebuild his empire the right way after prison—opening a sports bar and guiding his sons away from the game. But the streets aren't so forgiving, and the shadows of his past circle tighter as the money, bodies, and secrets pile up.

Mike Mike's kidnapping sets off a chain reaction, forcing old players and new enemies to reveal themselves. From Lil B and Lil Eazy chasing flashy dreams and dangerous money, to Felicia and Ms. Vickie managing cartel-level operations and executing street justice, the tension reaches a boiling point as federal agents close in. The women hold as much power as the men—moving money, raising babies, or caught in the crossfire of choices they never meant to make.

Brian's ex-wife, **Precious**, and her current man, **Cory**, both now targets in a massive WIC fraud investigation. With food stamps flipped for cash, fake LLCs, and over half a million wired under the radar, their attempt at a low-risk hustle has become a high-profile liability.

As bank accounts are frozen and indictments loom, everyone—from local dealers and baby mamas to dirty cops, hungry FBI agents, and long-standing bosses—must ask the same question:

who can you trust when the game flips and your past screams louder than your future?

Told with gritty realism, cinematic pace, and layered emotion, *Echoes of the Ghettos* is a raw, powerful portrait of a generation shaped by survival, hustled by dreams, and haunted by choices. This is more than a street tale—it's a symphony of struggle and ambition, echoing through every alley, every trap, and every broken promise.

The streets are talking. The feds are listening. And the echoes? They don't lie.

Book One ends... but the game is just beginning. Part Two is coming.

CHAPTER 1

GIRLS' NIGHT

The restaurant buzzed with laughter and clinking glasses, but at one corner booth, the night air carried a heavier weight of tension, relief, and unresolved emotion.

Precious sat at the dinner table with Kai, Mahsi, and Roxy—her sisters in spirit, if not by blood. Her smile was genuine, but the exhaustion behind her eyes betrayed her.

"I can't lie," Precious said, brushing her curls back from her face. "I needed to get out—the four walls were closing in on me. I've booked a section at Atlanta Live—bottles, the works."

Roxy nodded with a smirk and a touch of relief.

"Girl, you know we got you. I needed some air myself."

Kai sipped her drink, her eyes scanning the dim-lit room as if already halfway to the club.

"This is a much-needed girls' night out. Hell, I might get me a room. Nate's been so damn busy taking over things from your man. Girl, you really applied pressure on him. From what Nate's telling me, he's really getting out this time!"

The words hit Precious in a soft spot. Her smile curved gently, memories flashing across her mind like a slow, haunting slideshow.

"I can't lie—I miss my king so much it's killing me," she admitted, her voice low, fragile. "The kids constantly ask when Daddy's coming home, and… my body's aching for him. I've picked up the phone so many times but found the strength not to call him for a booty call."

Mahsi let out a scoff, standing from her chair with the flair of a woman who didn't even try to hide her vices.

"Girl, you're a better woman than me. I would have broken down by now. I gotta use the restroom."

Roxy chuckled knowingly.

"There she goes—her favorite place when we go out."

Precious cracked a small laugh, while Kai shook her head.

"I believe when she goes to the bathroom, it's her coke break," Roxy continued under her breath, only half-joking. "Cause everyone I know who lives in the bathroom? Cokeheads."

The women laughed again, the kind of laugh that masked secrets too deep to name.

In the Restroom – Night

Mahsi wasn't in there for long before her phone was pressed tight against her ear. The stall gave her privacy, but not innocence.

"Park by my car," she whispered. Her eyes scanned beneath the crack of the stall door. "She's directly across from me in a black Range Rover. We should be leaving in thirty to forty-five minutes. You'll have a small window."

The voice on the other end was calm. Precise.

"Got it," Reid replied. "Get them to take two shots, get them a little tipsy and off balance, and we'll handle the rest."

The line went dead.

Mahsi tucked her phone away and exhaled. Her heartbeat was steady—not anxious. This wasn't her first betrayal. She stepped out of the stall, adjusting herself in the mirror just as the bathroom door opened.

Precious walked in, concern evident on her face.

"Girl, I had to come check on you."

Mahsi turned with a practiced smile.

"I'm good," she said. "Just took some water pills." Then, as if it were a spontaneous confession: "But let me tell you—I've really looked up to you since I first saw you in the gym. The way you move, handle business… It's inspiring. You've been nothing but motivation."

The warmth in her voice was convincing—almost too convincing. Precious, always the empath, opened her arms and they embraced.

"Girl," Precious sighed, "sometimes it gets heavy and lonely. But we have to push on for these kids."

Mahsi nodded, playing her part to perfection.

Back at the Table – Moments Later

"Let's have a shot before we leave!" Mahsi suggested with a mischievous glint in her eye.

The women lifted their glasses in a quick, celebratory toast. The liquor burned, but the mood was warm.

As they laughed and prepared to head out, Mahsi's fingers slipped with practiced ease into Precious's pocketbook. The car keys disappeared without a trace, like a magician's sleight of hand.

Outside – The Trap Is Set

The night had settled cool and dark. They stepped out into the parking lot, laughter fading as Precious suddenly patted herself down.

Her keys—gone.

Before she could fully register the loss, two men appeared from the shadows, guns drawn. There was no time to scream. A van screeched to a halt beside them, the door already sliding open.

Precious froze.

Hands grabbed her, dragging her into the van with cold efficiency. The door slammed shut behind her. Tires squealed as the vehicle vanished into the night, leaving only the stunned echoes of betrayal in its wake.

The Storm Breaks

The hotel room pulsed with soft, amber light—silent except for the rhythmic creak of the mattress and Rain's whispered moans. Brian lay on his back, sweat glistening on his skin as Rain straddled him. She wore nothing but a G-string, her breasts bare, her hips moving with hungry rhythm.

He looked up at her, lost in the moment.

"Damn, baby," he groaned. "I see why they call you Rain. It's so wet."

She met his eyes and smiled—a slow, sultry smirk—before grinding down harder, faster. She was fully in control, and he was more than content to let her lead.

Then the phone rang.

Once.

Twice.

The third time shattered the mood.

Brian sighed, annoyed, reaching over Rain's body to grab his phone off the nightstand. He glanced at the caller ID. His whole mood shifted.

"Hello?" he answered, breath still heavy.

Kia's voice came through, shaky and urgent.

"Precious has been kidnapped."

Brian bolted upright, Rain sliding off of him, startled.

"What?" His voice cracked, the color draining from his face. He was already halfway out of bed, grabbing his jeans off the floor.

"Where are you?" he demanded, dragging his shirt over his head.

"I'm almost home," Kia replied. "Nate's waiting for me there. I'll be there in twenty minutes."

Brian didn't say another word. The call ended, and with it, the calm of the night. He was out the door in under thirty seconds.

Nate's House – Later That Night

Tension clung to the air like smoke. Nate's house was dim, quiet except for the low hum of a television in another room.

Brian stood over Kia, pacing as she recounted everything.

"So y'all were leaving the restaurant," he said, trying to piece it together, "heading to the club, saw her truck, but couldn't find her?"

Kia nodded quickly. Her hands fidgeted in her lap.

"Yes. It happened so fast. We were walking out, heading to our cars. It's like we were being watched—or they had intel. It was too perfect."

Brian clenched his jaw.

"You didn't call the police?"

"No," Kia said without hesitation. "Because I know you and Nate don't like involving them."

He stared at her, searching her face for anything that felt off.

"Do you trust Roxy and Mahsi?"

Kia hesitated. Just for a second—but enough to notice.

"Roxy, yeah," she said slowly. "But Mahsi… I mean, she seems cool. We met her at the gym a few months ago."

Brian didn't say it, but his eyes said enough. His instincts were sharpening like a blade.

The night felt colder near the West End, the kind of chill that slipped under jackets and gripped the spine. The I-20 bridge loomed above like a concrete beast, its underbelly dimly lit by flickering streetlights and the occasional glow of passing headlights. This was no place for mercy. It was a place people were taken to be forgotten.

Inside the back of a white panel van, the air was thick—sweat, fear, metal, and silence. Precious sat bound, wrists tight behind her back, a gag pressed firm across her mouth. Her body trembled not from the cold, but from the unknown.

She had no idea how long they'd been driving. Time lost all meaning when you were kidnapped at gunpoint. Her heart pounded against her chest like it was trying to escape her body. All she could do was replay it over and over again—the parking lot, her missing keys, the masked men, the guns.

Now she is here.

In hell.

A heavy door creaked open. A man stepped into view—Reid. His face was rough, eyes colder than the metal glinting in his waistband.

"Are you comfortable?" he sneered, like it was a joke.

Precious didn't respond. Couldn't. She stared at him, burning holes into his face with her eyes.

He stepped closer, crouching.

"You're gonna sit tight. We make a few calls, your man pays, and you live. Make it difficult?" He smiled, dead in the eyes. "And shit gets messy."

He slammed the door.

CHAPTER 2

UNKNOWN HOUSE – ROBBER CREW HIDEOUT – NIGHT

The room was dark, lit only by the glow of a grimy overhead bulb. Reid leaned against a table with two other men, maps and burner phones scattered across the surface. The energy in the room was electric, dangerous.

"We're gonna ask for half a million," Reid said coldly. "All hundreds and fifties."

Josh's face lit up like a kid on Christmas.

"Hell yeah, that sounds real good."

Reid's burner phone buzzed. He answered, voice low.

"Yeah?"

Mahsi's voice came through, sharp and tense.

"Don't hurt her. Just get the money. That was the plan."

Reid's expression hardened, his voice laced with venom.

"Look, bitch, you don't run nothing. But don't worry—it's under control."
 He paused, tone mocking.

"When are you getting here?"

Mahsi's voice was cautious now.

"An hour. I had to shake Roxy, making sure she wasn't following me."

The line went dead.

Reid chuckled darkly, tossing the phone onto the table.

"I'm gonna kill her ass," he muttered, mostly to himself. "She just doesn't know it yet."

The other men laughed, all cruelty and no conscience.

Outside, the night stretched on, heavy with betrayal.

The wind picked up, carrying the smell of wet concrete and exhaust. The city was sleeping—or pretending to.

In the shadows, something dangerous was unfolding.

And Precious?

She was out there somewhere, alone in the dark, surrounded by wolves.

INT. NATE'S HOUSE – SAME NIGHT

Brian stood in the corner, fists clenched, trying to breathe through a fury he couldn't control. Nate poured himself a glass of whiskey, but even that didn't steady his nerves.

"We gotta find her," Brian muttered, more to himself than anyone else.

Kia paced near the kitchen island, wringing her hands.

"We need a plan—something smarter than just storming the streets. If they know y'all, they'll be expecting that."

Brian's voice cracked as he spoke.

"That's my wife, Kia. My kids are asking for her.

They're expecting her home. And she's out there—somewhere—scared, cold, probably thinking I failed her."

Kia's eyes welled up.

"We didn't see it coming. We didn't think—"

"No," Brian cut her off, jaw tight. "But someone did. Someone knew where we'd be. What car she drove. What time we were leaving."
 He paused.

"Someone close."

The room went still.

Nate raised an eyebrow.

"You thinking what I'm thinking?"

Brian nodded, grim.

"We need to talk to Mahsi. Alone. Somewhere she won't see us coming."

The cold metal of the van pressed against Precious's back as she sat frozen, her breath shallow, fear etched across her face. Reid stood over her like a shadow cast in vengeance—hard eyes, steady hand.

"Give me your phone—but first, call Brian."

Reid cut the zip ties. Her trembling fingers hit three buttons. She handed the phone to Reid like a loaded weapon.

"Baby, you alright?" Brian's voice came through the phone.

"Depends how deep your pockets run," Reid said, calm and ruthless.

"I'ma kill you," Brian growled, furious.

"Shut the fuck up. Look—half a mill. Under the I-20 West End bridge. Two hours."

Click.

The line went dead. Brian stared at the phone, then turned to Nate, jaw clenched.

"They want half a mil. Meetin' under the I-20 bridge in the West End."

"Nothing but bums in that area…" Nate muttered.

"Good," Brian nodded. "Call Cold Drink—tell him the play. Tell him to go blend in. I'm about to get the money together. Meet you back here in forty minutes."

"You still got that good fake money?" Nate asked.

Brian cracked a dark smile.

"Yep. Just for times like this. Give 'em 150K real on top… rest fake."

Without another word, Brian disappeared into the night, a man with vengeance and deception in his veins.

INT. ROBBER CREW HOUSE – LATER THAT NIGHT

The room had grown darker, more tense. Reid paced now, clearly agitated, staring at his phone like it owed him money.

Josh sat on the couch rolling a blunt, unfazed.

The third man—Tone—cleaned his pistol on the table, humming to himself.

Reid finally stopped pacing, muttering,

"She should've been here by now."

Josh chuckled.

"Maybe your girl got cold feet."

Reid's jaw twitched.

"She ain't my girl. She's a pawn. And after we get the money— she's a dead pawn."

Tone looked up, amused.

"You really gonna smoke her?"

Reid didn't even blink.

"Loose ends get people caught."

INT. MAHSI'S CAR – NIGHT

Mahsi sat behind the wheel, her hands tight around the steering wheel, parked three blocks away from the crew's hideout. Her breath fogged the glass, her face lit only by the dashboard lights.

Her phone buzzed. A message from Roxy:

Where are you at?

Mahsi stared at the screen but didn't reply.

She was in too deep now.

Too many lies.

Too much money.

And no way back.

She reached into her purse and pulled out a small vial. Snorted a line off the back of her hand. Her nerves calmed, but her soul didn't.

"I didn't sign up for this," she whispered to herself, a tear sliding down her cheek. "I just wanted a come up… not this."

But deep down she knew—she crossed the line the moment she made that call under the bathroom stall.

EXT. WEST END – DAWN APPROACHING

Under the West End bridge, only two things waited: a test of trust... and a trap made of paper.

In the echoes of the ghettos, every move costs blood or bread— and Brian was ready to pay in both.

The city was beginning to stir, but for some, the nightmare hadn't ended—it was just beginning.

Inside that cold, dark van, Precious sat slumped against the metal wall, praying silently. Not for revenge.

Just to make it home.

Just to see her babies again.

To see Brian again.

To feel something other than fear.

And outside… the clock was ticking

CHAPTER 3

BLOOD FOR BLOOD

The wind howled beneath the West End bridge, swirling around scattered trash and sleeping bodies. Homeless people lay stretched out on flattened cardboard, some huddled near the orange flicker of a makeshift bonfire. The world ignored them, as usual—but tonight, something deadly lurked in the shadows of their forgotten corner.

A black SUV idled nearby. Inside, Brian and Nate sat in silence, their faces grim, eyes scanning every movement, every shadow. Beside a stack of pallets, Cold Drink blended in flawlessly, dressed in torn rags, his face buried beneath a hood and beard. He played the role of a sleeping vagrant, but his fingers were tense, gripping the handle of his concealed weapon beneath the blanket.

On the far end of the lot, a dark sedan flashes its headlights—three quick bursts.

Brian opened the passenger door and stepped out into the night air, gripping a black duffel bag packed with money. He raised it high, letting them see it under the streetlight's flicker.

From the shadows, Josh's voice rang out.

"Set the money on the ground. Leave it unzipped and back away from the car."

Brian didn't move.

"I want to see my wife first."

Josh barked again, this time colder.

"Do as you're told if you want to see her alive. Now back the hell up."

Reluctantly, Brian lowered the bag and slowly stepped back with Nate. The tension in his chest grew tighter with every step, his heartbeat pounding in his ears louder than the wind.

From the sedan, Josh dragged out a woman with a bag over her head. One arm locked around her throat, the other held a gun pressed to her temple. He walked toward the money, cautious, cocky.

A gust of wind tore through the lot, catching the edge of the unzipped bag. Loose bills flew into the air—fifties, hundreds—fluttering like leaves. The nearby homeless stirred. Then chaos broke loose.

Several people rushed forward, grabbing at the airborne money, yelling, falling over each other. The scene erupted into mayhem.

Brian's instincts kicked in. He sprinted toward the woman, shoving a man out of the way. He yanked the bag off her head—

Not Precious.

Confusion stabbed him in the gut.

Then, from the car behind Josh, a figure in a ski mask burst out—hands tied, mouth gagged, stumbling forward, running full speed.

Brian barely had a second to register it. The mask, the erratic movement, the panic.

His gun was already up.

Two shots rang out.

The figure collapsed mid-run.

For a second, time stopped.

Cold Drink opened fire from his position, hitting one of the robbers, who screamed and hit the pavement.

Brian and Nate rushed forward. Blood soaked the asphalt beneath the collapsed figure. Brian dropped to his knees, yanking off the ski mask—

Precious.

"No!" Brian cried out, voice shattered. "No no no no… Breathe, baby. Stay calm. We're getting you help. I'm so sorry—I fucked up!!!"

Precious coughed, blood leaking from her mouth. Her body trembled beneath him, life slipping through her fingers.

Nate was already on the phone, barking into it. Then he hung up.

"Help's on the way," he said, his voice strained.

Brian looked down at her—his whole world fading in red.

"It's gonna take too long. We have to take her ourselves."

But then—sirens.

Growing louder. Closer.

Precious's fingers reached for him, weakly gripping his shirt.

"Please… don't leave me… Why did you shoot me? Why?"

Her eyes filled with pain, betrayal, and heartbreak.

"Don't leave me… I'm hurting…"

Brian sobbed, his lips against her forehead.

"Please, don't leave us. I'll quit, I promise. I swear I'll change. Please, baby—please don't leave us."

The blue and red lights painted the street.

Nate grabbed Brian by the arm.

"B, if we don't leave, we're going to jail for a long time. Now get in the car."

Brian shook his head, tears streaming down his face.

"I can't, Nate... I can't..."

Cold Drink's voice cut in, firm.

"Boss, let's roll. Help's here, and Nate's right—we don't need to be here."

Sirens wailed. Lights flooded the scene.

With one last kiss to her blood-soaked forehead, Brian stood—legs numb—and staggered toward the SUV.

They pulled away just as police and EMTs swarmed the area, the lights chasing them through the darkness.

INT. SUV – MOMENTS LATER

The silence in the vehicle was suffocating.

Brian sat in the front seat, staring ahead, face blank, jaw clenched. Precious's blood was still on his hands. His eyes were red, lips trembling.

He turned slowly to Mahsi, sitting in the back seat.

His voice was low, lethal.

"You better start talking. And I mean everything. Right now."

Mahsi flinched, swallowing hard. Her lip quivered.

"Reid made me do it," she whispered. "He told me to join the gym, befriend her... I'm so sorry. He threatened to hurt me—and my family."

Brian's stare could've cut stone.

"I know where they are," she added quickly, voice shaking. "I overheard them—they're going to Josh's sister's house."

Brian blinked. His breath hitched. A flashback flickered in his mind—him and Reid as kids, back when life was simple and clean. Before the streets claimed them both. Before betrayal was possible.

"What's the address?" Brian asked, his voice now eerily calm.

"I don't know exactly," Mahsi stammered, "but I can show you. It's off Hightower Road."

From the back, Nate growled, eyes burning with rage.

"You know this bitch has to die. She crossed lines. She's the one who told Reid about my party. Had me followed."

Brian didn't respond. His mind was somewhere else, drifting into another flashback—Precious in a sundress, spinning in the sunlight. Laughing. Kissing his forehead. Hugging their kids.

Now she lay somewhere, maybe dying, with two bullets he'd pulled the trigger on.

Blood on his hands.

And war on his mind.

EXT. WEST END – NEAR I-20 BRIDGE – PRE-DAWN

The bridge sat still again, silent but stained with blood and betrayal. The city would wake soon—but for Brian, nothing would ever be the same.

CHAPTER 4

BLOOD DON'T WASH OFF

INT. JOSH'S SISTER'S HOUSE – DAY

Stacks of cash were spread out like trophies across the living room table. The blinds were halfway drawn, sunlight slicing through the space in angry beams.

Josh sat at the edge of the couch, hands covered in sweat and excitement, holding fistfuls of hundred-dollar bills. He looked like a kid at Christmas.

"Man, look at all this money!" he shouted, eyes wide, grinning like he just hit the lottery.

Across from him, Meat Man squinted, thumbing through a thick stack of bills. Something didn't feel right. He held one of the notes up to the light, then another.

"Hold up," Meat Man muttered. "Some of this shit's fake."

Reid stopped pacing. His body stiffened. The color drained from his face before being replaced with boiling rage.

"Hell naw," Reid growled, grabbing a stack and flipping through it. "Brian tricked us. Over half of this shit fake."

He threw the bundle across the room, bills scattering like feathers.

His voice dropped to a murderous calm.

"We're gonna kill everyone he loves behind this. I swear to God."

Josh slammed his fist on the table.

"This nigga been one step ahead every move we make."

He stared down at the table, frustration bubbling.

"How much do you think we really got?" he asked.

Reid shook his head.

"Hard to tell. We're gonna have to sort through it. Count every damn dollar."

But time wasn't on their side.

EXT. OUTSIDE JOSH'S SISTER'S HOUSE – DAY

The black SUV rolled to a stop two houses down from the target. Brian, Cold Drink, Nate, and Mahsi sat inside, the windows rolled down just enough to feel the air—tense and dry, like something about to crack.

They had eyes on the house.

Brian sat up front, phone still in his hand, his voice low and heavy. "Just got off the phone with Roxy. Precious lost a lot of blood. Police all over the hospital floor asking questions."

He didn't show it on his face, but his soul was fractured. Every breath hurts.

Nate leaned forward, eyes locked on the small single-story house with a blue door and peeling white siding.

"How do you think we need to do this?"

Brian didn't answer right away. His eyes were glass, thoughts dark. Vengeance had already taken root.

Before anyone could say more, a beat-up sedan pulled into the driveway of the house.

A woman stepped out—mid-30s, plain clothes, hair tied up, keys jangling in her hand.

Nate pointed.

"Is that Josh's sister?"

Mahsi nodded quickly.

"Yes. That's her."

Nate smirked, eyes narrowing.

"That's our way in—"

But Cold Drink was already gone.

Before Nate even finished his sentence, Cold Drink had cracked the car door and was halfway across the street. Smooth. Silent.

By the time the woman turned around, a pistol was in her face.

She froze, lips parting in a silent gasp. Cold Drink didn't say a word—just motioned with the gun. She nodded, terrified, and led him toward the house.

INT. JOSH'S SISTER'S HOUSE – MOMENTS LATER

Inside, the crew was still sorting money, tension rising by the second. Reid, Josh, and Meat Man were too focused on the fake bills to notice anything else.

Then—the door creaked.

Josh looked up, confused.

"Yo, you hear that?"

Too late.

Boom. Boom. Boom. Boom.

Four shots tore through the house like thunder.

Blood hit the walls. Bodies dropped before they even turned their heads.

Josh's sister screamed—but only for a second.

A fifth shot silenced her.

The house went still.

Only the sound of blood dripping onto hardwood remained.

The war had officially ended.

CHAPTER 5

FRAGILE LINES

The machines beeped steadily, a cold rhythm in a room filled with tension and quiet prayers.

Precious lay still, her body a battlefield. An IV snaked from her arm, tubes fed oxygen into her lungs, and bruises painted her skin like shadows of war. She was alive—but just barely.

Standing over her were the women who carried her name in their hearts. Her mother's eyes were swollen from crying. Kia stood silent, arms crossed, fighting guilt with stoicism. Roxy, red-eyed but strong, refused to cry anymore. And Jack's wife, stone-faced, watched over the scene like a quiet sentry.

The room smelled like bleach and despair.

Not a word was spoken. But every breath in that room begged God for the same thing:

Don't take her.

Across the hall, the waiting room felt like purgatory. Sterile, white walls. Plastic chairs. Vending machines humming like they knew secrets.

Jack sat with Cowboy, and the two little pieces of Brian's soul— Lil Brian and Milan.

Milan's feet swung just above the floor, her big eyes looking up with worry no child should have to carry.

"Why isn't Daddy here?" she asked softly. "Does he still love Mommy?"

Lil Brian didn't look at her right away. He stared at the tile floor, then slowly turned to his little sister.

"Yes," he said, voice firm—not for her, but for himself. "He's on the way. Uncle Jack talked to him."

Milan sniffled, curling into the crook of Jack's arm.

"When are we going to see her?"

Jack rubbed her back, his voice low, gentle.

"Soon. Real soon."

But no one in that room really knew what *soon* meant anymore.

Demo sat on the edge of his couch, palms sweaty, nerves shot to hell. His phone rang. He picked it up and hit redial.

It rang once before Nate answered.

"Hello?"

"Man," Demo said, trying to keep his voice steady, "I've been calling Brian, but no answer. My folks are in town—they want twenty."

Nate's tone was dry. "You've been MIA. What's up with you?"

Demo exhaled hard, shoulders sinking.

"Been going through it. Problems with the wife. Counseling… and my seventeen-year-old's pregnant."

The silence after that was heavy.

"I need this deal bad."

Nate softened a bit. "Truth is… we all have been going through it. Where are you at?"

"They're at the Holiday Inn, off exit 9."

"Cool," Nate said. "I'll be there in thirty. What's the room number?"

"319."

They hung up.

But Demo didn't relax.

He wiped his face, trembling. Across from him, a DEA agent leaned against the wall, arms crossed.

"You did real good," the agent said with a dry smirk. "Everything's going to be fine. Look at it like this—better them than you."

Demo didn't respond. Didn't have to.

His silence said everything: regret, guilt, and the weight of betrayal.

Steam drifted off Brian's shoulders as he stepped out of the shower. The mirror was fogged, but his reflection still stared back at him—haunted, broken, and colder than before.

His phone lit up.

Three missed calls: Jack. Roxy. Demo.

He hit Jack's number.

Jack picked up quickly. "Hello?"

Brian leaned on the sink with one hand, towel around his waist, voice heavy.

"How are things?"

Jack's tone was measured but real.

"She's stable… but she needs blood. They're looking for a match."

Brian shut his eyes.

Jack continued. "Your kids are asking for you. And her mom? She's not pleased that you're not here."

"I know," Brian said, almost whispering. "I had to shower… get my head right."

"You clean now?" Jack asked—not mocking, just checking.

Brian nodded to himself. "Yeah."

Jack sighed. "Police are still here. Place is crawling with 'em. Come on your A-game. I'll keep you updated. Everything's gonna work out."

Brian didn't answer.

He hung up slowly, heart still pounding.

He had washed the blood off his skin.

But not off his hands.

CHAPTER 6

THE COST OF LOYALTY

The motel room was dim and stale, its air heavy with the scent of old carpet and desperation.

Nate stepped into Room 319 at the Holiday Inn with that seasoned calm. A black duffel bag of drugs in one hand, a stack of fresh bills in the other. His shoulders finally started to drop—maybe for the first time in weeks.

Click.

BOOM.

The door exploded open behind him—DEA agents swarming in full tactical gear, guns drawn, voices loud and overlapping.

"Get on the ground!"

"Hands behind your back!"

The drugs hit the floor with a dull thud. Nate didn't even have time to flinch before he was tackled to the ground, a knee in his back, cuffs tightening around his wrists.

"You have the right to remain silent..."

He wasn't even listening. His ears rang with betrayal. His own.

Steam still lingered in the bathroom as Brian stood shirtless by the sink, his phone pressed to his ear, pacing slowly. His hair dripped. His eyes were sharp.

"So you meet me at the hospital, just in case them folks on some BS," Brian said.

"Yes, I'll meet you there," his lawyer replied over the phone. "I checked—nothing shows you as a suspect of anything. Plus, I need to show my respect. I'll be there in two hours."

Brian hung up, jaw tight. Something in his spirit wasn't sitting right.

Montage:

— Nate being dragged into a sterile interrogation room.

— Brian's kids sitting quietly at the hospital, waiting.

— DEA agents swarming through computer files, surveillance photos of Brian, Nate, Demo, Lou, Tig.

— Brian kissing a photo of Precious on his dresser.

— Jack and Cowboy holding Brian's kids as they doze off on their laps.

Nate sat across from Spencer, Hood, and Green in a small, white-walled room. A pitcher of water sat untouched in the middle of the table.

Spencer leaned in. "You help us, we help you. We know you've always been in Brian's shadow. And this—this is his drugs."

Nate's eyes were cold. Calculating. "What's in it for me?"

"Drugs and a gun charge—and you're a convicted felon," Spencer replied. "You're staring at twenty-plus years. And this is feds, baby. That's 85 percent, no parole."

"But…" Hood jumped in. "We can get it down to ten. Maybe seven. You give us something real."

Nate leaned back and let the silence breathe.

"What if I hand y'all the Caviar?" he asked, eyes locked. "The shot-callers of Atlanta."

That got their attention.

"Well, let's start with Brian," Hood said. "We hear he's out of the game. So how do we get him?"

Nate didn't even blink. "That's easy. I told him to come pick up his money—what Demo owed him. I'll give you Lou and Tig too. They were in that wreck a while back… with the drugs."

Smiles crept across their faces like wolves licking blood from their teeth.

"First," Nate added, "I need to call my wife. Second, I need out of here ASAP if y'all want this to happen. I'll have to make a call to Brian today."

Phone Call with Kia – Day

Nate's voice was calm, almost tender.

"Baby, listen. Do exactly what I say. Leave the hospital now. Don't say anything to anybody. Go to your mom's house and wait for me there."

Kia sounded confused. "Nate, why? What's going on? Precious had to fight for her life!"

"I messed up. Now I gotta save myself so I can still be there for y'all. Things are about to get real ugly. But we'll be alright. Just leave now."

"Okay, baby… you do what you have to do. I'm leaving. I'll call you when I get there."

Brian stepped inside Nate's house, tension walking in with him. He and Nate greeted each other like brothers—one last time.

Nate handed him a black bag.

"Man… this has been a journey," Brian said. "We've been through hell and high waters."

"Yeah, we have," Nate nodded. "That's what Demo owed. I bumped into him—200K. Clean my face up, bro. And thanks for everything. Some things… we takin' to the grave."

Nate didn't meet Brian's eyes.

"Yeah… let me get outta here," Brian said, his tone quiet. "'Bout to go see my Queen. She's a real fighter. Love you, bro."

They dapped up. One final time.

Brian stepped out of his car and bumped into Kia near the hospital exit.

"Are you leaving?" he asked.

Kia nodded. "Yeah, I need to help my mom with something. Precious is doing a lot better."

"Look, thank you for everything. Precious couldn't ask for a better best friend. You're the sister she never had. You and Nate—y'all family. Anything I can ever do, remember… I'm one call away."

Kia didn't say anything—eyes glossy. She turned, walking away fast, trying to hold in the tears.

Brian walked inside.

The waiting room lit up—his kids ran to him, wrapping their little arms around his waist, crying and smiling at the same time.

Jack was there. The lawyer too. So were the rest of his people.

He walked down the hall toward Precious's room.

But halfway there, he spotted something off.

Spencer.

Three men and a lady in suits stood beside his lawyer.

Brian's pace slowed.

He looked at Precious's room. She was asleep. His kids were by her side. His sisters too.

He looked back—Spencer was now walking toward him.

His lawyer opened the door.

"Brian, I need you to step out here for a moment."

Brian knew.

He *knew.*

And when the cuffs clicked behind his back, his kids screamed. The girls cried. The hallway filled with echoes of betrayal, broken trust, and sirens only he could hear in his head.

As they walked him outside, Brian caught a glimpse of the SUV.

His trunk was open.

The black bag—the one Nate gave him—sat on the hood.

All Brian could do was shake his head.

CHAPTER 7

THE WEIGHT OF DECISIONS

INT. COURTHOUSE CELL – DAY – MONTHS LATER

The cold walls pressed in. No windows. No clocks. Just time measured by thoughts and regrets.

Brian sat on a bench, hands cuffed in front of him, wearing a beige jumpsuit. His lawyer stood across from him, tie loose, voice low.

"There's an offer on the table," the lawyer said, glancing at the folder in his hand. "The DA said if you give up the properties… hand over the money in the business accounts… they won't supersede and bring charges against Precious and her mother."

Brian looked up slowly, eyes locked on the man's.

"You'll need to plead guilty," the lawyer added.

Brian nodded once, steady. "Alright. I'll hand over everything they're asking for and plead guilty. Plus… I don't want to risk taking it to trial and more people getting involved. What am I looking at?"

The lawyer exhaled, lowering his voice. "Good thing this is your first time. I'll make sure the offer stands at ten years. And they won't enhance the sentence."

Brian raised an eyebrow. "Enhancement?"

"That's when they stack points," the lawyer explained. "Four points for being a leader, two for laundering money, two more for stash houses. They'll keep building the mountain if we don't take the deal. Let me confirm everything with the DA—we'll push for a speedy trial."

ONE YEAR LATER

Sentencing Day.

120 months.

$2.3 million forfeited.

15 properties seized.

Businesses dissolved.

The judge read the sentence like it was math. Brian didn't flinch. Didn't speak. He accepted it with the stoicism of a man who'd already done his grieving.

Precious, now walking, healed but scarred, stood outside the courtroom holding their kids. She watched him nod to her—just once—as they led him away in chains.

INT. PRISON YARD – DAY

The yard buzzed like a small city—its own rhythm of survival. Men walked in circles, lifted weights, smoked rolled-up weed, and drank mystery liquid from water bottles. Dice clacked. Cards slapped on scratched tables.

Brian walked the yard with OG Smitty, a legend with salt-and-pepper dreads and wisdom in his eyes.

"You know," Smitty said, watching the chaos unfold around them, "this is all part of the plan. Take us away, leave our families to fend for themselves. We gotta start getting our priorities together."

Brian nodded. "Truth is… the first time I got real peaceful rest was when I got locked up. Felt like the world lifted off my shoulders."

He paused, voice thick. "Crazy part? The more I tried to get out… the more it pulled me back in. I went years with no fumbles. But soon as I tried to leave the game? All the bullshit started."

OG Smitty gave him a long look. "So… what's the move now?"

Brian cracked a faint smile. "Get my GED. And believe it or not, I've been reading. *As a Man Thinketh, Think and Grow Rich*—some of the realest shit I've ever come across."

He shrugged. "I lived on the streets at a high level. Now I'm focusing on getting my mind right."

OG Smitty grinned. "That's the key, youngblood. It ain't about just doing the time—it's about what you do with your time. And when you get out? Trust yourself. Be patient. Let it come together. You had a good run. Not many can say that."

EXT. PARK – DAY

Kids laughed in the distance. The sun hit just right on the metal of the swing set. But on the park bench, Nate sat stone-faced beside Spencer.

Spencer kept it straight. "Nate, best I could get the DA to agree on is you doing 90 months."

Nate looked away, jaw tight. Shame written all over him.

"All the people I helped y'all lock up… and now my name's trash in the streets," he muttered. "I crossed my best friend. And I still gotta do 90 months?"

Spencer watched a boy kick a soccer ball across the grass. "Nate… you were facing twenty. Easy. Trust me, I had to twist some wrists to get that deal."

Nate stood, tension stretching across his frame. "Okay. But can you hold it off another year? Kia's pregnant. I need to get her settled."

Spencer paused. "I'll do my best."

They walked off slowly, two men who had seen too much.

INT. NATE'S CAR – DAY

The silence between Nate and Kia was loud.

She stared at him, waiting for the truth.

"What'd she say?" she asked.

Nate dropped his head and couldn't hold her gaze.

"I gotta do 90 months."

Kia's eyes welled. "Ninety months?" She shook her head, voice trembling. "You should've never gotten in bed with those folks. They can't be trusted. I lost my best friend. And you're still going to jail?"

Nate didn't answer. He reached under the seat, pulled out a small sack of dust. He snorted hard, wiped his nose, and handed it to her.

Kia stared at it.

The silence said more than words ever could.

INT. PRECIOUS'S KITCHEN – DAY

Precious sat at her kitchen table, the soft daylight filtering in through gauzy curtains. The wine in her glass caught the light as she swirled it gently, her eyes focused on Roxy, who sat across from her.

"Girl," Precious said, her voice low but resolute, "I have a long road ahead of me. But I must say, Brian didn't leave us broke. The feds took a lot, but he still managed, as he says, to stay three steps ahead."

Roxy raised her glass with a nod of respect. "Toast to that," she said, her voice bright with admiration. "So, are you still thinking about getting a divorce?"

Precious exhaled, not in sadness, but in something closer to clarity. "Brian and I talked about it. We think it's best. I'm going to see him, see how he wants me to handle things. I'm always gonna have his back, but too much has happened. Divorce the thing."

INT. ASHLEY'S CONDO – NIGHT

The mood was different—quiet, intimate. Ashley bounced a baby on her hip while her friend Mona sat nearby, concern etched across her face.

Mona watched her for a moment before speaking. "Girl, you're not going to let Brian know about his baby?"

Ashley shook her head. "No. He has enough going on. Plus, he left me straight. I don't want to mess up his marriage. I know she's in control of everything. Don't want him to lose it. I'll let him know in time."

Mona frowned, her voice uncertain. "I don't know about that. I'm sure he'd want to know."

"He will," Ashley replied softly. "In due time."

CHAPTER 8

FRAGILE LINES & RECKONINGS

INT. PRISON TV ROOM – DAY Brian sat in the prison's TV room, taking it all in. The space buzzed with tension and noise—men played poker, some shouted over football bets, others just watched the television. The room was sharply divided: white inmates in one section, Black inmates in another, and Spanish-speaking inmates occupying the third.

His inner voice cut through the chaos, thoughtful and matter-of-fact.

The feds run off codes. The shot caller plays the most important role. Each state has a shot caller who represents the whole state. If he's a fool or careless, their car will stay crashing out.

If someone, like from Georgia, owes a Spanish dude or someone from Tennessee, they go to the shot caller of their car to get paid. Two things happen: either they pay it up for him, or they tell them to take it to the bathroom—fight one-on-one. But what won't happen, or it'll be a big brawl—Cars against Cars, meaning state against state—is putting hands on someone without permission from the shot caller.

You have to sit and eat with your cars. You also got Bloods, Crips, GD, South, Midwest, North DMV, and West Coast cars.

The tension snapped a few minutes later at the poker table.

Run stood abruptly, his eyes locked on Boo. His voice cut through the room like a blade.

"Not today. I've let it slide too many times. You're cheating. I'm not paying."

Boo leaned back, arms crossed. "Man, you trippin'. You just trying not to pay!"

The energy in the room shifted fast. Members of the Florida car and DMV car started to close in, sensing the storm.

Run turned, fire in his voice. "Y'all DC niggas really think y'all run something?"

Boo squared up. "So you're not paying me?"

"Hell naw!"

Chaos exploded in an instant. Three guys lunged at Run, fists flying and makeshift blades flashing. Blood sprayed, screams rose, and the Florida crew jumped into the fray.

By the time the guards stormed in, the room was a wreck. Bodies sprawled. Blood everywhere. And just like that, the brawl was over. Everyone was ordered back to their cells.

Brian sat on his bunk, staring at the wall. His cellmate, JB, leaned back with a weary look in his eyes.

Brian broke the silence. "How do you think this is gonna end?"

Big Wax chuckled grimly. "Not good. Them DC and Baltimore homies are crazy as hell. They live for this. The S.I.S is gonna have to call out the shot callers to work this out."

"Does it get that deep?" Brian asked, still trying to piece it all together.

"Man, you can get stabbed over $2 in here," Big Wax said. "The mindset's low around here. Guys mad at the world with all this time."

The next day, in the echoing prison hallway, the LT stood face-to-face with the shot callers from Florida and the DMV. His tone was sharp and no-nonsense.

"Can y'all work this out, or we'll be on lockdown for 90 days—no store, no phones, no visits?"

The two shot callers exchanged a look. It wasn't friendly, but it was necessary. Slowly, they extended their hands and gave each other a firm shake.

EXT. CLUBHOUSE – DAY Back on the outside, life went on.

At a clubhouse, music pulsed from the speakers as kids danced in circles and parents chatted over plates of food. A birthday party was in full swing.

Paris, a young girl with a birthday crown on her head and dollar bills pinned to her shirt, grinned as she moved through the crowd. It was her 10th birthday.

LIL B leaned toward LIL EAZY as they stood near the drinks table, watching the celebration unfold.

"I talked to KC," he said. "He said he'd charge us $3,500 for half a bag of purp."

"I got my half," LIL EAZY replied without hesitation. "When can we get it?"

"After the party. I'll set it up."

The DJ's voice suddenly boomed through the speakers. "Time for the dance-off! Girls against the boys!"

A crowd gathered. Kids whooped and hollered as two at a time stepped into the circle and danced with all their might. Parents clapped and laughed, pointing proudly.

As the party wound down, the family gathered to sing "Happy Birthday" to Paris. The candles on the cake flickered as she made her wish and blew them out.

Later, Paris tugged on her mother's arm. Precious looked down with a smile.

"I wish Daddy was here, Mommy," Paris whispered. "That's what I wished for when I blew out the candles. I miss him."

Precious knelt and pulled her daughter into a warm hug. "We all do, baby," she said softly. "We're going to see him next week."

INT. CITY STREET – NIGHT The night had settled heavy over the city, casting everything in a cool, metallic glow. Inside a parked car, Nate sat alone, his focus buried in a phone call. The soft glow from the screen lit up his face, oblivious to the danger creeping into his periphery. He didn't notice the figure approaching from the shadows.

A flash. A shot. And just like that, silence.

Nate's lifeless body slumped over the steering wheel as the unknown assailant disappeared into the night.

Soon after, flashing lights washed the street in blue and red. A crowd formed around the taped-off crime scene. Police officers moved methodically while a local news crew broadcasted live. Within the chaos stood three men in quiet conversation—SPENCER, GREEN, and HOOD—each looking more burdened than the last.

GREEN shook his head, his voice laced with regret. "Damn, we should've put him in protective custody. We might be in some serious trouble now."

"I tried," HOOD said. "He refused. Over and over."

SPENCER rubbed his temples. "How does this affect the few cases we still have open? There are people we haven't picked up yet."

GREEN exhaled. "We'll need to investigate. Maybe we can tie this to someone. Anyone."

HOOD hesitated before admitting the hard truth. "Can't lie, Boss. This could've come from anywhere. He set a lot of people up… and he was still in the streets."

GREEN's eyes narrowed. "Did y'all know?"

"Somewhat, Boss," HOOD answered.

GREEN scoffed and looked away, frustrated. "Just give him a free pass as long as he keeps turning people in… smh."

INT. PRISON TV ROOM – NIGHT In the prison's recreation room, BRIAN sat at a table, deeply focused on a game of chess. The board reflected his mindset—strategic, patient, always planning. OG SMITTY strolled up beside him with the calm swagger of someone who'd seen too much.

BRIAN didn't look up. "How much for a cell phone with a charger?"

"The Mexican is charging 10 stacks," OG said with a shrug. "Might get him down to 8500."

"Doesn't matter," Brian replied. "I need one. Put it together. What's the monthly charge for keeping it stashed till after four?"

"Two-fifty a month."

Brian nodded, eyes still locked on the board. "Cool. Let me know how they want their money."

SLIM approached, his tone low and deliberate. "Your once-best friend is no longer with us. His bad deeds finally caught up with him."

Brian finally looked up, meeting Slim's eyes.

"Nate got gunned down sitting in his car."

Brian didn't flinch. Not a twitch.

"Well," he said flatly, "I heard he was setting a lot of people up. Bound to catch up with him."

INT. PRECIOUS'S HOUSE – LIVING ROOM – DAY The TV played in the background as PRECIOUS and ROXY sat on the couch, sipping wine. The news covered Nate's murder, featuring footage of a distraught KIA crying on camera, blaming the Feds for forcing Nate to cooperate—claiming it led to his death.

ROXY shook her head. "Girl, she looks bad."

PRECIOUS nodded, somber. "Yeah. She reached out to me twice. I just couldn't talk to her. She left voicemails, messages… begging. But I had to cut ties."

"She hit me up too," ROXY said. "But I'm your friend first."

They both sipped again, the weight of shared loyalty and old scars between them.

CHAPTER 9

Visitor's Room – Day The energy shifted as PRECIOUS entered the visitor's room, flanked by the kids—PARIS, MILAN, and LIL B. They sat, waiting anxiously. When BRIAN finally walked in, accompanied by a couple of inmates, everything else faded.

The girls jumped up and ran to him, burying themselves in his embrace. LIL B stood and gave his father a dap, which turned into a tight hug.

Brian smiled, warmth radiating from him. "So glad to see y'all."

MILAN beamed. "Daddy, I made all A's."

Brian's face lit up. "You always do. How about you, Paris?"

PARIS, proud but a little shy, said, "Made 2 B's, the rest A's."

LIL B shifted awkwardly, looking away.

"Don't ask me, Dad. I'll get it together."

Brian placed a firm but loving hand on his shoulder. "I won't judge. But Lil B… you've always gotta put your best effort into everything you do. Don't settle for less."

"You're right."

Brian looked over the three of them, soaking in the moment. "So, how was your birthday party? Did you get everything you wanted?"

PARIS smiled, then hesitated. "Yes, Daddy. Thanks for my gifts. But… the only thing I didn't get was you coming home."

Brian's smile faded to something softer, deeper. "I know, honey. But soon… I'll be there."

The kids wandered over to the vending machine, leaving PRECIOUS and BRIAN alone.

"Brian," she said gently, "now that our divorce is settled, how would you like me to handle your money?"

Brian didn't hesitate. "Just give Tasha 150K. You can keep the rest. I know you'll flip it. You're a hustler—just not in the streets."

"And Tara?"

"She's good. I've had her set up for a while." He paused, voice thick with emotion. "I really hate it had to end the way it did, Precious. I'm forever sorry—and grateful—for you."

She placed her hand over his. "You're a good man, Brian. Just dealt some bad cards. But one thing I know about you—you never give up. You always find a way… and come back ten times better."

Brian nodded as the kids returned with snacks in their hands, laughter echoing softly in the room. For a moment, everything felt almost… normal.

But only for a moment.

Bloodlines and Blueprints

EXT. CITY. STREETS – DAY

Two years had passed. The streets hadn't changed much—same corners, same grind, same scent of hustle in the air. But the players had.

In a cramped apartment near the heart of the block, Lil B, Lil Eazy, and Mike Mike moved like veterans. Stacks of weed and dust lay divided on the counter, baggies disappearing into the hands of street runners every few minutes.

Outside, the neighborhood buzzed with life. Music blared from portable speakers. Smoke from joints and barbecue grills mingled midair. Kids darted between parked cars. Two candy-painted whips—belonging to Lil B and Lil Eazy—were being washed out front, their rims gleaming like polished trophies.

Men slid up to car windows, exchanged products for folded bills, and walked away counting stacks before handing them off to Lil B and Lil Eazy without saying a word. It was all clockwork now.

"I bet two hundred JD's faster than Charles," Lil B said, a smirk tugging at his lips as he flashed some cash.

"I take that bet," said Fat Gee, slapping $200 down on the concrete like it was war.

A small crowd gathered, buzzing in anticipation as JD and Charles lined up for a street race. Engines revved. Hearts beat.

Then—

A van rolled in slow, too slow.

Eyes darted. Feet scrambled. Within seconds, the scene scattered. Weed forgotten, money dropped, the crowd dissolved into alleys and doorways.

INT. HAIR SALON – DAY Across town, the world spun at a different rhythm.

Tara sat under the dryer, a fresh press and curl in progress, her nails tapping her phone screen. Her stylist, Nikki, worked behind her with quick, confident hands.

"Girl, are you going to the Young Jeezy concert?" Tara asked, her tone casually excited.

"Hell yeah!" Nikki grinned. "Me, Coco, and Pam are already locked in."

Tara smiled. "Al bought the clubhouse VIP booth. We comin' deep. I still gotta hit the mall though."

Nikki laughed. "Y'all about to be lit!"

"You know Al's always trying to put on," Tara said, rolling her eyes affectionately.

INT. TASHA'S HOUSE – DAY In a modest kitchen filled with the aroma of simmering stew, Tasha stirred a pot, frustration simmering just beneath the surface.

"Your brothers and cousins out there, messing up," she muttered, more to herself than to her daughter. "If my brother was home, they wouldn't be out there trying to sell drugs."

Bre, her teenage daughter, leaned against the wall, arms folded.

"Mommy… you know they're just doing what they saw Uncle Brian do. That's what all of them out there are doing—trying to make money."

Tasha sighed heavily. "That still doesn't make it right. Easy and Brian made sure those boys didn't need nothin'. All they had to do was go to school, learn something, make better choices. Instead, they learned the street. Made soft asses."

The phone rang. She wiped her hands and picked it up.

"Hey, Bro, how are you doing?"

"I'm A1. How about you?" came Brian's voice on the other end.

Tasha didn't hesitate. "I'm good, but I'ma tell you straight. Your son, Lil Eazy, Mike Mike, and Cam are out here dealing drugs. Can't tell them nothin'. They quit school. Just a mess, Bro."

There was a pause. A long one.

Then Brian answered, voice tight with frustration and disappointment. "That's a blow to hear. I'm in here gettin' my mind right, thinking' about how Imma show them how to turn a negative into a positive… and they out there following' my old footsteps."

INT. TARA'S CONDO – EVENING Later that evening, Tara stood in front of her mirror adjusting her outfit—fitted dress, heels, a hint of gloss. In the background, Al lounged on the couch, drinking, smoking, and counting thick wads of cash with casual ease.

Her phone rang.

"What's up, nephew?" Tara answered.

On speaker, Lil B's voice came through. "I need you to hook me and Lil Eazy up with your boyfriend. We tired of going through middlemen."

In the background, Lil Eazy chimed in loud and clear. "Hell yeah, Auntie! Put us in the game, coach!"

Tara sighed. "Your daddy gon' kick all our asses."

"Auntie, look… we've been out here hustlin' for over two years now," Lil B said, his voice steady, mature beyond his age. "We stacked up 25 Gs. Either you gonna look out, or you gonna let us keep dealin' with these suckers."

Al heard everything from the couch. His demeanor shifted. He stood, took the phone from Tara, and spoke directly.

"Tomorrow, come down to Tara's condo. We'll sit down and put it together. Y'all not going to the show tonight?"

"Hell naw. Jeezy already paid. We trying to get paid—stayin' down in the trap."

Al smiled, amused but impressed.

"Okay, like that! Get that paper. We will meet tomorrow." He hung up and turned to Tara.

"Baby, it is what it is. Them young niggas gon' get their money. Their feet are already wet. Might as well put 'em in good hands. They are their daddy's DNA… products of the ghetto."

Tara looked at him, uncertain. The game hadn't changed. It just changed faces. And her family—Brian's sons—were stepping in deeper.

47

CHAPTER 10

YEARS LATER

The yard buzzed with noise. Shouts, laughter, weight benches clanging. But for Brian, everything had faded into background static. Sweat darkened his t-shirt, forming an abstract map of pressure and perseverance. He dropped into another set of push-ups, elbows slicing sharp angles into the air, his focus honed and fierce. The dust beneath him soaked in his effort.

Brian was a man of medium build, but there was nothing average about the way he moved—each motion deliberate, his breath controlled like a man with something to prove not to the world, but to himself. At thirty-eight, prison hadn't broken him; it had revealed him.

His thoughts ran deeper than the surface grit of this place.

Information only turns into knowledge when you start to apply it. It's not about how you start but how you finish.

He'd learned that the hard way. The system had convinced him that he was only good for one thing: pushing poison. But now, knowledge was his hustle. Not just gathering it—applying it. That's where the power was.

He paused his set, looking around the yard—some men were lifting weights like they were preparing for war, others simply paced in that caged aimlessness. He'd been both those men. But no more.

Being prepared is only half the battle, he thought, the words surfacing like scripture. You still need some luck. Some favor.

He dropped again, arms burning, but he welcomed the pain. It reminded him he was alive, still in the fight.

The system had me thinking all I was good for was selling drugs. But now, I understand—information, and how you use it, makes all the difference.

That was the real product now. That was what he'd sell when he got out. No more crumbs off another man's table. Brian was building his own.

The Night Belonged To Tara.

Inside the packed nightclub, the air pulsed with bass and joy. Strobe lights flashed across smiling faces as friends and family danced in celebration of her 30th birthday. Al, her boyfriend, stood posted in the VIP booth, a drink in his hand and opportunity heavy on his mind.

"This is a big week," he said, leaning in to Lil Eazy and Lil B, both nodding like they already tasted the future. "I'm getting plugged in with a heavy Mexican who's got a warehouse full of work. Our numbers are about to get lower, and the work? Plentiful."

Lil B grinned, clinking his glass. "Music to my ears. That void since BMF and Westside/Southside got picked up? Ain't been right since. I'll drink to that."

Lil Eazy smirked. "I've been lusting for something like this. Time to run the check up!"

As they toasted, Tara glided through the crowd, radiant and buzzed on love and attention. She slipped her arms around Al, kissed him, and tugged him toward the dance floor. "Come dance with the birthday girl."

The DJ called for everyone to raise a glass. People cheered, clapped, shouted Tara's name. Just when the energy peaked, Al held up a hand, stopping the music. Silence dropped like a velvet curtain.

He turned to Tara, dropped to one knee, and pulled out a ring that sparkled under the club lights.

Gasps. Cheers. Laughter.

Tara screamed, hands over her mouth, then nodded wildly. "Yes! Yes! This is the best birthday party ever." The DJ dropped "Ain't No Stoppin' Us Now." The floor erupted in celebration, bodies moving in rhythm, champagne spraying, joy spilling over like a wave doing the electric slide.

Back inside the prison, things were calmer, but no less strategic.

Big Brian sat across from Turtle in the TV room, a chessboard between them. Turtle moved a pawn with patience, eyes steady.

"You're on countdown," he said, not looking up.

"Six weeks to go," Brian replied, gaze locked on the board. "It's been a journey. Can't lie... this might be the best thing to happen to me. I hate that it cost me my wife, time with my family... but my mind's never been so tight. Time to put my plan in motion."

Turtle nodded. "I believe you're one of the few who won't become a product of the system."

"I can't afford to. My son, nephews, my sister—they're all knee-deep in this game. If I can't reach them, who will? I just gotta use my brain, plan, execute."

Turtle leaned back. "Just remember the golden rule on a plane— when shit goes down, secure your mask first. Can't save anyone if you can't breathe."

Brian's eyes narrowed in thought, but before he could speak, Von walked up holding a thick stack of stamp books, betting sheets, and parlay tickets.

"The whole compound's playing, Boss," Von said, handing the items over. "Hope you don't take a hit."

Brian grinned, flipping through the tickets. "If I do, I can pay. That's all that matters. That's why they play with me."

"You're right," Von said. "Best bookie on the compound. I still have more to pick up. Chow time—they ran us in."

Brian nodded. "I got Glover making fifty big pizzas and nachos for everyone spending with me. Make sure everyone playing gets slices and nachos."

"You know how to treat your people," Von said, walking off. "Feeding the whole compound."

Brian leaned back, pride flickering behind his eyes.

My new hustle: I'm the bookie, his thoughts narrated. Each book of stamps equals ten dollars—that's compound money. When I get out, I'm doing this legit. People love to bet on games. The great part is, it brings no heat—hell, it's legal in Vegas. Now I see why the mob was so big on it.

Brian had found clarity where most found despair. He wasn't just doing time—he was building a blueprint. And when that gate opened, he wouldn't be stepping out as a free man. He'd be stepping out as a made man.

Sunday's energy was easy at Al and Tara's house.

The game was on, the blunt rotation had just begun, and the boys were vibing like they had no worries outside the walls of the living room.

Al was kicked back in his recliner, eyes locked on the screen. Lil B lounged near the edge of the couch, tapping a rhythm on his thigh. Lil Eazy sat with a smirk like he knew something no one else did, while Mike Mike leaned forward, fully engaged in the game but not above some casual conversation.

Mike Mike turned to Lil B. "I know you're happy, Unk's coming home next month."

Lil B nodded, though there was a flicker of caution in his expression. "Yep. He claims he's not selling any more drugs."

Al laughed, leaning in, drink in hand. "They all say that behind them walls. Hell, I said it."

The room erupted in laughter, the kind that carried both truth and understanding. No judgment—just lived experience.

Lil Eazy chimed in, shaking his head with a grin. "Can't wait to see what he has up his sleeve. Unk ran circles around most of these niggas."

Al leaned forward, nodding with a kind of reverence. "Hell, your dad was the Don. Niggas still talk about him from the 80s. Both of them—legends. Y'all's DNA? Cut from the cloth."

Lil B's smile faded, his tone shifting as the weight of old wounds surfaced. "Silk and Nate messed everything up."

Lil Eazy laughed but with an edge of warning. "Hell, Silk's kids act like they want some smoke. Watch his daughter though—Terri. I heard she's ruthless, like the Black Widow."

Just then, Tara entered the room with a tray full of neatly rolled blunts, her presence light but commanding. She handed one to Mike Mike with a playful scowl.

"Nobody wants to smoke behind you, Mike Mike," she teased. "You stay wetting the blunts."

They all laughed again as lighters sparked. Tara smiled, proud of her role in this moment of peace.

"Oh—and the fish and grits are ready."

That was all it took. The room emptied faster than a club at last call, everyone rushing toward the kitchen.

Across town, in the calmer corners of the city, dinner had a different tone.

Precious and her daughters sat around the table, plates full, conversation gentle but pressing. The evening carried a quiet tension, the kind only children could cause when they ask questions that touch the grown-up heart.

"Mom," Malin started, her voice curious and uncertain, "are you and Dad getting back together when he comes home?"

Precious exhaled gently, her expression soft but resolute. "Baby, we've talked about this—no. But we're like best friends. And we're going to make sure you're all good."

Paris, even the heart-driven one, frowned. "I think you should forgive Dad and try again. God says we should forgive, Mom."

Precious smiled at her, reaching for her hand. "I have, baby. I have forgiven him. But we both agreed to move on. Once you're grown, you'll understand."

Malin narrowed her eyes, playful but probing. "Do you love Cory?"

Precious grinned, pushing her plate aside. "Now, where is all this coming from? Feels like I'm on trial or something."

Laughter helped ease the moment, but the truth lingered in the air like perfume—warm, familiar, and just a little bittersweet.

Back inside the prison walls, game day meant more than touchdowns.
 It was economy, excitement, and tension—especially in the TV room where inmates gathered around the television, yelling at the screen, reacting like investors on the trading floor.

Brian sat near the back, calm amid the chaos, speaking to a small group.

"Man," he said, voice low but firm, "I lost over five million—money, assets, my wife, my son to the streets. But what's crazy is what I learned reading, about how the CIA allowed drugs into the U.S. to fund foreign wars. All on the backs of us Black men. And then they lock us up, throw away the key."

Joe shook his head, eyes dark with history. "They have been taking us from the house since slavery. Left the women to raise the kids. It's all a project. A test. To see what kind of products come out of the projects. Open your eyes."

Suddenly, shouts echoed from the front of the room.

"Damn!" ATL Fat hollered. "I shoulda known better than putting them Falcons on my ticket. Gotta stop betting with my heart!"

The room cracked up.

"If your ticket is dead, go to bed!" Tuby screamed from across the room.

Von leaned in, shaking his head. "The Cowboys are the compound killer! Down 14. If they on your ticket—tear that shit up!"

Moe wiped his brow dramatically. "City just sweated me out. The sweat box is real!"

Turtle chuckled, getting up. "Don't know about y'all, but I'm going to the window. All I'm waiting on is the 49ers."

Brian didn't say much. He just observed, absorbing everything like a general in a war room. Every bet, every reaction—it all fed into the bigger picture he was building.

Elsewhere, in a dimly lit lounge laced with smoke and whispers, Terri and Apple walked in with deliberate grace. Ross sat alone in a corner booth, heavy-set, drink in hand, and eyes already scanning.

Terri sauntered over, her voice velvet and venom. "I hope you don't mind. I brought my friend. Don't worry—she won't be a third wheel. We share everything."

Ross grinned wide, gold tooth catching the light. "The more, the merrier. What y'all drinking?"

"Shots of tequila," they said in unison. "With salt and lemon."

They drank. They laughed. They smoked. The tension was a game, and everyone knew the rules.

As the night wore thin and the buzz got heavy, Terri leaned close.

"We're gonna follow you. The night is young."

She rubbed his belly, teasing but with a predator's charm.

Later, inside Terri's car parked near a gas station,

She sat in the driver's seat watching Ross through the windshield.

"How much you wanna bet he stopped to get rubbers and Red Bull?" she asked, smirking.

Apple laughed without hesitation. "Nothing niggas so predictable—'cause I know that's what he's doing. Niggas always think with the wrong head."

Their laughter filled the car, light but laced with game.

They weren't just out for fun.

They were playing too.

Only difference?

They knew exactly what they were playing for.

CHAPTER 11

There are seasons in the streets when the lines between ambition, loyalty, and survival blur so much that no one remembers where they started. Everyone becomes a player in a game with no scoreboard, just stakes. And this chapter? This was one of those seasons—where every move had a cost, and every silence echoed louder than truth.

The hum of conversation and the clink of silverware filled the air of the upscale restaurant, but at one secluded corner table, business was being served more than food. AL sat across from two stone-faced Mexican associates, his demeanor calm, assertive. Beside them sat Santiago—a sharp, calculating man with a tone as smooth as the suit he wore.

Santiago lit a cigarette slowly, eyes never leaving AL. "I heard great things about you, my friend," he said, voice low and deliberate. "How many can you buy? I charge you sixteen apiece."

AL leaned forward, locking eyes with him. No bluff. No hesitation. "I can buy twenty."

Santiago grinned. "Good, my friend. I'll match you with twenty when you're ready to deal."

AL didn't blink. "Now."

Santiago chuckled, impressed. "Like that, huh? You're about business." He leaned back, tapping his ash. "Now show me your license. I need to know who you really are… considering you owe me three hundred and twenty thousand dollars, my friend."

AL reached into his wallet and slid it across the table. Santiago took his time inspecting it, as if reading into the soul behind the ID.

"Santiago," AL said, voice steady, "I'm about to make you a lot of money."

"I like making money," Santiago replied, handing the license back. "I really do."

Meanwhile, over in the trap house, the energy was different—but the anticipation was just as real. The walls smelled of smoke and sweat, with a steady stream of customers filtering in and out like it was a convenience store.

Lil B sat at the table, focused, thumbing through a thick stack of cash. His eyes never left the money, his fingers working like they'd been born to count.

"Can't wait till AL hits us with the good news," Lil B muttered, half to himself, half to the room. "Tell us what the new plug talkin' 'bout. We 'bout to run our check up."

Lil Eazy, lounging on the couch, controller in hand and eyes on the screen, smirked. "This is our time to shine. 'Bout to make our mark—step out from under our dads' shadows."

Mike Mike worked the door, handling customers like clockwork, but his ears were on the conversation too. Everyone in that room felt it—the momentum shifting. They were ready.

In contrast, Ross's condo was drenched in decadence and danger. He sat on the couch in nothing but boxers, sipping Hennessy, smoke curling around his head as if trying to warn him. He watched Terri and Apple dance for him, bras and G-strings glowing under the dim lights, bodies swaying in sync.

Apple moved toward Ross, her touch slow, sensual, rubbing his chest and neck, making him sink deeper into the leather cushions.

Terri, always the one playing chess, strolled over to her purse casually, pulled out her small two-shot Derringer, and turned back without hesitation. Before Ross could react, the cold barrel was pressed to his forehead.

"Where is the money at?" Terri asked calmly.

Ross didn't say a word—just pointed to the bedroom. His body froze, but his eyes screamed.

"Get up," Terri ordered, stepping back.

They moved into the bedroom. "Look behind that chair," he said.

Apple strutted over, lifted the chair's edge, and pulled out a heavy bag. She opened it, peeked inside.

"Bingo," she said, smiling.

Terri stared into Ross's eyes—no hate, just clarity. "Night-night."

They wiped the place down like professionals. No prints, no loose ends. Before leaving, Terri caught sight of a photo on the dresser—Ross, AL, Lil B, Lil Eazy, and a few others, arms around each other like brothers.

"One by one," she whispered, eyes cold, "I'm gonna get y'all."

And then they were gone, heels clicking against the floor like punctuation.

Later that day, sunlight poured onto Bo's driveway as AL and Bo pulled up to the house. The moment AL stepped out, his energy was different—like he was already living two moves ahead.

"This is the break we've been looking for," AL said as he walked up to the door. "We are about to have a run. Gotta call Ross and Lil B."

Bo nodded. "Yeah, with these numbers, we can control the market."

They slapped palms, locked in, visions of power swirling behind their eyes.

Back in the penitentiary, Brian sat in his cell surrounded by silence and stamps. His fingers flipped through the little paper books like a banker thumbing bonds.

"Eighteen hundred made," he muttered to himself. "After paying out twelve... not bad for two days of work."

He grabbed the phone, dialed out, his tone softening as the line connected.

"Hey, daddy," Paris said on the other end.

Brian leaned back, smiling. "How's my baby girl?"

"Doing my homework," she replied proudly.

"Are you doing your best?"

"Yes."

"Where's your sister?"

"She went out with some friends."

"Okay," he said, letting a pause settle between them. "Love you. Always strive for greatness."

As he hung up, Brian looked back at his books of stamps. To anyone else, it was just a prison hustle. But to Brian? It was the foundation. Strategy. A future unfolding. Every dollar, every call, every lesson he whispered into the phone—he was building something.

Something real.

The streets were loud with hustle, the prison walls buzzed with strategy, and the families left behind were caught in a strange balancing act—half surviving, half waiting. Everyone was playing a game. Some didn't even know it.

At a modest corner Food Mart—one of those lowkey WIC-authorized spots that flew under radar but made serious bank—Cory stood with his arm around Precious. A few stock boys moved quietly behind them, putting up cereal boxes and canned goods, none aware of the quiet power play being discussed right next to them.

"This the new million-dollar run, baby," Cory said, his voice filled with confidence and a slick kind of street wisdom. "Trust me, my uncle made millions riding around in his fruit-and-vegetable truck. Bought food stamps at half price—straight from the people."

Precious raised an eyebrow, still piecing it together. "How though? I still don't get it."

Cory grinned, breaking it down like it was algebra and he was the professor. "The government pays us full price for every dollar in stamps. So let's say we buy five hundred dollars worth? The government kicks us back a thousand. Double-up money—no corners, no re-up. Just government-funded profit."

Precious leaned in, smiling like she'd just seen the bigger picture. "Baby, you are a genius."

They kissed, the kind of kiss built more on ambition than love. This wasn't romance—it was partnership. And like many before them, they were stepping into the underbelly of the system with eyes wide open.

Meanwhile, just down the block outside some rundown apartments, a whole different kind of business was going bad.

Lil Eazy stood over Mario, who was trying to explain why he was short again. His tone was pleading, eyes nervous. "I swear, Lil Eazy, it wasn't my fault. The police came, I had to run, and a junkie must've stolen my bomb."

Lil Eazy wasn't buying any of it.

"That's the problem," he snapped, stepping closer. "Guess you already copped them new J's, huh? Must think I'm sweet or stupid."

And just like that, Lil Eazy clocked Mario right in the mouth. The man dropped, face to concrete. A quick kick to the ribs followed as people watched from doorways and balconies—but no one intervened. Cam stood close, watching the crowd, making sure no one stepped out of line.

They didn't.

Lil Eazy and Cam walked off like it was just another day. For them, it was.

Inside prison, the lunchroom was alive with backdoor trades, chatter, and business. Stamp books were exchanged like cash, and Von sat with ATL Fat, managing payouts from the previous day's bets.

"I love the way y'all handle business," June Bug said as he passed them. "Next-day payouts? That pizza last night was smashing."

Von gave a slight nod. "Only one way to do business—the right way. We don't play with y'all money, so don't play with ours."

Across the chow hall, tensions flared. An inmate snapped, shouting about the half-cooked food, slamming his tray before getting rushed and twisted into a chicken wing by two officers.

"Von!" South Carolina Bell called from a distance, lifting his shirt to reveal food stashed beneath. "Tell Brian I got him tonight."

Von chuckled. "You better hope you get out of here with all that. That fool Bama just made it hot."

Bell smirked. "I got a décor. We are eating fried chicken tonight."

But minutes later, Bell was stopped, searched, and had all his food tossed into the trash. Fried chicken and hope thrown in the same bin.

"Crazy how they throw away food," Von muttered as he left the chow hall. "Rather let it rot than let us eat it."

ATL Fat shook his head. "Who you tellin'? Look at that trash can. My mouth was watering for that chicken."

Outside, back in the free world, Lil B was playing big brother. At Meke's house, he handed off fresh clothes and new Jordans to his younger brother, Doc.

"You about to be the freshest kid in school," Lil Brian said, ruffling Doc's hair. "Only one with these J's. Just keep your grades up."

"Thanks, big bro. You are the best!"

Meke popped her head in, eyes already searching. "You got some money for me? These kids are eating me outta house and home."

Lil Brian rolled his eyes, but pulled out some cash. "Hey to you too, Mom." He handed her a small stack.

Meke smirked. "When is your daddy coming home? I might get my man back now that that lil college girl left him."

Lil Brian shot her a look. "He will be home soon. And no—he is not hooking back up with you."

"You a hater," Meke said, striking a pose. "Look at this fine body. I look better than your little girlfriends."

The boys cracked up. Lil Brian leaned toward Doc. "That's your mommy," he said with a half-smile. Doc just laughed harder.

At the barber shop, Brian sat in the chair, getting his weekly shape-up. It wasn't just about the cut—it was about staying sharp mentally, too.

"Tennessee Mick made some good clean white," Barber 1 said, "had me tipsy as hell."

Barber 2 raised a brow. "How much for a water bottle?"

"Hundred bucks. Worth every drip."

"I'ma pull up on him. Maybe he cut me a deal."

Brian grinned. "I'll get you two bottles. Just keep my cut crispy all year."

"Bet, ATL B. Good lookin' out."

Detroit Mike spoke from the corner. "The Mexicans outta hand with them phone prices—seven-five now."

Brian nodded, eyes narrowing. "You know what they say—it costs to be the boss. If we came together as a people, we could make our own moves. But they control the market… they set the prices."

Everyone went quiet for a beat. Truth has a way of echoing in the right room.

Later that day, Brian was on the yard, walking with his close circle—Joe, OG Head, and two others.

"Crazy how the cycle keeps repeating," Brian said, eyes scanning the horizon. "My son and Easy's son deep in the streets. And the crazy part? They are getting fueled by my sister's fiancé."

Joe nodded solemnly. "That's how the system works. That's why it's important for heads of the house, the ones who get a second chance, to get out and do right. 'Cause the feds will hide you forever if you let 'em."

He sighed. "This my second time around. And each time, the longer you are in, your record becomes your worst enemy."

Brian looked up at the sky. "I got a plan. I know the streets are gon' call when I get out. Old buddies gon' try to hand me bricks. But I'm staying strong. I like being a bookie. I like playing smart."

OG Head smiled but shook his head. " That's the hardest part. Saying no to fast money—especially when they are dropping bricks on face card."

Brian exhaled. "Only time will tell."

Then he spotted the gathering. Two inmates were lining up for a foot race, and a crowd was forming.

"Looks like they about to race," Brian said. "Let me go get my bet on."

He jogged over, pulling out his stamp books.

"Everyone, bets made!" the announcer yelled. "Going once, going twice—"

"Hold up," Brian called. "Twenty books on Miami Black!"

Chi Town grinned. "Bet! You ain't said nothin'."

Brian looked around. "Anybody else got South American?"

The Spanish Dude stepped forward. "I do. Fifty books."

Brian smiled. "Bet."

The race popped off. Miami Black flew down the yard like a blur. Brian smirked—money well placed. More races followed, stamps changing hands like Vegas chips

Sometimes the people at the top don't fall by force—they rot from within, slow and unnoticed, until the empire crumbles. Power gets passed like a virus: from father to son, from old rules to new plays, from silence to a shot in the dark. In this game, the checkmate doesn't always come from the front.

Sometimes, it walks in wearing heels.

CHAPTER 12

The weight of leadership never slept—not in the streets, not in prison, not in the silence of a shared bed where plans were built on pillow talk. And in Al's house, as the sun dipped below the edge of the blinds, those quiet pressures were stacking fast.

Al sat on the edge of the bed, counting cash with muscle memory. His face was tight, focused, brows furrowed. This wasn't just money—it was movement, it was power, it was protection.

Tara stepped into the room, already sensing something was off. "See you've hit our stash spot," she said, nodding toward the duffle bag half-emptied on the floor. "What's going on?"

Al sighed and looked up. "Bae, I found a new plug. Empty all the stash spots, but I'm still short. Ross owes me... but he hasn't hit me back yet."

Tara's tone softened. "You want me to go to the bank?"

Al shook his head. "Nah, baby. If all else fails, I'll get Lil B and Lil Eazy to loan me. I'll give them a player deal. They'll jump."

Tara smiled faintly, trying to keep him grounded. "Okay. The food's ready. I'm about to take a shower—watch out for Allen, he's asleep."

Al gave a slight nod, his fingers going back to the stack like a casino dealer. His mind was already twenty moves ahead.

Back inside the prison walls, hustle came in a different form—but it still came hard.

Brian sat in his cube, surrounded by stamp books. It wasn't flashy, but in this world, it was currency. He and Von quietly sorted them, stacking them into neat bundles.

At the door, an inmate appeared. Tall, gold fronts flashing, South Florida Kane leaned in.

"ATL B," he said casually, "can you sell me a hundred in flats?"

"Yep," Brian replied, reaching into his stack and handing them over.

"Same deal?" Kane asked.

"Same everything," Brian said. "Have your people Western Union the money to Tasha. Again."

Kane nodded. "Okay, thanks. You did good out there, huh?"

Brian smirked. "And you know this, man."

As Kane disappeared, Brian passed another stack to Von.

"Here. This is for Miami Black. Tell him good job and to rest up— folks gon' want a rematch. I cleared 800."

Von looked surprised. "How did you know to bet with Miami Black? South Americans have been smoking everything lately."

Brian grinned like a chess player after checkmate. "Miami Black caught three rabbits before, bro. You know what they say—if a man can catch three rabbits, he can play in the lead. It's all about intel."

Von walked off laughing, shaking his head, pointing back at Brian like, *that man don't miss.*

Over at Terri's condo, the night was laced with sex, smoke, and secrets.

Steam rose from the bathroom as Terri ran the shower head over Apple's body, her other hand roaming with control and affection. Apple moaned softly, eyes closed, letting Terri take the lead.

Later, in the bedroom, Apple gave Terri pleasure, licking her whole body with slow intensity until reaching her clit and started licking fast but with purpose until Terri released her fluid, Terri collapsed in silence. They lit a blunt, the room heavy with smoke and satisfaction.

"Have you talked to the rest of the girls yet?" Apple asked, exhaling.

Terri nodded. "Texted them. They'll be over tomorrow. We have two parties this weekend—some big fish will be there."

Her phone rang.

"What's up, twin?" she said, putting it on speaker.

Toni's voice came through. "Sis, y'all sliding to Magic City tonight?"

"Nah, we're already in bed, bro."

"Aight, well I'll swing by tomorrow. Need to run something by you—me, and Charlie Mo."

"Cool," Terri said, glancing over. Apple was already asleep, her chest rising steady in the dim light.

Terri laid back, her mind never fully at rest. Power plays had to be made, but they had to be made *quietly*.

That same night, Brian was back in his cube, phone pressed to his ear.

"Sis, you get the Western Union?" he asked.

Tasha's voice was clear on the other end. "Yep. Total $2,500."

"Good. More's coming, but I'm sending it under Bre's name this time. I need more names. Everything else good?"

Tasha's sigh came through the phone. "I'll get you more names. Everything's good… except these boys running the streets. Not listening to me. Think I don't know what I'm talking about."

Brian shook his head. "That's how it goes. Still disappointed in Tara. Can't believe she flipped on everything we planned. But that's life. Can't cry over spilled milk."

"I feel you, bro," she replied.

Before they could say more, an inmate shouted in the background:

"Mask up! Mask up!"

Brian tensed. "Look, I'll call you tomorrow. Officer's walking."

He hung up, tucked his phone away, and laid back like he was already asleep. Around him, other inmates scrambled to do the same putting up their phones

A female officer passed by the cubes, pausing at him.

"Brian," she said, smirking. "Stop playin' sleep. I heard 'mask up.' Now get up, empty my trash and take some bags out."

Brian sat up, blinking innocently. "Didn't know you were working tonight."

He followed her out.

Inside The Officer's Office, The Energy Changed.

Ms. White, confident and clearly familiar with the game, leaned against the desk. "Me and my sister are going to ATL next weekend," she said. "Outkast, T.I., Young Jeezy, Killer Mike. Think you can get us tickets? I know you were a boss out there."

Brian nodded like it was light work. "Yeah, that's nothing. How many?"

"Six."

He didn't miss a beat. "Cool. Look—you need to stop playing and bring some phones and cigarettes in. I pay you $2,500 a load."

Ms. White raised an eyebrow. "I like your style. I need some extra cash. Kids' daddy don't help me, period. But you can't tell nobody."

Brian smirked. "You think I'm gonna mess up my meal ticket by running my mouth?"

That was the difference between Brian and the rest—he didn't chase noise. He moved in silence and collected outcomes.

Brian was balancing two worlds: one built on razor wire and cement, the other on fragile connections and whispers across phone lines. His empire wasn't flashy—it was structured, controlled, low-risk. While others chased fast money, Brian was calculating longevity.

He sent money home like child support for a community he still felt responsible for. His sister Tasha, overwhelmed by the new generation, tried her best to hold the line. His daughter still answered his calls with joy. Even in his cell, he was more of a patriarch than many men walking free.

And yet, trust didn't come easy. Tara's betrayal still cuts deep. That wasn't just business—it was blood.

Every phone call. Every book of stamps. Every silent alliance.

Brian wasn't just surviving prison. He was preparing to *own* his second chance.

The real question wasn't whether Brian would win. It was whether his world would let him *walk away* clean.

CHAPTER 13

Every city breathes differently after midnight. The laughter grows louder, the intentions more slippery, and the rules? They blur. In Atlanta, the parking lot outside a nightclub could tell just as many stories as the dancefloor inside—and on this particular night, Toni and Charlie Mo were center stage.

They stood near a steaming BB⁸Q truck, the smell of ribs and late-night sauce luring in the crowd like clockwork. A few other hustlers flanked them, joking, sipping, staying alert. Two women approached, dressed like they knew they looked good and moved like they weren't surprised by the attention.

"Give them what they want. I'm paying," Toni said, eyes roaming, chin tilted.

"Thank you," the girl with the blonde hair replied, polite but guarded.

Toni gave her a half-smirk. "That's nothing. So… where are we going after this? The Hotel?"

Blondie turned to him, unimpressed. "You think buying a $10 plate gets you a hotel invite?"

Toni leaned in, undeterred. "Hell yeah feed you and beat that thing to sleep"

Charlie Mo, already laughing, co-signed. "Hell yeah, sounds about right."

The girl stepped back, chin high, her tone shifting from polite to fed up. "That's what's wrong with y'all niggas. Not every female is some cheap trick."

Toni wasn't fazed. "Shit, if it's good, I'll take you to Houston."

She reached into her purse, pulled out some cash. "You just don't know. But here, *sir,* I'll pay for me and my girl's food. He's tripping."

As she handed the money to the vendor, Toni muttered under his breath. "Unappreciative trick. Better be glad I stopped slapping whores."

The girls walked away, heels clicking, dignity intact. And yet, the tension in the air stayed like barbecue smoke—thick, lingering, and dangerous.

Elsewhere in the city, the night felt softer.

Bo lay in bed with April, their limbs tangled, the glow from the TV casting light across the room. It was pillow talk hour—the time when real plans start spilling out, loose and honest.

"Today was a good day," Bo said, voice mellow. "Met a real Mexican plug. Things are really about to go up from here."

April shifted closer, her tone part teasing, part serious. "'Bout time. You've been loyal to Al since day one. We could use some upgrades around here."

Bo nodded. "Don't worry. This is our run now. I'm gonna get out from under Al's shadow. Still work with him, but I'm doing my own thing now—gonna catch my own people."

April bit her lip, eyes gleaming. "Been telling you this. You're getting me hot and wet talking like a boss."

Bo laughed, pulling her close. "You've been acting funny with it. Come give daddy some."

They didn't talk after that. Their bodies did the rest.

By 3 a.m., across town, Waffle House buzzed with neon and hunger. Lil B and Lil Eazy slid into a booth, hunger in their stomachs and just a little liquor in their veins.

As the waitress dropped menus, the door chimed. Three women walked in, fresh out the club—heels high, hair laid, energy still humming.

Lil Eazy caught eyes with one of them. She smiled. So did he.

"Y'all must be coming from Magic City Monday," he said.

The one with the brown skin and bold lip gloss—Leah—shrugged. "Nah, we should've gone. The club we went to was lame."

Lil Eazy grinned. "happens sometimes but I'm sure I can show you a good time my name. Lil Eazy. What's yours?"

"Leah."

Just like that, they locked in. Numbers were exchanged. Smiles traded like secrets. Lil B grabbed their food and nodded toward the exit. It was all smooth—a quiet game. The kind that sets up longer plays.

But not everything in the night moved so gently.

At a gas station not far from the city's edge, Toni and Charlie Mo were at the pump. Toni headed into the store, and Charlie stood outside when a black dude walked up—thin, nervous, holding a small stash.

"Got that loud," the man said, eyes shifting.

Charlie Mo raised a brow. "Let me see how fat your pack is."

The man shrugged. "It's four in the morning. Can't be too choosy."

He opened his jacket and revealed the stash. Before he could blink, Charlie pulled a gun from under his hoodie.

"Don't run. Don't say a word. Just drop it all and empty your pockets—if you wanna make it home."

Panic hit the man's face. "Man, I'm just trying to feed my kids. Please… this is all I got. I haven't even paid rent yet."

Charlie's face didn't shift. "Sounds like a *you* problem. Now take off before I change my mind."

The man didn't wait for a second warning. He bolted around the corner like his life depended on it—because it did.

Toni stepped out of the store moments later, bag in hand. He spotted Charlie Mo at the car, counting weed sacks and a stack of bills on his lap.

"No, you didn't," Toni said, half laughing, half shaking his head.

Charlie Mo just grinned. "He was asking for it. Better be glad I ain't bust his ass."

Life After Dark

The deeper into the night these characters go, the more their truths leak out. Toni plays big but hides insecurities behind bravado. Bo is stepping out of Al's shadow, but loyalty lines are starting to blur. Lil Eazy is finally feeling seen outside his father's name. And Charlie Mo? He's a ticking time bomb, unchecked and too reckless for his own good.

It's a city pulsing with ambition, lust, ego, and pain. Every character is chasing something—respect, power, freedom—but most of them are running blind, chasing shadows in the dark.

Some are plotting their rise.

Others are counting their sins.

And when the sun comes up?

Only a few will be left standing with clean hands.

The city moved fast, but the women behind the men weren't just keeping up—they were training for it. In a sunlit gym thick with energy and sweat, Tara, April, and Shan were just wrapping up another morning workout. Each of them carried stories on their shoulders, but inside this space, they left all the drama at the door and focused on staying sharp, strong, and sexy.

"Girl," Tara huffed, wiping her face with a towel, "that workout almost killed me."

"Who are you telling?" Shan said, wobbling on sore legs. "My legs are still shaking like Jell-O in a car crash."

April smirked, adjusting her ponytail. "I finally gave Bo some last night. That man was bouncing up and down like a kid on a trampoline."

They all laughed—hard, loud, and free.

Tara shook her head. "I don't think Al's gonna go for me making him wait months like you did."

April raised her brows knowingly. "You gotta train them how to act right."

Shan nodded, already pulling her hoodie over her sports bra. "Are we eating after this?"

"Yeah," Tara said, grabbing her gym bag. "Let's hit Thumbs Up. Just hope they ain't slow. I gotta get Allen."

The girls headed out, still glowing from their workout and the freedom of moving in a world that constantly tried to slow them down.

Back behind the walls, Brian was in motion too—jogging the prison yard in steady strides, mind sharper than his breath. Around him, inmates played chess, ran basketball games, jumped rope, or did pull-ups on rusted bars. It was a twisted kind of peace—routine chaos.

It's not about doing time; it's how you do your time, Brian's thoughts echoed in his mind. *We won't have this much free time again.*

Some men wasted their bids getting high, losing themselves in clouds and cliques. Others joined gangs for protection—acting hard to hide the fear in their chests. A few studied the law and fought back against the system with brains instead of brawn.

Then there were the ones hiding in plain sight. The ones who dipped both ways, pretending one thing in here, living another out there. Brian had seen it all. And judged none—except the liars.

Then you have my type, he thought. *Come in, see a system built on supply and demand, and run the check up. I've changed, yeah... but I'm still a hustler. I just refuse to do anything that'll cost me ten more years of my life.*

As he slowed to a walk, he noticed a large circle forming in the yard. Something was brewing.

He walked over to Joe, who was posted at a chess table, never missing a move on or off the board.

"What's going on out there?" Brian asked.

Joe barely looked up. "PR and DC cars 'bout to clash. Word is, a DC dude got caught stealing from a Puerto Rican."

Brian sighed. "A lot of blood is about to spill."

"Who are you telling?" Joe said. "Lockdown coming. Just hope the shot callers squash it before it gets too ugly."

But it was too late.

A fight exploded from the circle—fists, knees, boots flying. Officers hit the deuces. Alarms screamed through the yard. COs—both men and women—swarmed like ants. Smoke guns popped. Orders were shouted. Inmates not involved dropped spread-eagle to the ground as the chaos got contained.

Brian laid down with the rest, face in the dirt, arms stretched wide.

"I'll be so glad when this foolishness is over," he muttered.

Joe, flat on the ground beside him, answered, "Who are you telling?"

At the trap house later that night, things weren't much calmer. Lil B stood in front of Lil Eazy, eyes sharp, tone low.

"What did you do to Mario?" he asked. "His people called me, saying you were dead wrong. They want to see you."

Lil Eazy shrugged like the whole thing was light. "Man, Mario tried to play me like a lame. Said someone stole his bomb—but he was rocking new Jordans and a fresh sweatsuit."

Lil B nodded. "Word. Some of them will never get it. Anyway, Al wants us to pull up around 1."

"Yeah, I talked with him earlier. Sounded excited."

"Probably the new plug got him hype."

Mike Mike, half paying attention from the couch, chimed in. "We down to nine zips. Man, I met a freak the other day. She let me hit every hole."

Lil B gave him a side-eye. "Cuz, you just a cum freak. How much did you give her?"

"Light hundo," Mike Mike said proudly.

The room erupted in laughter.

At Cory's WIC store the next day, money moved as quietly as footsteps.

Customers lined up, swiping food stamp cards. Cory stood near the register, passing out crisp bills like it was nothing.

"It ain't even noon," he said, grinning, "and I already swiped thirty-five hundred."

Ta leaned on the counter, shaking his head. "Just got off the phone with Tammy—she done seventeen hundred already. Man, these stores are a gold mine."

Cory smirked. "I talked with Precious. She got some properties we need to check out. When Bush crashed the market, real estate got dirt cheap. We damn near could buy up a whole neighborhood for half a mil."

Ta nodded, eyes lighting up. "Lead me to the water, I'll drink. Hell, you taught me how to fish—I'm with it. We need to move some of that bank money anyway."

Cory hesitated a beat, then said, "Man, Ashley cut me off."

TA blinked. "Why? What'd you do?"

"She tried playing a side piece, but wanted more."

Ta laughed hard. "She's still gonna let Boston play for us? He is a dog on the field."

Cory smirked. "Yep."

They both knew the streets weren't the only game they were winning.

Hustles & Crossroads

Every circle is moving now. Tara's trying to hold her home together while keeping her self-worth intact. April is tired of being the passenger—she's ready to drive. Brian watches the whole machine from the inside, picking apart the gears, trying to create an exit route that doesn't end in a body bag or another cell.

Meanwhile, Bo's carving his lane. Lil B and Lil Eazy are still chasing a fast come-up—but they're doing it smarter now, picking up patterns. And Cory? He's shifting from game to legacy, playing with politics, real estate, and respect.

But the thing about every empire—whether it's built on food stamps, street corners, or inside a prison yard—is that it always attracts attention.

And attention?

That's how kings fall.

CHAPTER 14

There were levels to the street game—surface money, hustle money, plug money—and Al's workhouse was where those lines blurred and fortunes were sorted. The smell of rubber bands, residue, and ambition hung thick in the air as Al, Bo, Ant, and Stone stood around the kitchen counter. It was cluttered with cell phones, scales, stacks of cash, and baggies ready for sealing. This wasn't just a spot—it was a pipeline.

Stone glanced up from the cash he was counting, locking eyes with Al. "When do you think these numbers are gonna get better?"

Al didn't hesitate. "Working on it now. Could be next time you come."

"That'd help out a lot. I can finally start catching my folks again," Stone said. "They claim they are paying twenty-nine."

"Don't worry," Al said, his voice smooth, quiet confidence. "A massive event is about to happen. Trust me on that."

"Sounds good. I'll hit you up." Stone slapped palms with Bo and started gathering his cut.

Al's phone rang. He checked the screen and answered. "Hello."

KK (on phone): "Daddy, I'm seeing you tonight. My son is with his daddy for the week."

Al grinned. "Oh yeah? I'll be over later. Tell your mommy I'm bringing her favor."

KK: "Okay, Daddy. You know I can't wait 'til you get me my own spot. I'm about to get my hair done. I'll call you when I'm back."

Al leaned on the counter. "Told you—get your baby daddy to take his son, and I'll get you your own spot."

Bo turned to Tay, who was zipping up a black bag. "Tay, stay safe and away from the haters."

Tay nodded. "You know that's my motto." They dapped up, and Tay dipped.

Bo leaned into the moment, excited. "Bro, just think—once we start getting straight from Santiago, the game is ours. I'm on a mission to stack my check up."

Al nodded, focused. "Yep. Santiago told me to pull up around eight tonight. I'm still a few dollars short, but it'll all work out."

At the hair salon across town, Precious sat with foil in her hair and business on her mind. The gossip swirled around her like the hair dryers: who was beefing, who was up next, what crews were outside tonight. But she wasn't just listening—she was calculating.

Liz turned toward her. "Precious, you got a house for rent?"

Precious smiled. "Actually, I got two—one off South Fulton, the other on Cascade. I'll send you the address and the lockbox code. Check them out and let me know."

Liz nodded. "I'll check it this weekend. My man and I broke up."

Right then, KK walked through the door, smiling and waving at a few stylists. Precious didn't look up—but she definitely noticed.

Back in the dorm cube, Brian and Von were deep in discussion. The dorm was alive with motion—guys pacing, lounging, arguing, reading, or nodding off from cheap highs. A few leaned against bunks in half-sleep, rocked off K2, dozing while standing.

Brian kept his focus.

"I heard they're gonna bring the PR and DC shot callers out today. Try to squash the beef," he said.

Von leaned in. "Hope so. Can't move around like I need to."

Brian nodded. "I'm putting something together for you—something that can make you six figures. You just gotta stay solid. You know I'm leaving soon, but for keep it real and loyal? I got you."

Von's voice cracked slightly. "Man, I can't lie—you're the best thing that's happened to me here. Meeting you? Changed me. You taught me how to hustle, stack money, handle business right, keep my face clean. I came to prison at twenty. Now I'm twenty-seven, got three more to go, and I'm taking care of two kids. Still sending money to my baby mom. She has savings waiting for me."

Brian smiled. "Key to life look, listen, and learn. We got two ears, two eyes, one mouth. If you're always talking, you're never learning. I hear these guys bragging about what they used to do. Most of that stuff? I did as a teenager. But it ain't about what you *did*. It's about what you're *doing*, or what you're *about to do*."

Just then, Columbia approached—one of the most respected, quiet power brokers in the dorm.

"Brian, you got a minute?"

Brian nodded. "Yep."

Columbia's tone was respectful. "I know you're going home soon. And you said you're done with the streets. But I like how you move. I can have five hundred kilos—low numbers, best stuff—delivered to your front door."

Brian didn't hesitate. "Columbia, I promised myself, God, and my kids I'm done. I've lost too much—especially time, which I can't ever get back. I appreciate you considering me, but my heart's not in it anymore."

Columbia nodded, no offense taken. "I can respect that. You got my number. If anything changes, hit me."

They dapped, and Columbia walked off.

Von looked stunned. "Man... I don't know if I could've turned him down. That man got boats and planes. He is real cartel-level."

Brian exhaled. "Everything that glitters ain't gold. He pulled my jacket, saw I kept it a hundred. Saw how much the feds took from me—and I'm still standing tall. That's why he wants to deal with me. Atlanta's a hub."

Meanwhile, over at the car wash, Lil B and Lil Eazy kicked back while their whips got cleaned. A light breeze blew through, junkies wandered by with random goods, and music thumped softly from the speakers inside.

Lil Eazy leaned on the hood. "That girl Leah I met at Waffle House? Her dad's the mayor of Atlanta."

Lil B paused. "You mean *the* mayor? Like, the man who runs the city?"

"Yup. And Leah goes to Spelman."

Lil B laughed. "Damn. You're about to get some royal pussy."

Just then, a couple of dusty street walkers stumbled up.

"Fifty for two boxes of Tide and 24 Pampers," one said, eyeing the cars.

Lil B waved him off. "I'll give you ten for the Tide."

The junkie thought for a second. "Deal. You got any rocks?"

Lil B handed him the cash. "Nah. Now move before you make the cops spin the block with your hot self."

The junkies dipped.

Lil Eazy leaned back. "Man, I really think I like shawty though. She's different. Our convo hit different."

Lil B shook his head. "Bro, you just met her twelve hours ago. Don't start that Mike Mike shit. As soon as you meet a girl, you are in love."

"Man, forget you," Lil Eazy said with a grin. "Our cars ready—let's dip."

Before they could pull out, four teens approached on foot, fresh-faced and hungry.

"Kurt," one of them said, stepping up, "Lil B, you need to front me some work. It's jumping out here."

Lil B studied him for a beat. "If you come with two hundred, I'll put a zip on your face. That'll show me you're serious. Here's my number. Call me when you're ready."

The young hustler nodded.

Lil B and Lil Eazy pulled off with the music loud, exhaust trailing behind them like a wake of ambition.

But the streets don't care about your intentions. Only your actions.

And in a city where loyalty is currency and betrayal is always an option—
Everyone's next move could be their last solid one.

CHAPTER 15

Tasha's house was the kind of place that stayed alive with voices—card tables and loud music, the scent of seasoned meat in the air, and laughter layered with the truth. On this particular afternoon, Bre was working the kitchen while Tasha and her crew huddled around the spades table, trash-talking and letting secrets slip through wine-soaked lips.

"I told that man," Tasha said, smacking a card down, "if he wanna come up in here, I need to see some pay stubs. I don't need no leech around here. Definitely don't need no broke man trying to break my back like that's his way in."

Laughter echoed through the room.

Tina leaned back in her chair, grinning. "Girl, I can't lie. Every now and then, I *need* some broke wood. They are humping for survival—somewhere to live, driving my car while I'm at work. That desperation fuck hit different."

The ladies howled, nodding in agreement.

"Not me," Tasha said, fanning herself. "Been there, done that. I need a grown, independent man who can lay that wood. The *whole package*. I'm not cheating myself anymore."

Vanessa jumped in, eyes full of mischief. "Girl, as soon as Black Rick hits your line in the morning, I bet your stuff gets moist."

Tasha didn't miss a beat. "Rick, don't count. He will be back at his mama house in two days. That doesn't qualify."

In the kitchen, Bre stirred a pot while her friend Jessica leaned on the counter.

"They talk like this all the time," Bre said, half-laughing.

"They're funny," Jessica replied.

"They're lonely," Bre said, more serious now. "I don't wanna be by myself in my late forties or early fifties."

Jessica nodded. "You got a point."

Just then, Mike Mike walked in.

"Sis," he said, "can you fix four to-go plates?"

"Food not ready," Bre replied. "Give me thirty more minutes."

Mike Mike shrugged. "Cool. I'll wait in my room. I'm not about to sit around and hear Mommy and them talk."

"You got some weed?" Bre asked.

"That gas. I put it in your room. Follow your nose—you'll find it."

He strolled past the spades table, catching the attention of two of Tasha's friends.

"Cam done grew up looking good and stuff," Vanessa whispered.

"Leave my son alone," Tasha said without looking up. "Stick with your bar dates."

At 8-Ball Bar, the night was buzzing—liquor flowing, pool tables cracking, the jukebox humming low in the background. Old heads filled the corners like veteran soldiers off-duty. Among them, Jack and Cowboy sat talking over shots, eyes steady, history thick between them.

"Cowboy," Jack said, leaning in, "I really believe Brian's done with the game. I taught him regularly."

Cowboy smirked. "They all say that when they in there. But you know, like I know—everything changes when you walk out the doors."

"Nah," Jack said. "That boy got his mind right."

Cowboy nodded slowly. "I'm just trying to plug him back in with Julio. Lotta money can be made. I just don't have the same juice no more. But Brian got Al, Lil Eazy, his son—they were making some noise."

Jack's eyes narrowed. "After all this time, is this your plan for him?"

"Man," Cowboy said, shrugging, "not many move the way Brian moves. He's Eazy times ten."

"I hear you," Jack muttered.

Just then, Jonny and a partner walked up.

"Jack. Cowboy."

They both nodded in greeting.

"I hear Brian on his way home," Johnny said.

"Yep."

"Well, let him know I need to talk with him," Johnny said, voice low. "I can put him right back like he never left."

Jack chuckled. "Johnny, get in line. Everybody is happy their prizefighter is coming home. But y'all know just like I know—Brian chooses who he deals with, and on his *terms.* Good luck."

In his cube, Brian sat alone. The dorm was busy with movement—music in the air, the distant sound of dice hitting tile. But he wasn't in the noise. He was deep in thought, staring into the middle distance like it was holding answers.

BRIAN (V.O.):

Crazy how the closer I get to getting out, the more old feelings pop up—feelings I thought weren't there anymore.

Why does the opportunity for my first love keep coming, but no one wants to invest in my new ideas?

Do they only see a drug dealer? Is this the hand I gotta play?

How is it the CIA can pump drugs into this country and face no consequence? Why are prisons full of Black and brown people, when we're only thirty percent of the population?

So many questions. So many problems. And nobody's solving them.

America is a business. We're all products in some form.

Von entered, breaking the silence with a stack of parlay tickets and stamps in hand.

"Word on the compound," Von said, "the leaders of PR and DC getting shipped. They don't have control of their cars."

Brian shook his head. "They don't. On other yards, you won't see PR smoking K2. DC? Most of 'em crash dummies—messing up money."

Brian's phone buzzed. He answered.

"Hello?"

TICKET JERRY (on phone): "Got your VIP suite box tickets—ten people, free food and drinks included."

"My man! I'm giving her your number. Y'all go from there. My sister is paying you already?"

"Yep. We're good."

"Cool. She'll be in touch."

Right after, South Carolina stepped in, holding a bag.

"ATL B, here's your chicken—ten quarters, legs crispy."

Brian grinned. "Hot and fresh, huh? What do I owe you?"

"Hundred."

Brian handed him a wad of stamps. "And here's a tip. Keep me at the top of the list."

"You already top tier."

A small crowd started forming. Inmates approached with tickets and bets.

ATL Fat stepped up first. "You my city homie, but I'ma pop your ass this Week 6."

Brian smirked. "I'm here for all the smoke!"

ATL Fat laughed. "For sure. You heard they picked Black Boy up?"

"Yeah," Brian said. "Good dude. Hope his past is clean—no guns involved."

"Twenty of them things," ATL Fat said, walking off.

Big Hurt came up next. "I'm going to the window this Monday, Jack."

"You better," Brian said. "You've been swinging at air for three weeks straight."

Then came N.O. Ric, holding a half-crushed ticket. "One game keeps killing me."

Brian clapped him on the shoulder. "This week gotta be your week."

Temptation, Transition & Trust

Outside those walls, old players like Cowboy and Jonny weren't waiting for Brian to come home—they were already strategizing around him, like he was a chess piece that belonged to *them*. But what they didn't understand was that Brian wasn't anyone's pawn anymore.

He was evolving—deep in thought, deep in purpose. Not immune to the temptations. But stronger now. Sharper. He still had the juice. The respect. The leverage.

The streets were watching. The players were circling.

But Brian?

Brian was preparing for a new kind of war.

CHAPTER 16

The soft hum of conversation filled Precious' living room, where the girls—Pairs and Malin—were curled up on the couch, talking in that teenage tone that danced between playful and painfully real. No phones in their hands, no music playing—just words, eye contact, and dreams unfolding.

"Sis," Pairs asked, tilting her head, "who would you stay with if you had to choose—Mom or Dad?"

Malin thought for a second. "I'd go back and forth."

"I'd stay with Dad," Pairs replied quickly, "but visit Mom often."

Malin turned to her sister with a sly smirk. "Are you still a virgin?"

Pairs blushed, but kept it honest. "Yeah. But Pac Man almost had me. The only thing that stopped us was he didn't have protection."

"I can't believe you let it get that far."

"Pac Man is gonna be my husband," Pairs said confidently. "He's going to the NBA, and we're going to the same college."

Malin raised her brow. "You're only sixteen. You know how much can change in just one year? Five years from now? No telling what'll happen."

Pairs shrugged. "We're in love. That's what it's going to be."

Changing the subject, Malin lit up. "Lil B said he's got some new shoes for us. I can't wait till he brings them."

Pairs leaned in again, her voice softer. "How do you feel about Cory? You like him?"

Malin shrugged. "He's alright. He's not Dad."

"Right. But he's nice to Mom, buys her things, and looks like he makes her happy."

Malin nodded. "Yeah… for now."

In the trap house, the energy was different—raw, hungry, and loud. The kitchen table was covered in food containers, sauce-stained napkins, and loud conversations. Lil B, Lil Eazy, Mike Mike, and Cam were mid-meal and mid-strategy, locked in like brothers before battle.

"Man," Cam said, licking his fingers, "Sis can cook her ass off."

"Hell yeah," Lil B agreed. "These oxtails, rice, and black-eyed peas—banging. We might need to open a restaurant."

"For real," Lil Eazy said with his mouth full. "I don't even *eat* peas, but all this fire. And the cornbread—oh my God."

"Told y'all," Mike Mike said, leaning back. "Bre got down in the kitchen like her name Annie Mae."

Lil B pushed his plate aside, serious now. "We 'bout to head over to Al's—see what he got going on. I think our big break 'bout to happen."

Lil Eazy raised his glass. "A run in the making. Let's make a toast—to us. Let no man separate what we are building. We bros for life. Money over everything."

They clinked their glasses. Cam rolled up a few blunts. Lil B filled bookbags with cash. Mike Mike was texting a play, and Lil Eazy was on the phone, already plotting the next move.

At the WIC store, business was booming like any legit corner hustle. Precious stood behind the counter with Roxy, both working with precision and speed. Customers came in, handed over cards, and walked out with cash and dignity.

"What's the count for the day?" Precious asked.

Roxy checked the register. "$4,500. Can't lie, girl—I've been thinking about stacking my money and opening one up myself. This is a win-win."

Precious smiled, already proud. "Work here for six months, and the next one we do together."

Roxy lit up. "I like that. Thanks, friend. You are the best."

Precious turned, placing a few bills in the drawer. "You always come through for me. Had my back, gave me a shoulder to cry on. Sister for life."

In the car, smoke curled from a blunt as Toni and Charlie Mo sat still, watching the street, eyes scanning but minds spinning.

"Man," Toni said, voice tight, "we gotta get Lil Eazy and them. That's all I think about."

"Yeah," Charlie Mo agreed. "For Unk. They think they making noise. We'll see."

Toni stared through the windshield, stone-faced. "Let's head to Sis' house—see what she got going on."

Charlie chuckled. "Hell, I wanna see them bad females who are always around. I want Amy's white ass."

Toni shook his head. "Cuz, I'm ready to get some real money. Selling dope ain't it for me anymore."

Back in the federal prison TV room, the mood was heavier— wiser. Brian, Jeff, Joe, and OG sat around a table. OG and Joe focused on chess while others played poker nearby. The space was segregated in its own way—Mexicans in one group, whites in another, Blacks holding their corner. The television mumbled in the background, mostly ignored.

Brian leaned forward, voice low but sharp. "That crack law is crazy as hell. How can five grams of crack get you more time than five hundred grams of powder?"

Joe scoffed. "They know *we are the* ones selling crack. Whites? Mostly selling powder."

Brian nodded. "Yeah, but crack comes *from* powder. Just feels like they sit around brainstorming ways to keep us locked up."

OG jumped in, his voice filled with fire. "America was built on the Black man's back. They're scared we'll take their women. Scared of our strength. They know when we ruled Egypt, we were gods—building pyramids without tools they still can't recreate today."

Brian rubbed his chin. "You gotta learn the game to play the game. Only problem is… they move the goalpost every time we get close."

The room fell into silence for a moment, the weight of those words hovering like smoke.

****: Legacy, Lies & Loyalty**

Brian was growing sharper by the day—less reactive, more reflective. Precious was stepping into her own power. Bre was quietly earning her respect. Even Lil Eazy and Lil B were beginning to recognize that what they were building had weight—had the potential to last if they didn't fumble it.

But tension was mounting. Toni and Charlie Mo weren't just watching. They were circling. Calculating.

And the game?

The game doesn't wait.

INT. PRISON SHOWERS – DAY

Steam swirled in the tight shower room like smoke rising off a battlefield. It clung to the walls, heavy and hot, blurring outlines and softening sharp edges. Inside the mist, life continued in its own coded rhythm.

One inmate sat on a bucket in the corner, a makeshift barber giving him a low fade with a buzzing contraband clipper. Another hunched over a mop bucket, scrubbing clothes with institutional soap, hands raw and methodical. A group of men shared cigarettes and rolled-up weed, the scent thick and unmistakable.

And tucked near the back, a crew worked quietly—brewing jailhouse hooch in soda bottles, one man always standing watch, scanning the fog for guards.

Brian stood still beneath the falling stream, his eyes half-lidded, head tilted back, water running down his face like the weight of memory. His muscles were tense, but his soul felt heavier.

BRIAN (V.O.)

The little things matter.

Just taking a hot shower in peace... It's priceless.

It's crazy how we risk everything for money—yet, here, you'd give every dime just to get out.

How we use our time... that's the most valuable thing we got. So many waste it. Doing time ain't the worst part. It's what you do with your time that really matters.

He dragged his hands through his hair, water dripping down to his shoulders. The water washed over him, but it couldn't touch the weight he carried inside. No soap in the world could rinse regret.

INT. AL'S WORK SPOT – DAY

Stacks of cash lined the table like trophies of a war not yet won. Rubber bands, scales, and weight surrounded AL and Bo like tools of a calculated madness.

AL's voice was clipped, tight with frustration. "Man, I've been calling Ross since last night. Nothing. No answer."

Bo chuckled. "You know how he is—a big freak. Get with them girls, go MIA."

"That's cool," AL said, eyes still on his phone. "But I need that change he owes me. Santiago's waiting on me. First impressions matter."

He looked at the table, at all the money... and yet, it still wasn't enough. Not yet.

"He'll call," Bo said, half-confident. "Probably making something up now."

INT. TERRI'S CONDO – DAY

The condo smelled like money and marijuana. In the soft light filtering through the windows, Terri and Apple stood in their bras and panties, stacks of cash spread across the table like a designer display.

Apple snapped a rubber band around another thick bundle. "$100,000, bitch."

Terri leaned on the window frame, her eyes watching the world below. "I bet he had more. Gave that up too easily. But it's cool—a free pick."

Apple strutted into the kitchen. "We need to go shopping. When we popping out with them matching Maseratis? I can't wait."

Terri smirked. "Soon."

INT. AL'S SPOT – DAY

The front door opened. Lil Eazy and Lil B entered, both rubbing their hands like cold couldn't touch them.

"There go my nephews," AL greeted, arms open, "trappers of the year!"

"And you know this, man!" Lil Eazy replied. "What's good? What's the plug talkin' 'bout?"

AL grinned slyly. "Do you love pussy?"

Lil Eazy laughed. "Hell yeah. Only thing that comes before pussy is money."

They all cracked up.

"I need a favor," AL said. "But it'll benefit y'all. I need to use your money upfront. I'm a little short from what I told Santiago I wanted to buy. But I had to make an impression."

Lil B didn't hesitate. "No problem. Hell, you the reason we got it in the first place."

He handed over the bag.

"Cool," AL said, counting. "This about to be a game changer. Santiago got work and great numbers. I'm going down on y'all—doubling the load."

He sorted through the money with precision. This wasn't just business—it was strategy.

INT. TASHA'S HOUSE – DAY

Tasha walked into the den, already raising her voice.

"Y'all run red lights and stop signs," she said, shaking her head. "Slow down. Go get your GED. Get a trade. The streets ain't your friend—they build you up just to tear you down."

Mike Mike sat back, smirking. "Ma, don't worry. We just picking up where Unk left off. Keeping the family business going. It's in our DNA."

Tasha's eyes narrowed. "Boy, you sound like a damn fool. Remember—a hard head makes a soft ass."

Before more could be said, Tara walked in from the kitchen doorway.

"Hope you got some food left," she said.

Tasha softened. "Girl, I fixed you two plates. They are in the Kroger bag. Bre cooked."

Tara's eyes lit up. "Thanks, sis. Bre throws down!"

Mike Mike and Cam breezed by, each planting a kiss on Tara's cheek before darting out the house.

Tara watched them disappear, then turned back to Tasha. "Have you talked to Brian lately?"

"Yesterday."

"Think he's really done with the streets?" Tara asked, her voice a mix of doubt and hope. "I mean, that's all he really knows."

Tasha took a breath. "I believe he's done with drugs. His new lane is sports betting. Being a bookie. That's his hustle now—even inside. And he's making good money."

Tara nodded slowly. "Well, with Brian... where there's a will, he finds a way. He makes gold out of dust. I just hope me and him get on better terms."

Tasha smiled faintly. "He is not mad at you, sis. He's disappointed you didn't follow through with the plan. But like I told him—you are a grown lady now. You make your own decisions."

Decisions & Dividends

The game was tightening, the players picking their corners, their next moves already loaded. Brian, buried in reflection, found peace in the heat of the water. Al was leaning heavy into the Santiago deal, gambling everything for a bigger slice of the pie. Terri and Apple were stacking like queens building a silent empire. Meanwhile, Lil B and Lil Eazy were proving their loyalty, putting faith in the man who gave them the keys.

Back home, the women—Tasha and Tara—were standing in their own truths, raising boys who didn't know how to slow down and wondering about men who might never change.

Everyone had chosen a path. Some clear. Some muddy.

But one truth rang louder than all:

Loyalty pays. But it also costs.

And the bill was coming due

CHAPTER 17

INT. TERRI'S CONDO – DAY

Toni and Charlie Mo stepped into Terri's condo like they owned shares in it. The smell of incense and cash was thick in the air, and so was the energy—powerful, feminine, and expensive. A stack of money was casually sitting on the glass coffee table like it belonged there.

Toni grinned. "Right on time! Sis, I need a loan."

Terri didn't even look up from her phone. "Bro, when do you *not* need a loan that you will never pay back?" She glanced at Charlie Mo. "Hey, Mo."

Toni smiled wider, playing it cute. "Sis, you know I love you. Brought some bad work this time."

Terri rolled her eyes. "That's a new one. So... how much you lose gambling? How much do you need?"

"Ten K," he said quickly. "See? Didn't hurt your pockets too bad."

Terri put her phone down and sat up straighter. "This year, we are going to Daddy's gravesite for the balloon release, right? For his birthday?"

Toni nodded. "Yep, I'll be there."

Just then, Apple walked into the room with a towel wrap around her. Charlie Mo's eyes locked onto her like a magnet—no shame, just hunger.

"What's up, Apple?" Toni said with a smirk, catching the moment and making it awkward on purpose.

Apple winked, sauntering off. She knew the effect she had. And she liked it.

INT. AL'S HOUSE – DAY

Al's phone buzzed on the counter. He picked it up.

"Yeah?" he answered.

Derrick (on phone): "Have you talked to my brother in the last 24 hours?"

Al shook his head. "Nah, been calling him. No answer."

Derrick: "His baby mom hit me—been blowing his line up. He was supposed to come get his son for a haircut. Nothing."

Al's voice got serious. "Something's definitely not right."

"I'm going by his place," Derrick said. "I got an extra key."

"Let me know what's up," Al said, his gut twisting.

INT. PRISON COMMON AREA – DAY

Brian, Turtle, and Jeff sat at a plastic table, locked into a casual game of Scrabble, but the conversation was far from surface-level. Jeff, a white man with a calm demeanor and a mind like a calculator, leaned in as he broke things down.

"Compound interest," Jeff said, "is how you build wealth. It's about making your money work for you—not you working for money."

Brian looked curious. "Tell me more about that. I have been hearing it, but never really understood."

"Have you ever heard that old question?" Jeff asked. "Would you rather get a million dollars up front or a penny doubled every day for 31 days?"

Brian grinned. "Sounds like a trick question. Still—give me the million. I'll flip that like gymnastics."

Jeff smiled. "That's where you'd be wrong. A penny doubled daily for 31 days turns into over lil over 10 million. Do the math."

Turtle leaned forward, intrigued. "Yeah, by day twenty-two, you're already at over 100K. Then it just takes off. That's cold."

"Exactly," Jeff said. "Now picture this—start with $10K, put it in S&P 500 stocks. Add to it every paycheck. Do that for 20 years. You'll hit millions. You might've only put in $250K over time, but compound growth? It builds on itself."

Brian shook his head, lowkey frustrated. "Man… I wish I knew all this years ago. I was too busy burying cash instead of letting it grow."

Jeff nodded. "And that's just one lane. You can pull money out every quarter once you're deep enough in. You can borrow against your stock portfolio, get loans without touching your investments. That's the wealth game. Quiet power. My ancestors' way."

Brian's eyes sharpened. He was listening now. Not just hearing—*listening.*

INT. SANTIAGO'S WAREHOUSE – DAY

The hum of cold air conditioning mixed with the faint scent of chemicals and cash. Santiago sat at a steel desk, cool and calculated. Al placed a thick bag on the table. Santiago pointed to a duffel behind him.

"See you soon," Santiago said with a nod.

They shook hands.

Al turned and loaded the SUV, then hopped into another one parked outside with Bo already behind the wheel.

Al's face was lit with fire. "Man, we're locked and loaded. I just saw *hundreds* of bricks. It's on! We about to go hard in the paint—fuck the city up."

Bo just grinned and hit the gas.

INT. ROSS'S CONDO – DAY

Derrick pushed the door open with caution, stepping into the stillness. He called out once—no answer.

And then he saw him.

Ross. Lifeless. On the floor.

Derrick's heart dropped. He reached for his phone, hands trembling, and made the call.

INT. TERRI'S CONDO – EVENING

The vibe had shifted. The lights were dimmed, tequila poured, smoke in the air. Apple lounged on the couch, a blunt between her fingers, a shot glass in her hand. Four other women were sprawled across the room, already half-lit and smiling.

"It's time we make plans," Apple said. "Hit a resort, get some tans."

Amy, the only white girl in the crew, raised her hand. "I could use a tan to get me through the winter."

The door opened, and Asia walked in like the party had been waiting on her.

"Where's the party at?" she asked, tossing her bag on the table.

April slid her a plate. Not of food—but a plate lined with coke and straws. Asia took a quick hit like it was just part of the dress code.

Then Terri walked in. All eyes shifted.

Dressed in all black Prada, she moved like a boss—heels clicking against the tile, presence undeniable.

"Glad y'all are here," she said. "We have a party tonight. High rollers. Dress sexy. Play the role. Find the mark."

They all raised their glasses and toasted as music flooded the room. The energy shifted. Game time.

Power Moves & Dead Ends

The temperature of the streets was changing. Al had just leveled up—locked in with Santiago and ready to flood the city. But in the shadows, bodies were dropping. Ross was dead. Derrick found him too late, and now a ripple effect was about to begin.

Brian was growing—mentally, financially, spiritually. Every conversation behind bars was a brick in a new foundation. Meanwhile, Terri's circle of women was setting traps with beauty and strategy. They weren't just eye candy—they were bait with brains and teeth.

Tasha was watching her boys drift deeper, knowing the cost. Tara was wrestling with guilt. And Toni? Still broke. Still needing help. Still not ready to change.

Everyone was playing a part.

Some were making moves.

Others were making mistakes.

But all of them were running out of time.

INT. AL'S WORK SPOT – DAY

The room buzzed with low tension. Stacks of money sat like monuments on the table, and the smell of fresh plastic from vacuum-sealed packs hung in the air. But the tone was somber. Al stood with his phone pressed to his ear, pacing slow.

"I just got off the phone with Derrick," he said, voice tight. "He found his brother dead. Only in his boxers. Looks like he got cleaned out—no money, no jewelry, nothing."

Bo, sitting at the edge of the couch, shook his head. "Damn. We gotta start asking around, dig into this. Ross was family. You don't let just anybody get that close."

Al nodded, his jaw clenched. "I bet a female's involved somehow."

Before more could be said, the doorbell rang. Bo answered it to find Lil B and Lil Eazy walking in, all energy and street confidence. Hugs were exchanged, palms slapped with love and respect.

Bo didn't waste time. "They just found Ross dead in his apartment—half-naked."

Lil B's face dropped. "Damn. Any idea who did it?"

"Not yet," Al said. "But I'm not waiting around for detectives. I'm doing my own digging."

Lil Eazy rubbed his hands, changing the subject but clocking the weight in the room. "I see the plug came through. How's it doing in the water?"

Al smirked. "Great. 28 is coming back at 28. Here—ten for y'all. Four already paid for."

Lil B grabbed the work, already thinking plays ahead. "Say less. We are about to be on—buying twenty in no time."

The two younger hustlers dapped up and dipped, their momentum unshaken, even as shadows moved behind the scenes.

INT. RESTAURANT – NIGHT
Tara and Shan sat at the bar, hookah smoke curling through the

air like secrets. Drinks clinked. Music played low. But the conversation was sharp and sober.

"My brother's coming home," Tara said, exhaling a thick cloud. "And we haven't really been talking like that."

"Not Brian mad at his favorite girl," Shan teased.

Tara shook her head, serious now. "Long story short—he gave me money to start a business. Instead, I invested it with my man... bought some bricks."

Shan's eyes widened. "Damn, Tara. That's bold. Disrespectful, too—knowing your brother. He wanted you to clean that money, not flip it in the streets."

"I get it," Tara admitted. "But the route I took worked. We flipped it. Bought two houses—renting one, living in the other. Got cars. I even got money waiting for him."

Shan sipped her drink. "All I can say is, talk to him. He loves you. Y'all'll bounce back."

Tara nodded. "Yeah... but he's serious about not touching drugs anymore. And now that Al just hooked up with a major Mexican plug? Brian could've fit in perfectly. But that's another story."

Shan gave her a look. "Girl, you sound like you are in it to win it. Brian probably wanted y'all to move differently. Now you, Lil B, Mike Mike, Cam, Lil Eazy —y'all deep in the hustle. He might feel like he sacrificed for nothing."

Tara didn't reply. She just exhaled slowly, letting the silence speak.

INT. ROSS'S CONDO – DAY

Yellow tape stretched across the entrance like a final boundary. Inside, detectives snapped photos, lifted fingerprints, and cataloged everything. A lieutenant picked up a framed picture from the table, one of Ross with Al, Bo Lil B, and others.

He slipped it into his pocket.

INT. TONI'S WORK SPOT – DAY

Toni was already moving heavy, his voice full of frustration as he unzipped a bag and inspected the work.

"Man, I hope this batch is better than last time. 28 was coming back 22. That almost took me out of the game."

G Mack raised his eyebrows. "Why didn't you hit me? I would've straightened it out." He handed over a zip. "Here—extra. On me."

Toni nodded. "I had to move it to people who don't cook. Couldn't risk it coming back short again."

G Mack leaned in. "You hear about Ross getting killed? In his condo. They say he was shot twice. I gotta find a new plug. Ross was cool."

Toni blinked. "Damn. I ain't even heard about that. I ain't really know him though."

G Mack added, "He ran with Al and them."

Toni's face turned cold. "Well, you know I don't mess with them suckers anyway. Long-standing family beef."

He dipped out, heart steady, but thoughts racing.

INT. PRISON YARD – DAY

The weight room echoed with bags filled with dirt and low murmurs of game being shared between sets. Brian spotted up on a bench, pressing heavily while the conversation moved from muscle to money.

"I've been reading up on compound interest," Brian said, racking the bar. "It's how you make money in your sleep."

Joe nodded. "We grew up thinking shoe boxes, safe deposit boxes, or the ground were good places for money."

ATL Money added, "But rich folks say money that's sitting is *dead*. Waiting to fly away or get lost."

Brian grabbed a towel, wiping sweat from his brow. "That's why assets matter. Things that grow. Stocks. Real estate. Stuff that makes your money work for *you*."

Jeff chimed in from a nearby incline bench. "Look at the Federal Reserve. They got America by the nuts. Every ten grand you deposit? They can loan out *a hundred* of that."

Brian raised an eyebrow.

Jeff continued, "And most people think the government owns the Fed. Wrong. It's privately owned—by the Rothschilds, Rockefellers, JP Morgan, and a few more. They control interest rates. They can flip the economy like a light switch."

Joe looked stunned. "Wait, what?"

Jeff nodded. "Read *The Creature from Jekyll Island*. It's all in there. That's where the Fed was born—off the Georgia coast, in secret."

Turtle shook his head. "Man, y'all talking above my pay grade. Y'all keep this up, the CFR, Bilderberg Group, and Jason Society gon' knock y'all off for spreading all this secret knowledge."

They all laughed. But Brian didn't.

He was filing it all away—building new blueprints while doing reps. Freedom wasn't just physical. It was financial, mental, and generational.

Pressure, Principle & Power Shifts

The weight of Ross's death sent tremors through the circle. Al and Bo were scrambling for answers while pushing forward with a massive deal. Lil B and Lil Eazy didn't skip a beat—but under the surface, loyalty and legacy were being tested.

Tara, deep in a game she once swore she'd avoid, sat on the line between independence and betrayal. Brian's absence loomed large, and she knew it.

Meanwhile, behind bars, Brian was building. Not with bricks, but with books. With dialogue. With insight. He was turning knowledge into capital—and preparing to come home *different*.

And while bodies dropped, deals formed, and fortunes shifted—one truth became clear:

The streets were evolving. And so was the war.

CHAPTER 18

INT. LIL B AND LIL EAZY'S HOUSE – NIGHT

The house pulsed with bass and laughter. The air was thick with the smell of Hennessy, weed, and body spray. Lil EAZY, Lil B, Mike Mike, and Cam lounged with seven girls scattered between laps, couches, and the floor. They were in the middle of a drinking game—some version of "Never Have I Ever" or Truth or Dare—with one rule: if you lose, you take a shot.

The room echoed with cheers and groans as someone downed their third shot in a row. Cam was already leaning back, giggling with two girls whispering in his ears, while Mike Mike fake-grimaced and knocked another shot back.

Lil Eazy slapped the table. "Don't tap out now! We are just getting started!"

Laughter filled the house, but underneath all the noise, the energy was clear—business was good, spirits were high, and the trap was running smoothly.

EXT. PARK AND RIDE – DAY

Tasha and Bre sat in the parked car, engine running, windows cracked. The sun was beating gently on the windshield, but the mood inside was all business.

Tasha looked over, tone direct but warm. "Bre, you're 23. What are your plans? You're smart, creative, and a hard worker."

Bre gave a small smile. "I love investing in stocks. Uncle Brian's been showing me the way. And Mommy and I love cooking. One day, I want to open a restaurant."

Tasha nodded, impressed. "You definitely got the touch. Your seasoning? Next level. But stocks? Baby, that's still considered a white man's game."

At that moment, a car pulled up beside them. Tasha glanced over and straightened up.

"That's her."

The door opened, and a correctional officer stepped out in plain clothes.

"Wander?" Tasha asked through the window.

"Yes," the woman replied.

"Hey. I'm Tasha. Get in."

Wander climbed into the backseat.

Tasha reached into a bag. "Here's your money, the tickets, and the package for bro."

Wander nodded. "OK. Thanks."

As they were about to pull off, Bre side-eyed the rearview.

"Ma... she works at the jail, right?"

Tasha smirked. "Yep. You know Brian—always got something up his sleeve."

INT. LIL B'S TRAP HOUSE – DAY

The table looked like a mini cartel setup. Bags of weight, scales, bundles of cash, and pre-rolled blunts. Lil B and Lil Eazy sat across from each other, focused and dialed in.

Lil B leaned in. "The world's in trouble now. We got a real plug. He put us in *position*."

Lil Eazy lit his blunt and blew smoke. "We are about to be on some real big shit. The *new and improved* Easy and Brian. Put your money where your mouth is, Jack."

Mike Mike stumbled in, holding his head. "Man... I got a hangover that feels like death."

Cam laughed from the couch. "Nobody told you to take all them damn shots last night."

Mike Mike groaned. "Man, I was trying to keep up with them girls. Should've known better."

EXT. PARK – DAY

The local park was full of life—kids running drills in football pads, parents chatting from their folding chairs or waiting in cars. Cory stood in the middle of the field, blowing his whistle, commanding the space.

"Run two laps!" he shouted. "Last one, give me ten push-ups!"

As the kids took off, Cory and TA made their way toward the stands. Ashley was sitting there, arms crossed, watching Boston and Mal run.

Cory gave a little smile. "I was thinking of coming over... We need to talk."

Ashley didn't even look at him. "Cory, we have nothing to talk about."

"So you're really cutting me off like that?"

"Yep. It's time I move forward."

Boston and Mal ran up just then, interrupting the tension.

"Mom, can we go to Wendy's?" Boston asked.

Ashley shut it down quickly. "Boy, I already cooked."

Cory smiled. "What do you cook, Mom?"

"Meatloaf."

Cory's eyes lit up. "My favorite."

Boston tugged his arm. "You coming over, Coach?"

Cory's smile faded. "Not tonight."

The kids ran off. Ashley didn't say a word. Cory just watched her, knowing the door was closing—and fast.

INT. LIL EAZY'S TRAP HOUSE – NIGHT

The trap was quiet but energized. Lil Eazy, Lil B, Mike Mike, and Cam sat around discussing moves over open bags and glowing ashtrays.

Mike Mike leaned back. "Man, we just went *ham*! The streets love the new work and numbers."

Lil Eazy nodded. "I gotta agree. This is only the beginning. Time to spread our wings—new territory, new cash."

Lil B was already there. "Great minds think alike. We need some of that Bankhead money."

Lil Eazy shook his head. "Bro, you are thinking local. I'm talking *globally*. The world's our attitude."

Mike Mike grinned. "Well, I think I'll drink a cold one and look at some hot ones."

Cam laughed. "Which strip club are you hitting, bro?"

"Blue Flame," Mike Mike said, standing.

Lil Eazy stood too. "I got a hot date with Leah tonight."

Lil B stayed seated, locking eyes with Cam. "Y'all dip. Me and Cam'll hold it down here."

Business never slept. And neither did ambition.

Vision & Vices

Every scene played like a different room in the same mansion—the trap boys celebrating their growing empire, Bre laying quiet bricks toward a future in stocks and food, Tasha handling business with the precision of a seasoned general.

But behind every celebration, there was pressure. Behind every play, a risk. The women held the glue. The men pushed the weight. The kids? They were watching everything.

And Brian?

Still orchestrating it all from a cell, stacking knowledge like bricks, and betting on minds instead of muscles.

One thing was clear:

The empire was expanding. But so was the target on their backs.

INT. CUBE CELL – NIGHT

The prison dorm buzzed with late-night noise—metal clinks, low conversations, and the hum of TVs behind sheets used as curtains. But in Brian's cube, it was strategy hour.

Brian leaned back on his bunk, a deck of parlay tickets and paperwork spread out across his lap. Von, seated on the plastic chair beside him, looked at him with admiration and curiosity.

"You pulled a real rabbit out of the hat, B," Von said, shaking his head.

Brian cracked a half-smile. "Always remember—we walk down the hill and fuck *all* the pussy. It's not what you know, Von... it's *who* you know."

Von laughed, leaning forward. "What are you selling them phones for? That's the hottest commodity on the compound."

Brian sat up, speaking low but sharp. "I'm only dealing with three people. Selling eight phones for four racks apiece. Letting you rent two of 'em out for $25 an hour. And I'm pushing a carton of cigs for $2,500."

Von's eyes popped. "B, you're giving it away at them prices! Phones go for seventy-five hundred easy. And one pack of cigs costs a grand."

Brian looked unbothered. "How's that giving it away? I spent $2,500 for the mule, $2,500 for ten phones, and $600 for ten cartons. You do the math. But more important than profit? I'm making sure the *team* eats. If you play it right—only deal with the two people I linked you with—when I'm gone, you'll be able to move lowkey and still eat until you go home."

Von shook his head in awe. "Man, you surprise me every day. How you move in silence... all chess moves."

Brian nodded once. "Only way."

INT. RESTAURANT – NIGHT

The restaurant buzzed with conversation, sports highlights flickering on flat screens, and hookah smoke dancing in the air. Lil Easy and Leah sat at the bar, drinks in hand, low lighting wrapping them in intimacy.

"Who's your favorite team?" Lil Eazy asked, sipping from his glass.

Leah blew out a thick cloud of smoke. "Dirty Birds all day, every day—win or lose."

Lil Eazy raised his eyebrows. "Oh, you a fan-fan."

"All day," she confirmed proudly. "So, what do you do for a living?"

Lil Eazy smirked. "I'ma keep it real—I'm a hustler. I got it out of the mud."

Leah's face stayed neutral, but her eyes sharpened. "I don't judge. But I like to know what I'm getting into. Glad you told the truth so I can make my own choice."

Lil Eazy leaned in slightly. "So, what's your choice? You rocking with me or what? 'Cause I'm really into you. You all I think about lately."

Leah laughed softly, tilting her head. "I'm sure you have plenty in your stable. You're too confident. But to answer your question—yeah, I'm rocking with you. I like your style. I like your honesty."

Lil Eazy looked impressed. "What about your pops?"

"He'll be alright," she said with a shrug. "What else have you got planned for us tonight?"

Lil Eazy grinned. "Have you ever been to amateur night at the Blue Flame?"

Leah's eyes widened. "I've never even been to a strip club."

"Never?" he asked, half-joking. "Oh yeah—that's where we are going."

"Can I invite my girls?" Leah asked, excited now. "They'll kill me if I go without them. We have been planning to go."

"Cool," Lil Eazy said. "I'll hit up a few of my bros."

The night was young, and the vibes were just beginning to cook.

INT. KK'S HOUSE – NIGHT

The house smelled like fresh air freshener, weed, and perfume. Al walked in like he owned the place—because he did, in a way. He handed KK's mom a bottle of vodka and a bag of loud.

"Thanks, AL," she said, grinning. "Don't know how you knew, but I was out of *everything*."

"No problem," he replied coolly. "You know I got you."

KK walked in, her eyes sparkling. "Where are my treats?"

Al smiled, pulling her close. "Don't worry—you gon' get yours."

KK poured drinks, and they walked into the den, leaving her mom to enjoy her vices.

"Long, busy day," Al said as he settled into the couch. "Good, but long."

KK climbed onto his lap with a mischievous look. "Don't worry, Daddy. I'm about to relieve some of that tension."

"You always do," he said, eyes heavy. "Can't wait."

She looked up at him, serious now. "You for real? You'll get me my own place if I let my son stay with his dad?"

Al stared her in the eyes. "You know I don't play. Just keep me happy. Don't ever try to compete with Tara—and I'll make sure you're straight."

KK nodded eagerly. "Yes, Daddy. All I wanna do is keep you happy."

Al sipped his drink, lit up, and leaned back as KK slowly knelt in front of him start giving him head

Leverage & Loyalty

Moves were being made from all angles. Behind prison walls, Brian operated like a general—feeding his soldiers, building an exit plan, and ensuring Von had a lane once he left. It wasn't just about survival. It was about legacy.

Lil Eazy was evolving too—testing honesty, vulnerability, and trust with a woman who came from power. But even that had its risks. One wrong move with Leah, and he could find himself under scrutiny from more than just her father.

Al, meanwhile, was living in excess—balancing KK and Tara like a man juggling fire. The loyalty he demanded was heavy, conditional, and transactional.

But for each of them, one truth loomed:

Power comes with pressure. And pressure exposes character.

CHAPTER 19

EXT. OUTSIDE CLUB – NIGHT

The parking lot was chaotic—cars double-parked, people pre-gaming on hoods, a long line stretching from the door to the end of the sidewalk. It was the kind of night that felt alive before you even stepped inside.

Lil Eazy strolled up like he owned the building. Leah was by his side, flawless in a two-piece dress, with three of her girls trailing behind her—all heels, hair, and heat. Heads turned. Whispers followed.

Lil Eazy reached into his pocket and peeled off a few bills, handing them smoothly to the security guard.

The guard nodded and parted the rope. "VIP treatment. Go ahead."

Inside, the music was blasting, the crowd hyped, and an amateur performer was mid-twerk on stage while the host cracked jokes over the mic, keeping the energy high.

A waitress walked over, recognizing the power walk.

LIL EAZY (Turning to the waitress) "Take us to the VIP."

As they moved through the crowd, Lil Eazy dapped up everyone he knew. Half the club seemed to be someone he'd done business with. G Mack stopped him with a firm handshake.

G MACK "Hey, I heard about Ross. I used to shop with him heavily. I need a new plug."

LIL EAZY (Confidently) "For sure. Come to the VIP, have some drinks. Let's chop it up."

Leah and her friends exchanged curious glances. They were starting to see what "hustler" really meant.

As they entered VIP, hands tried grabbing at the girls—strangers taking liberties. Leah pulled her arm away quickly, her eyes sharp.

Lil Easy turned his head but kept walking. He wasn't about to cause a scene—yet.

EXT. RENTED HOUSE – NIGHT

Elsewhere in the city, a different kind of party was in motion.

Inside a suburban rented house, a PJ party was in full swing. Guys in polos and business-casual slacks mixed with girls in lingerie, booty shorts, and robes barely tied. The music was vibing, weed smoke swirled in the air, and two hookahs hissed from the corners. On the kitchen counter—coke lines and half-empty bottles of tequila.

Terri sat on the armrest of a leather chair, watching like a queen pin overseeing her court.

TERRI "We have to play our cards right. These guys tonight? All 9-to-5 business owners. All we have to do is give them a good time."

APPLE "I told the girls—don't be too aggressive. Let the guys be touchy-feely first."

TERRI (Laughing) "Just don't let Amy get too drunk or high. You know how she gets."

APPLE "You did good by bringing in other girls for the tricking."

TERRI "Wait until the weed, cocaine, and alcohol kick in. The show they're about to put on? These guys won't know what hit 'em."

She grinned, watching the energy of the room turn from party... to opportunity.

INT. CLUB – NIGHT

Back at the club, the energy was electric.

Leah's friends were lost in the vibe, getting lap dances and giggling, while Lil Eazy made it rain from the VIP section. Ones fluttered through the air like confetti as strippers danced in sync with the pounding bass. The DJ shouted Lil Eazy out over the mic, bringing attention straight to their section.

By the bar, Toni and Charlie Mo were observing. Silent. Calculated.

CHARLIE MO (Spotting someone) "That your man G Mack with Lil Eazy. Toni, look."

TONI (Smirking) "That's him over there. Look at him, chillin' with that lame."

CHARLIE MO "We need to touch him up. He's running with the OOPS now."

TONI "You might be right."

Their eyes locked on the VIP like snipers behind enemy lines.

Suddenly, the host grabbed the mic and stopped the music.

HOST "Hold up, hold up! Frank-O just gave me $50 to slap Peaches' ass as hard as he can!"

The crowd roared. Peaches strutted to the stage in a G-string and turned around, presenting her cheek with a grin. Frank-O stepped up, wound up, and SMACK!—the sound echoed across the club.

Gasps. Laughter. Mouths covered. Some stood up out of their seats.

Lil Eazy used the moment.

LIL EAZY "Everybody in here, grab a shot glass! We are about to get lit!"

The waitress moved fast, handing out shot glasses to everyone in VIP. Lemons. Salt. Liquor. The crowd leaned in.

MIKE MIKE (Raising his glass) "Raise your glass!"

LIL EAZY "Three, two, one!"

Cheers. Shots. Shouts.

The strippers clapped cheeks to the beat, and the DJ screamed over the speakers:

DJ "They know how to party over there—Lil EAZY and crew!"

From across the room, Toni and Charlie Mo mean-mugged the whole section. Plotting. Burning.

INT. RENTED HOUSE – NIGHT

The scene had evolved. The living room was now a grown-up jungle—lap dances happening in corners, girls sitting on laps, talking games, or whispering in ears. Music played low, creating that seductive buzz between business and pleasure.

In the back bedroom, three girls—one White, one Black, one Asian—were with two corporate white guys. Laughs, drinks, and things better left to the imagination.

Billy, in a silk robe, walked back out into the living room, adjusting his collar.

BILLY (Taking a drink) "Terri, you're really showing my bosses a good time. Big bonus coming my way… which means a bonus for you too."

Terri raised an eyebrow, half-smiling.

TERRI "I told you I have your back. I got the best party girls in town. But Billy—why didn't you say a big bonus for me?"

Billy smirked. "You know I have your best interests at heart. And this? This is just the beginning. Plenty more coming your way."

Terri stepped close, her energy calm but commanding.

TERRI "Don't disappoint me."

Billy gulped the rest of his drink. He wouldn't dare.

Influence, Image & Enemies While Lil Eazy played king of the club, Terri was quietly building an empire off the desires of rich men who wanted to escape their straight-laced lives. Each play was calculated. Each conversation is a transaction. Each move—profitable.

But shadows were forming.

Toni and Charlie Mo weren't just watching. They were studying. Waiting. Jealousy brewing with every shot taken and every dollar thrown.

Brian might've been locked up—but the moves his circle was making had real-world consequences.

And in this game?

Attention is power. But power makes you a target.

CHAPTER 20

The sun cut through the narrow prison window like a blade, landing across the tile floor of Brian's cube. He leaned back on his bunk, cool and collected, but always calculating. Von sat across from him, legs bouncing, notebook in hand.

"I'm betting five grand on today's softball game," Brian said. "Super Dave thinks we're sweet. But watch this—pass out the new cleats right before the game starts. Let 'em see us clean, organized, ready. They'll be defeated before the first pitch."

"You're playing mind games," Von replied.

"Chess moves only."

Just then, ATL Fat approached the cube with urgency. He and Brian dapped up.

"B, when are you going back straight?" ATL Fat asked. "I can't keep those phones—they move like hotcakes."

"Any time now," Brian said. "I told you—we control the market with those numbers and still walk away with clean profit."

"Word is, the Mexicans are trying to drop their prices. Gotta keep 'em in a chokehold."

Brian gave a knowing smirk.

"Eazy always told me—when you create the market, you control the game. Checkmate."

Money covered the table like a new layer of wallpaper—rubber-banded stacks, half-counted piles, digital scales, and a quiet TV in the background showing the news on mute. Bo and Al were halfway through counting when something on the screen caught Al's eye.

"I can't believe nobody on the street's hasn't said a word about who killed Ross," Al said. "I put out ten grand for info."

"Strange," Bo said. "We usually hear something by now."

Al exhaled and leaned back, eyes sharp.

"Man, we ran through those forty packs fast. Santiago liked that. I paid for twenty, he gave me fifty. We're on our way—to the top."

Just then, the garage door creaked open. Lil B and Lil Eazy stepped in, both with oversized bookbags. They dropped them on the table—money spilling out like a waterfall of paper.

"That's how y'all young fellas feelin'? Love the energy," Al said, laughing.

"We got them noddin' off and throwin' up," Lil B said. "The SWAT's ours now."

The room buzzed with momentum. The empire was expanding by the hour.

The sun beat down on the concrete, but spirits were high. Precious, Cory, TA, JP, and Tammy stood outside a row of worn-down houses with faded siding and crooked porches. They passed around a sheet of property listings, marking prices and scribbling notes.

"Most of these houses are going for under fifty grand—depending on the rehab. Couple of 'em are fifteen," Precious said.

"Fifteen K? Wow, I never would have thought you could be buying a house in the 2000's in Atlanta," Cory replied.

"They really crashed the market," TA added. "We need to scoop as many as we can. This feels like Monopoly in real life."

"We'll set up a trust. Buy under an LLC, then put the LLC in the trust. That way, we're protected three times over," Precious explained.

"Bet. Pull the numbers for those ten. Let's break down the renovation costs and get to work," Cory said.

They didn't just see rundown houses. They saw legacy. And freedom.

Tasha sat behind the wheel of her car, engine running. Black Rick sat shotgun. Three women filled the back seat, each dressed casually but clean—no one wanting to draw attention. It was all business.

"We're going five minutes apart. Inside—we don't know each other. Don't make eye contact," Tasha instructed.

"Why do we gotta act like strangers?" Tina asked.

"Stop acting slow," Black Rick cut in. "People get suspicious. Think we runnin' a scam, and then—bam—police."

Vanessa got out first and headed toward the Western Union entrance. Tina followed two minutes later.

"Your brother's a genius with this. You think he'd put me on when he gets out?" Rick asked.

"You drink too much," Tasha said. "You get drunk and act like a fool. Brian doesn't move with liabilities. Just get your $250, Rick."

"I'm just sayin'—I can change. Put in a word for me."

Tasha didn't answer. She just stared forward, waiting for her cue.

The bleachers were packed, the buzz of side bets and side-eyes filling the air. The Supreme Team stood out immediately. Von and Big Chunk were passing out brand-new cleats, and heads were turning.

Brian stood by the dugout, calm, arms folded.

"The key? Stay away from drugs. That's what brings heat. Phones and cigarettes—you can make six figures clean here," he said.

"I'm following your lead, B. You ain't missed yet," ATL Fat replied.

Joe leaned in, whispering. "Words are brewing. They say Twin's hot. And claims Crip, but it's been over thirty days and no paperwork."

"He should've checked in. That's protocol," Brian said.

"He thinks he is tough. Burpees and dips got him feeling Superman. Might go down after the game."

Von walked up, holding a folded sheet and a bundle of stamps.

"Here. $3,700 in bets—names, amounts, and how they wanna get paid," Von said.

Brian took it, looking it over like a CEO reviewing quarterly earnings.

"They really believe."

Brian's grip was tightening, not just on the yard—but on his legacy. He wasn't just making plays. He was setting systems in place. He was teaching Von and ATL Fat how to build, not just hustle. He was showing them how to eat without drawing heat, how to make power plays with strategy, not ego.

Al's empire was growing in kind. Between Santiago's plug and the SWAT neighborhood folding, he and his nephews were stacking like kings—but not without shadows creeping. Ross's silence still echoed through the streets, and Al's gut told him it wasn't over.

In the free world, Precious and Cory were flipping real estate plays into long-term wealth, building trust structures the same way Brian built loyalty behind walls. And Tasha? She was moving like a capo—smart, silent, and surgical.

But the winds were shifting. Tensions were brewing. And enemies were watching.

Because in every empire—someone's always plotting.

Hidden Lines & Softball Wars

INT. TARA'S HOUSE – EVENING

Tara stood in front of the mirror, adjusting her earrings with a confident smirk. Her hair was laid, outfit hugging all the right curves. Her phone buzzed on the dresser.

TARA "Hello?"

TASHA (voice crackling through) "Hey, sis. What are you getting into? I'm bored and need to get out—me and a couple of the girls."

TARA "Me, Shan, and April are hitting the happy hour and karaoke at Smoke Room. Allen's over at Al's mom's."

TASHA "Say less. I'll be there. I think Tina and Vanessa want to come too."

TARA "Cool. We got a table already. Hookahs, drinks, and drama—what more could you ask for?"

INT. WANDER WHITE'S APARTMENT – DAY

The apartment was filled with the light clatter of kids playing in the next room. Wander White and Janelle sat at the kitchen table, red cups in hand, the air thick with whispered truths and unsaid worries.

JANELLE "Girl, Jimbo got me all the way fuck up. Behind on child support, have behind on my car note—I'm thinking of hiding my ride at your place for a minute till I figure this out."

Wander leaned in, her eyes locking with Janelle's like a vault closing.

WANDER WHITE "I'm about to tell you something. But it stays between us. I mean graveyard type."

JANELLE "You know me and you already got secrets we takin' to the dirt."

WANDER WHITE (stands) "This one's heavier. Follow me."

They walked to the bedroom. Wander opened her nightstand and pulled out three thick stacks.

WANDER WHITE "How much do you owe?"

JANELLE (blinking) "With interest? $2,500."

Wander handed over the money like it was light work. No hesitation. Just family.

INT. SMOKE ROOM – NIGHT

The atmosphere sizzled—live band vibing, hookahs flowing, drinks clinking. The table was full: Tara, April, Shan, Tasha, Tina, and Vanessa all deep in girl talk, laughter breaking out between puffs and sips. The energy was feminine and powerful, the kind of evening that recharges souls and strengthens bonds.

Tara wasn't just out—she was reclaiming space, celebrating herself in the midst of chaos and money moves.

INT. JP'S WIC STORE – DAY

Cory pushed through the door, dap-ready as always. JP stood by the front, posted like a boss in his own right. Imani was behind the counter, running cards like clockwork, cash slipping out like an ATM on overdrive.

They stepped into the office.

JP "Bro, you saved me. This game you put me on? I'm seeing more now than I ever did in the streets. Moving weight"

CORY "We've been tight since third grade, bro. When you came home, I wasn't gonna watch you crash out. This WIC hustle? It's clean. Smart. And most importantly—safe."

JP pulled a small box from his drawer and handed it over.

JP "To show my respect—take this."

Cory opened it. A Rolex. No words. Just smiles.

INT. WANDER WHITE'S APARTMENT – EVENING

JANELLE (laughing) "You've been showing out. You meet a baller or something?"

WANDER WHITE "Something better."

She leaned in.

WANDER WHITE "I've been smuggling phones and cigarettes in for Brian. He pays me $2,500 a trip. Plus tips. Real tips."

Janelle's eyes widened.

JANELLE "You?! Miss. Play-it-safe? Damn, they need a second mule? 'Cause I got bills, and doing the right thing ain't doing enough."

Wander smirked.

WANDER WHITE "Stick with me. I'll plug you in."

EXT. SOFTBALL FIELD – DAY

It was game time. The crowd buzzed like a casino floor. Bets flying. Pressure rising.

The scoreboard glowed: 7-7. Last inning. Brian's team had its last at-bat.

Von moved through the crowd like a bookie in motion, collecting bets and passing out folded slips.

BRIAN (to his squad) "Compound interest! Compound interest!"

The chant caught on, his crew repeating it like a war cry. "Compound interest!" louder and louder.

The pitcher threw the ball.

Crack.

The bat sent the ball soaring over the fence—two runners on base.

Game.

The field exploded in cheers. Von hugged Brian, fists in the air.

VON "Let's go, B! It's about to go down!"

But then—shifting energy.

A quiet signal passed.

A pack of CRIP inmates moved toward another man. Before he could brace, two bodies closed in. Shanks flashed. Blood spilled.

Chaos.

Screams.

The guards didn't move fast enough. By the time they noticed, the yard had already cleared.

Blood was left behind.

**

Loyalty, Lessons, and Limits

In every empire, the bricks are laid by those who understand timing.

Brian was teaching more than betting—he was schooling men on the economy of war, the art of presence, the science of silence. Whether it was compound interest or compound control, he had it figured out.

Meanwhile, the women—Tasha, Tara, Wander, and even Janelle—were finding their power in the margins. Some clean, some not, but all calculated.

Al's team was moving weight. Cory's was buying real estate. But while some were stacking bread, others were stacking bodies.

The streets never rest.

Because when money, loyalty, and ego mix—blood always follows.

CHAPTER 21

SMOKE, PAPERWORK, AND PERFECT SETUPS

EXT. SMOKE ROOM – NIGHT

The crowd inside the Smoke Room was alive—hookahs glowing, drinks flowing, laughter thick in the air like perfume. On stage, Vanessa held the mic, belting out "I'm Going Down" like it was her personal therapy session. The room roared with cheers, Tasha leading the applause like a proud auntie.

Moments later, April stepped up with her drink in hand and selected Lauryn Hill's "Ex-Factor." As her soulful voice cut through the haze, everyone raised glasses in quiet respect.

Back at the table, the girls leaned in close, the night wrapping them in that familiar, dangerous warmth of freedom.

TASHA "Girl, I can't lie—I'm feelin' some type of way. I'm gonna call Black Rick tonight, scoop him on my way in."

VANESSA (laughing) "I met somebody at the bar. He's comin' home with me."

TASHA "No, you didn't. The bar pick-up working for you tonight?"

VANESSA "They are the best. No strings attached. I give a fake name and a wrong number—every time."

They cackled like teenagers sneaking out.

A man approached.

GUY FROM THE BAR "Michelle, you ready?"

VANESSA (turning smooth) "Yes, Dan. Just had to grab my pocketbook."

TASHA (trying not to choke on her drink) "That girl don't miss."

INT. FBI HEADQUARTERS – DAY

Agent Schwartz stood in front of Captain Agent Hill's desk, holding a manila folder fat with heat.

AGENT SCHWARTZ "Look at this, Boss."

CAPT. AGENT HILL "What am I looking at?"

AGENT SCHWARTZ "Six WIC stores in metro Atlanta. Typically, a store pulls in maybe ten grand monthly, tops. These are ranked in thirty to fifty. Each."

CAPT. AGENT HILL "What brought this up?"

AGENT SCHWARTZ "The welfare department flagged the numbers."

CAPT. AGENT HILL (sitting upright) "Send someone in. Scope the business flow. Ownership?"

AGENT SCHWARTZ "Two are linked. The other four are different LLCs."

CAPT. AGENT HILL "Keep digging. Build enough for wiretaps and poles. Maybe even plant someone inside."

The silent war had begun.

EXT. TASHA'S CAR – NIGHT

Black Rick hopped into the passenger seat, reeking of whiskey and Red Bull.

BLACK RICK "I knew you were gonna call Daddy. Couldn't resist."

TASHA (deadpan) "Start talking like that again and I'll put you out on this curb."

BLACK RICK "Your loss. I'm Trojan Man — popped a pilled, few shots, I'm powering up tonight going eat that sweet pussy all night then beat you to sleep."

Tasha speechless and Black Rick turned up the radio and started crooning a 112 slow jam like he was on stage at the Apollo. Tasha shook her head, fighting a laugh.

INT. TRAP HOUSE – NIGHT

Cam stood in the corner with a mic and passion. His verses bounced off the walls, blending into the smoke and grind of the hustle. Lil Eazy, Mike Mike, Lil B, and three girls vibed with him, heads nodding in unison.

LIL B "Cuz, you got it. You sound better than half of them industry clowns. You need to hit them open mics."

CAM "I've been thinking about it. Big showcase is coming up. Might slide in."

LIL EAZY "That's how Joc, D4L, all these boys did it. Let's make a label. Push you to the top."

MIKE MIKE "I'm down. bra got the bars, we got the bread. Let's go."

INT. BRIAN'S CUBE – NIGHT

Brian leaned back on his bunk, phone in hand. Von sat across, the weight of a bloody yard incident still heavy.

VON "You think dude gonna make it? He got hit badly."

BRIAN "He knew his paperwork was shaky. Should've checked in. I got no sympathy for snitches. Do the crime, do the time."

He dialed.

BRIAN (into phone) "Sis, everything went smooth?"

TASHA (on the line) "Yep. All good. $25K, no hiccups."

Brian smiled.

BRIAN "Cool. Sounds like you and Black Rick having a good time?"

In the background, Black Rick emerged dancing and naked. Tasha laughed.

Brian ended the call, still grinning.

INT. WANDER WHITE'S LOCATION – NIGHT

WANDER WHITE "Hello?"

BRIAN "Are you good for Friday? Macon drop."

WANDER WHITE "Yeah, that works. I got another one who wants in. You said you wanted more."

BRIAN "Perfect. Line her up. You'll get a fat tip for that."

WANDER WHITE "I'll call Tasha tomorrow and set it up."

Brian hung up, his grin turning more calculated.

BRIAN "Things lining up. Double load incoming. Buckle up. Put your shades on—the sun shining on us now."

VON "I ain't the captain, but I'm on this ship. Gotta admit, I'm happy for you—but I'll miss having you here."

BRIAN "Stick to the script. Same people. Same rules. Stay silent, keep moving. This empire runs itself now."

Behind the Smoke, Beneath the Moves The trap house was humming with beats and dreams. The clubs were full of laughter and lust. The WIC play was printing money, and the prison yard was under control. But beneath all the motion—chess. Real moves.

Brian's system was airtight, built not just on hustle, but discipline. Al was stacking through Santiago. Cory and Precious were flipping housing. The ladies—Tasha, Wander, even Janelle—were sliding through cracks, playing roles once reserved for men. The hustle had evolved.

But so had the heat.

The feds were circling, and someone was bound to slip.

Because when everyone eats, somebody always starts talking.

CHAPTER 22

SMOKE, PAPERWORK, AND PERFECT SETUPS

The streets were buzzing with quiet moves and louder distractions, but behind closed doors, everybody was leveling up. The hustle wasn't just about product anymore—it was about paperwork, positioning, and power plays.

INT. TARA'S HOUSE – NIGHT

Tara and Al were tangled in sheets, their passion as thick as the silence afterward. No words, just heavy breathing and old wounds layered under skin.

INT. LIL B'S CONDO – NIGHT

Lil B and Aaliyah sat on the floor, back against the couch. The blunt passed between kisses. Their laughter was low and lazy, the kind that only happens when love and kush meet under dim lights. Clothes came off. They disappeared into each other.

INT. PRECIOUS' HOUSE – DEN – DAY

Precious clicked through her laptop while Cory sipped coffee beside her.

"The whole budget—buying the ten houses, repairs, taxes, all in—comes to about $850K," she explained. "When they're finished and the market shifts, they'll be worth between $1.5 to $2 million."

"We need to move now," Cory said. "What's first?"

"We start with the LLC, create a trust, and put down earnest money. I already know the sellers personally."

"Why not just run it through your company?"

"I can't mix it. Brian still has a stake in my business. I need this clean and separate."

EXT. CAR – DAY

Bo and Tyrone sat in a parked car. The engine was off, but tension stayed on.

"Look," Bo said. "I'm fronting you a brick. Play it smart, and Myrtle Beach will be yours. Today it's one—months from now, it could be twenty, maybe fifty."

"Man... I'll be back in three days," Tyrone said. "My wife dipped. I got $1,500 to my name, and I'm still all gas, no brakes. Appreciate you, Bo."

"Just don't crash," Bo replied. "Text me when you touch back down."

INT. LIL EAZY'S CONDO – EVENING

The smell of garlic was in the air. Hannah stirred a pot while Lil Eazy rolled up.

"We need a getaway," he said. "Me, you, Lil B, Aaliyah—Miami."

"You already know I'm in," she smiled. "When?"

"Couple weeks. Look up flights, hotels—let's plan something nice."

"Food's ready," she said. "You want a plate?"

"Yeah. Fix it with love."

INT. HOTEL ROOM – NIGHT

Mike Mike laid in his boxers, smoke curling around him. Sonya strolled around in a bra and G-string, sipping Hennessy.

"Are you still giving me the down payment on that car?" she asked.

"How much did you say again?"

"Five grand."

"I got you tomorrow."

"Michael... I think I'm falling for you. We should get our own spot."

"I feel you too. Start looking."

They kissed. Lust took over.

INT. DORM – DAY

Brian was knocking out burpees with two others. Down the hall, three inmates nodded off from 2-K, looking like ghosts in skin.

"You getting butter from the duck today?" Joe asked.

"No pain, no gain. Look at them fools high as a kite," Brian replied.

Other inmates watched, laughed, and filmed. Von, meanwhile, was in his cube talking business.

"Best I can do is five books per hour," Von told DC Jay.

"That works," Jay said. "Gotta call my lady, check on my kids. Pay him, boo."

Jay's partner handed over the stamps. Brian stepped into the cube.

"Man, I don't judge," Von said. "But DC dudes? Hardest hitters— yet some sweet as pie."

"The Wire warned us," Brian said. "Remember Omar? Killer... and gay."

"They say they keep both—a girl and a dude. I don't even know."

INT. STUDIO – NIGHT

Cam stood in a booth. Wiz stood beside him, lined with plaques.

"Cuz and Lil Eazy said they'd invest," Cam said. "But I need to get serious. What's the first move?"

"Record," Wiz said. "Find your hit. Do showcases, strip clubs. Feedback comes quick."

"How much for 20 tracks? Beats included?"

"Five bands. Normally 25K, but I believe in you. Plus, I'll bring in Midnight Black."

"That's love," Cam said, handing him two bands. "When do we start?"

"Now."

INT. TASHA'S HOUSE – DAY

Bre sat on her laptop, tracking stocks. Tasha walked in.

"You wanna ride with me?" she asked.

"Where to?"

"Macon. Meet up with Wander."

"I'll pass. Gotta track these stocks. Already made $2,500."

"Okay, do your thing, Warren Buffet."

"Mom! How do you know about him?"

"Girl, he's one of the richest men alive. I pay attention."

INT. SANTIAGO'S WAREHOUSE – DAY

Santiago and AL stood face to face. Ms. Vickie walked in, poised and powerful.

"AL, you're impressing me," Santiago said. "But Ms. Vickie? She's the truth. When I'm gone, she's who you deal with."

"Heard your name. Never seen the face," AL said.

"Best way to stay in the game," Vickie replied.

"Trucks will be here in days," Santiago said. "Drought's coming. I doubled the load."

"Say less," AL nodded. "We're ready."

INT. DAY ROOM – PRISON – DAY

Brian and Jeff were mid-chess. Turtle and Joe watched. Dominoes slammed nearby. Scrabble clacked in the back.

"My niece is learning stocks," Brian said. "Calling plays like a vet."

"I'll teach her options," Jeff said. "Make or break moves."

"I'm a high-risk guy," Brian said. "If the read is right, I'm in."

Lou approached.

"Thanks for getting them Bloods off me," Lou said.

"You good?"

"Yeah. Uncle's a big sportsbook guy. He's hyped. Wants to meet you."

"Say less."

Joe looked up.

"Boy's still on life support. We're about to be locked down."

Brian sighed.

"That'll slow the currency flow. Tighten cell block arteries."

A bang echoed. An inmate was pounding on the door—check-in signal. Von strolled in, dapping guys up.

"What's the fuss?" Brian asked.

"KB checking in. Owes for K2. Word is, $500 tab," Von said.

"Junkie-ass gonna get poked," Turtle said.

"That's why I say leave drugs alone," Brian said. "We can make a million off phones and cigarettes."

He pointed to the board.

"Get caught with a phone, 100 shots in 40 days. Cigarettes? 300 shots. But you live to fight another day. Get caught with dope? Whole new case."

Joe nodded as officers escorted KB out.

"Ain't no insurance policy for stupidity."

Brian leaned back.

"That's why I move how I move. Quiet. Sharp. With structure. Let 'em chase highs—I'm chasing legacy."

Everyone was leveling up.

Money moves in silence.

CHAPTER 23

"BURIED MOVES AND WELCOME BACKS"

The sun sat low behind a stretch of grey sky as Brian and Jack stood side by side at Easy's gravesite. The grass had grown in around the headstone, but time hadn't softened the weight in Brian's chest. They stood next to Brian's SUV, not saying much at first, just letting the silence speak.

"Jack, so much has changed… but really, nothing's changed," Brian said finally, eyes scanning the city skyline behind the cemetery's fence. "New buildings. New clubs. A few new faces. But the streets? Same old rules."

Jack nodded. "That's why I stay out of the way. These young dudes, they are different. No respect. The numbers game died when the lottery went legal. Now I'm just slow-rolling at the pool hall, keeping it quiet."

Brian glanced over. "You don't fool with sportsbook?"

Jack chuckled. "Nah. My bankroll can't back it."

"That's my new lane," Brian said. "Got into it inside. Made seventy-five thousand over two years. Really more, but that's what I stacked and came home with."

Jack raised a brow. "How'd you cash that out?"

"Stamps," Brian said. "Currency on the compound. You need 'em for everything—haircuts, kitchen food, phones, gambling. Folks send money to your people, who then buy 'em. Me? I was the bookie. Had stacks of stamps high as your head."

Jack shook his head, grinning. "You are a hustler for real. So what's next?"

"The game changer," Brian said. "Most bookies have people filling out slips by hand. I met this Asian kid, who knows a guy who builds apps. I'm talking about putting the sportsbook in the palm of your hand. Millions to be made."

"That's genius," Jack said. "What's the hold up?"

Brian looked out across the headstones. "I'm opening a sports bar too. Calling it The SweatBox. I'm thinking of close to a million startups. The app alone's gonna run a quarter mill."

"You still got that kind of money?"

"It's buried. Just waiting for the tenant to move out of the house."

Jack laughed. "You a bad man, Brian Jordan."

Brian smirked. "Was taught by the best. Good teachers make great students."

At the warehouse, Bo pulled up and backed into the garage, with Al right behind him. They moved like clockwork, unloading boxes and breaking down shipments. Inside, the air smelled like hustle and fresh cardboard.

"Dog," Al said, wiping sweat from his brow, "a few months later, we bought fifty, getting a hundred on face card. Santiago said he loves how we're stepping up."

Bo nodded. "We've been rocking. Locked in with some of the best in the city, and out-of-state money flowing heavy. I see us moving a few hundred a week easily. The city's becoming ours."

Al's phone rang. He picked up. "What's up, my Queen?"

Tara's voice came through, smooth. "I'm good, my King. Just calling to remind you about my brother's dinner tonight."

"I remember. Just waiting for Lil Eazy and them to pull up, then I'm headed to shower."

"Okay, I'll be here waiting." They hung up.

Al turned to Bo. "Tonight I meet the man, the myth—Brian Jordan."

Bo smiled. "I've heard nothing but good things. How his crew handled the Miami boys set the tone for all of us in the A."

Al nodded. "I heard stories even before I met Tara. He's a living legend."

The garage door opened again. Lil Eazy and Lil B walked in with gym bags full of money.

"This is for the twenty we owe," Lil Eazy said.

Lil B handed over another bag. "And this is us buying fifteen."

Bo handed them two bags in return. "Y'all been putting in work. What time are you pulling up?"

"We're just gonna put this up, get dressed, and head to Auntie's. She's cooking soul food and seafood."

They dapped up and dipped.

At Precious's house, the kids scrambled around getting dressed.

"Y'all about ready?" she called out.

"Yes, Mom!" they answered in unison.

"Good. I got one stop before we hit Tasha's."

At Tasha's house, the kitchen was alive with motion. Music played, food simmered, and Bre stood over a pot while Tasha placed a banner that read Welcome Home.

Mike Mike walked in, kissing his mom's cheek.

"Mmm, it smells good in here, Mommy."

Tasha grinned. "Your sister did most of the cooking."

Mike Mike turned to Bre. "Okay, Bre! Always showing out."

Elsewhere, at an upscale indoor pool party, Terri, Asia, Apple, Blu, Amy, and Sonya were turning heads in their own cabana. Hookahs blew smoke like fog machines while shots were slammed and laughs echoed.

Asia leaned into Terri. "Girl, Peanut all touchy-feely. Talking like he's wanted me forever."

Terri tossed back a salt lick and shot. "Reel him in. I heard his pockets run deep."

Three iced-out guys approached.

"I like y'all vibes," said one, locking eyes with Blu. "Y'all really know how to party."

Blu, dark-skinned and striking, stood to greet them. The room shifted. Every move she made commanded attention.

Back at Brian's place, he stood in the mirror, adjusting his shirt. On the bed behind him were a copy of The Wall Street Journal and a Donald Trump book. He gave himself a nod and headed out.

Meanwhile, in a crowded trap house, dice clattered against concrete. Toni shot, the room erupting in cheers—until he rolled a seven.

"Man, I'm done," he said, scooping nothing off the floor. "'Bout to lose my re-up money again."

In every corner of the city, moves were being made. Quiet ones. Loud ones. Buried ones. Some hustled for power, some for freedom, others just for a meal and a piece of peace. Brian Jordan was back—not with noise, but with precision. While others played checkers, he was building a board no one had seen yet. One app. One sports bar. One shot at rewriting his legacy.

The streets hadn't changed—but the player had. And now, the game was on his time.

The weight of change didn't feel heavy in the air; it felt casual, like an old song fading in and out of memory. At the POLICE STATION, LT sat behind his desk, the photo from Ross's house clutched in his hand like it held answers. Officer Blake stepped in, closing the door behind him.

"Sir, Ross is from Southside. Cleveland Ave. Zone 3 to be exact," Blake said. "Been to prison once. But nothing since. Clean for ten years."

LT leaned back in his chair. "Was he affiliated? Gang ties? Drugs? That condo and car of his were more than a 9-to-5 flex."

"A few street whispers, but nothing solid, sir."

"Keep digging," LT ordered. "We're starting with smoke. I need fire. I'll talk to the family this afternoon."

In every corner of the city, moves were being made. Quiet ones. Loud ones. Buried ones. Some hustled for power, some for freedom, others just for a meal and a piece of peace. Brian Jordan was back—not with noise, but with precision. While others played checkers, he was building a board no one had seen yet. One app. One sports bar. One shot at winner it all

CHAPTER 24

Inside Tasha's house, laughter and soul food filled the air. Music played low, kids ran around the table legs, and dominoes clacked in the background.

Brian stepped in with a grin and announced, quoting *The Color Purple*, "I don't know y'all no more!"

Everyone burst out laughing. Tasha walked up and wrapped him in a tight hug.

"Brother, so glad you're back with us. You're looking real good."

Precious moved through the crowd, drink in hand, and raised her glass. "The President is back! How you feelin'?"

"Great," Brian said, his voice grounded. "Unbelievable, really. Seeing y'all, my kids—just everything I've missed."

"We missed you and your girls too," Precious said. "They're glowing. One day this week, let me take you to dinner. Just us."

"I don't mind being treated by my beautiful lady," Brian teased.

Outside, Brian and Al stepped onto the porch. The night air cooled their conversation.

"Glad they released a real one," Al said. "Heard nothin' but great things. I'd like to hold out my olive branch."

Brian nodded. "Appreciate that. But you probably heard—I'm done with the streets. I see clearer now. I don't knock the next man. Not my son. Not my nephews. Everyone finds their own light."

"True," Al said. "I love your sister. Being part of this family is real to me."

Lil Eazy, Lil B, and Mike Mike joined them, forming a semi-circle around Brian.

Brian looked each of them in the eyes. "Understand something. When you own a business or work a job, you write your own script. Nine out of ten, it plays out that way. But with the streets? A new script gets written every day—and you don't get to choose your role. You might think you're in control. But trust me—you're not. The only question worth asking is: *What's your endgame before the game ends?*"

Silence. They felt the weight.

Tara came out and hugged Brian tight. "So glad you're home. I love you. We missed you."

His daughters ran out next. "Daddy, can we spend the night with you?"

"Sure," he said, voice cracking with emotion.

Tasha yelled from inside. "Cam, come help me with the fireworks."

Allen echoed her, "Yeah! Fireworks!"

They stood together, watching the night sky light up.

Hours later at the cigar bar, everything oozed class and danger. "Grown and sexy" vibes. Cigars. Hookah. Suits. Sparkles. Old-school records spinning.

"Brian," Cowboy said, "the streets ain't been the same since you left."

"Streets don't change," Brian replied. "The players do. Some make it weak. Others make it profitable."

Jonny approached, hugging him tight. "Glad you're back. I got a move in motion. One piece away—you'd make it complete."

Brian's smile faded. "Truth is, maybe if you'd tossed Jack some funds—just a little something to look out for me when I was down—I'd consider it. But I was left for dead, Jonny. Didn't hear from you once."

Johnny looked stunned. "I feel that. Maybe we'll see eye to eye down the road. Toast to your return."

Outside, Lil B, Lil Eazy, Mike Mike, and Cam smoked and posted near the cars.

"Unk gets back in?" Lil Eazy said. "It's over. All-star cast."

"Old money crew returns," Lil B nodded.

Inside, Al and Bo watched the crowd from the bar.

"Brian brought the streets out," Al said. "Real money is here tonight."

"Ain't seen some of these cats in a minute," Bo added.

"I'm tryin' to pull my brother-in-law in," Al said. "He'll come around. Especially if that money becomes funny."

On the dance floor, the DJ shouted, "Make some noise for Brian Jordan!"

Joyce walked up, stunning in a curve-hugging dress. "You brought the whole city out."

Brian kissed her. "That dress? Say less. You're mine."

The DJ dropped *Step in the Name of Love* and the crowd stepped in rhythm.

At the pool party, Terri and her girls took command.

"Ready to set it off?" she grinned.

They stripped to their bikinis and cannonballed into the pool. Volleyball followed. Music thumped. Men watched. Women whispered.

Ike nudged Stone. "That chocolate one. She's mine."

"Brian's home," Stone said.

"Drought's coming. I sent Johnny to bring Brian in. He's a game changer."

"He's gonna rock with you over Al?"

"Man, lie. Women, lie. Numbers don't."

Outside the cigar bar, Ms. Vickie and four stunning women stepped out of an SUV. Heads turned.

"Brian," Jack said, handing him a shot. "They treat you like a lottery pick."

Brian smirked. "I dance to my own beat. Do I look broke to you?"

They laughed.

Ms. Vickie entered, her daughters flanking her. Al froze.

"That's her," he whispered.

"Who?" Tara asked.

"The woman I told y'all about. Santiago's right hand."

Brian greeted her with a warm hug.

"You haven't aged," she said.

"Neither have you," Brian replied. "Thanks for what you did for Jack."

"You took your lick to the chin. Didn't say a word. That's why."

"The only way I know."

Felicia grinned. "Glad you're home, Brian."

Across the bar, Al whispered, "Your brother rubs shoulders with giants."

"Brian's different," Tara replied.

"He'll be an asset," Bo added.

Al walked over.

"Al? Small world," Ms. Vickie said. "You know Brian?"

"Future brother-in-law."

"Not Tasha?"

"No. Tara."

"Damn. I was about to sic my daughter on you."

They laughed.

"You still like to keep it in the family," Brian teased.

"Why change what's not broken?"

Back at the pool, money stacked in front of Terri as they played Blackjack.

"You're fine," Stone told Blu. "Dark skin, perfect teeth. You're real."

Blu blushed. "Been watchin' you too."

"Trips, shopping, might even put a baby in you," Stone winked.

Terri called for another card. "Hit."

Ike stayed. Je busted.

Terri revealed two kings. Ike had two nines.

"Lady luck's with you," he said.

"You could say that."

"Let's toast," Ike said. "Night's young. Roll up."

Back in the cigar bar, the younger generation was soaking it in.

"Feels good having Unk back," Lil Eazy said.

"All I hear is legends," Mike Mike added.

"We got work to do," Lil B said. "Big shoes to fill."

"Where's Cam?"

"Studio. I might slide."

Brian walked over.

"What y'all drinking?"

"Tequila."

"Shot time. Listen. It's not what you make—it's what you save and invest. That's the key. Compound interest. I wish I'd known sooner."

"You the Don," Lil B said. "We just follow suit."

"Son, that was never the plan. That's the government's plan. The scariest part of the game? The people. They smile, laugh, and eat with you. Then stab you. I can't give anyone the power to take me from my family ever again."

"That's deep," Lil Eazy said.

"It's true," Brian said. "It happened before me. To me. And it'll happen after me. I'm gonna keep askin' y'all: What's the end game?"

Mike Mike came back with shot glasses.

"Hold up!" Al shouted. "Bartender, make 100 shots. Hail to the Don!"

The next morning at Joyce's house, Brian laid in bed, phone to his ear.

"Bre, I'm taking you to lunch. Gonna meet Jeff. He put me on options trading. He's sharp."

"Bet, Unk. I'm ready," she said.

Joyce entered with breakfast.

"Now's the time to buy. Prices are low."

"Put together a $250K list," Brian said.

"They'll need rehab," Joyce replied. "But that's an easy mil when the market bounces."

The king had returned, but he wasn't looking to wear the crown the same way. Brian moved differently now—smarter, sharper, calculated. The people, the deals, the streets—all still there, waiting. But the question wasn't who missed him.

The real question was: **Who feared what he might become next?**

Because the game had changed. And Brian was no longer just a player.

He was the blueprint.

CHAPTER 25

THE DAY HAD A HEAT TO IT

One of those sticky southern waves that seemed to slow time down. But in Atlanta, business didn't stop because of the weather. Especially not for the ones playing behind the scenes.

Outside WIC Store – Day Two FBI agents sat parked in an unmarked vehicle with tinted windows. Cameras on the dash, coffee in the cupholders.

"In two hours, seventeen people were there," Agent Miller said.

"That's a lot of early traffic for a small shop," Agent Moore replied.

"We're going to have to get someone inside."

They exchanged a knowing look. The case was building itself.

Car Dealership – Day Cory, TA, and JP sat in a glass-walled office across from Blake, the dealership owner. Cory slid a folder across the table.

"When will they be delivered?" Cory asked.

"Three weeks tops," Blake replied.

"Here's the down payment. We'll pay the balance when we pick up."

"Appreciate it, Blake. We'll be back real soon," TA said.

They shook hands. Business handled.

Lil Eazy's Trap House – Day Money spread across the table like a fan. Gmack counted it with precision, licking his fingers with each stack.

"Fourteen thousand," G-Mack said.

"Cool. I'll give you a whole one. You owe me fifteen," Lil Eazy replied.

Bags exchanged. The motion was smooth.

"Cam went crazy in the booth last night. I think we should hit that open mic tonight," Lil B said.

"I'm with it. G-Mack might be the next big asset. He used to get his weight from Ross—had Dill Ave booming," Lil Eazy responded.

"Everything's lining up. Mike Mike and Cam sliding through too. Man, Ms. Vickie's daughter? Felicia? She was all over me last night."

"Nigga we saw with her with that big fine ass she grown grown. How old is she?"

"Twenty-seven. We are hooking up later."

They smirked. A good night was shaping up.

Brian's Car – Day Brian sat parked, sunlight creeping across his face. He was on the phone with Precious.

"When Betty says she is moving?"

"This weekend. I had to break the lease and throw her extra. You must be hiding something in there the way you rushed me."

Brian chuckled. "I left you straight, you good."

"We need to talk about the business. I was thinking about buying you out."

"You're straight for now. If everything moves how it's supposed to, I won't need it. But call me as soon as Betty's out."

Derrick and Ross' Momma's House – Day Lt. sat across from Derrick. The room was quiet. Derrick held back frustration, answering carefully.

"You said some jewelry was missing—got any photos?"

"Yeah, I can get those. He flipped cars, too. We were heading to the auction that morning. I know he had cash, but I don't know how much."

"Anything else? We've got nothing right now. Waiting on prints and phone records."

"Last thing he told me? He had a hot date. Didn't say her name, but it felt new. He just split from his son's mom."

The officer scribbled a note.

Outside a Mall – Day Terri, Apple, Blu, Legs, and Amy stood by their cars, all with shopping bags. Stylish, confident, loud.

"What's the play for tonight?" Apple asked.

"Ike said he'd hit me up later," Terri answered.

"Stone has been blowing up my line," Blu added.

"We gotta play this right. They are seasoned. If we play it cool, we walk away with more than just attention," Terri said.

"Let's eat and drink," Amy chimed in.

"I'm craving Ruth Chris," Terri smiled.

The girls laughed. The streets weren't ready.

Tasha's House – Day Brian, Tasha, and Bre sat around the table, a laptop open in front of them. Business being handled—quietly, strategically.

"I still got that play with Ms. White and her friend. Fifteen grand packages. I'm running a 60/40 split with you," Brian said.

"Bet. I can work with that. That every week?" Tasha asked.

"Every two. Could be slow or flooded with product, but that's the motion for now. What is the count?"

"You got 75k in the safe deposit boxes, 38K in the bank, and Bre is working 25K in the stocks you told her."

"That 25 is now 33 and climbing," Bre added.

Brian cracked a proud smile. "That's what I'm talkin' about. We're finally compounding the interest. Jeff told me options trading can flip six figures in a day. Money while you sleep."

"Unk, thanks for believing in me. I've been reading Stocks for Dummies like you told me. I think this is what I want to do for real—for life," Bre said.

Al's Workhouse – Day Bo and Tyrone stood in the back of the work spot, hands full of product and ambition.

"You said you'd be right back," Bo said.

"And I am. Back like I never left—the haters shook," Tyrone laughed.

They dapped up, and swapped bags.

"Next time, I'm grabbing a whole one. Myrtle Beach? It's about to be mine. Tourist money is sweet."

"I put two on you. Told you it's ours for the taking," Bo replied.

Al walked up mid-convo, ending a call.

"Y'all building a solid team. We're down to our last 30. I told B they could get 10 till I re-up. I gotta call Ms. Vickie. Santiago's still overseas. This drought? Watch what happens—numbers going through the roof."

"Just what we need. Let the city dry up—we're about to flood it," Bo said.

They grinned. War was coming—just not the kind with guns.

FBI Headquarters – Day A spotless whiteboard. Four agents stood in front of it, tension in their stances.

"Six stores and counting, two hours apiece. Constant traffic. Some walk in, leave with nothing," Miller noted.

"We need names. Faces. We're running the LLCs now," Schwartz added.

"Still want us watching the stores?" Moore asked.

"Yep. Warrants for taps, surveillance, banking records—all in motion."

"Good work. Keep me updated. We're getting close," Hill ordered.

G Mack's Spot – Day Money hit the table. Drugs sat next to it. The vibe was thick.

"That last pack? Fire. I need a 9-piece," Toni said.

"I told you I gotcha. They're loving this work. I'll even give you a better number," G Mack replied.

"Yo, can I use the bathroom?" Charlie Mo asked.

"First door on the left," G Mack said.

Charlie Mo vanished but kept his eyes open—checking exits, layouts, everything.

Toni's Car – Day They hopped in. The windows up, music low.

"He's done. Let me get a hit of that," Charlie Mo said.

"He won't see it coming. His ego is too loud," Toni replied.

They both laughed and sparked up. The countdown had started.

Tara's House – Day Tara paced, phone to her ear. Energy pulsing through her words.

"Girl, I'm putting together a plan. Everybody is moving, and I'm standing still."

"You know I'm down. Tell me when," Shan said.

"I wanna pay Brian back somehow. Maybe bring him in on the business, but he's really done with the street game."

"Mommy, can we go to G-Mommy's? I wanna play with my cousins," Allen called out.

"In a little while, baby."

She looked at the whiteboard in her kitchen filled with notes and plans. Her time was coming. Just needed the right play.

The city was simmering—under pressure, under watch, and under fire. Every corner had a hustle, every hustle had a crack. The Feds were tightening the rope, while the streets chased expansion, loyalty, and legacy. Everyone had a plan. But the deeper truth? Not all plans survive the pressure of the game. The drought was coming. The moves were already made. And soon, Atlanta would feel the shift in the air. The kind that only happens before a storm.

CHAPTER 26

Real Ones, Real Games

EXT. FOOTBALL FIELD – SATURDAY AFTERNOON

Fourth quarter. The scoreboard glared: 0–0. It was now or never.

TA jogged up to Coach Cory, eyeing the defensive lineup.

"Coach, let Boston run a Power 5. That's their weak side."

Cory turned to the young running back. "Boston, you want the ball for the win?"

"Yes, Coach," Boston replied, fired up.

"Power 5. I need y'all to block hard. Boston, run fast. TD on three—one, two, three!"

"TD!" the team shouted.

The snap came quickly. Boston took the handoff, found the gap, and exploded downfield. Touchdown. The crowd erupted. Ashley stood, shouting with joy.

"That's my baby! Good job, team!"

After the celebration, Boston ran to Ashley with another kid trailing.

"Mommy, Coach is taking us to get pizza. Can Mal ride with us?"

"Where are his parents?" Ashley asked.

"They're not here," Mal said. "Coach picked me up."

She nodded. "Okay. That's fine. Let Coach know."

Cory walked up moments later.

"I'm lost without you," he said softly. "Did you get your gift?"

Ashley folded her arms. "Yes, and it was nice. But I'm still standing on my words."

"You really play hardball."

Before he could say more, another mom approached.

"Coach Cory, can you drop Man Man off? I can't take him with y'all."

"No problem," Cory replied with his usual charm.

Ashley nodded toward the bleachers. "You better walk on before your other girlfriend gets mad. They have been watching us since you walked over."

"You trippin'. I'll see you at Yellow Mushrooms," Cory said with a grin.

INT. JACK'S SUV – DAY

Jack and Brian pulled into the dealership lot.

"Been thinking," Jack said. "I want to open a brewery."

Brian turned, intrigued. "Gambling and alcohol? That's a billion-dollar play."

"Double fold—food, beer, real estate."

"When?"

"Couple months. After I help get your lounge running."

"I like it. I'll have Joyce pull some comps and land info."

"Not Precious?" Jack asked.

"Nah, Joyce. I'm running moves through her now."

They climbed out and browsed the lot.

"Cash for the SUV?" Jack asked.

"Nope. Financing it. Build credit, write-off for the business. Jews got rich being best friends with bankers—then became the banks."

Jack nodded. "I feel you."

INT. PRECIOUS'S HOUSE – BATHROOM – NIGHT

Pairs hovered over the toilet, vomiting. Milan stood behind her, arms folded.

"I'm never drinking again," Pairs groaned. "Should've listened to you."

Milan rolled her eyes. "That stuff is nasty. I don't know why y'all do it. Plus, y'all smoke way too much."

Precious entered.

"What's going on?" she asked, alarmed.

"Think she got food poisoning," Milan said.

Precious leaned closer, concern deepening. "How long has she been sick?"

"We got in late. She came home with me."

"I'll go grab something for her stomach," Precious said. "Be back."

INT. DEALERSHIP – DAY

Brian sat inside a black-on-black Cadillac SUV, arm out the window.

"This is me," he said, smiling.

Jack nodded. "Like you never left."

Brian's phone buzzed. He looked at the caller.

"Cowboy again. He says Julio wants to meet up."

Jack raised a brow.

"Julio's broke," Brian muttered. "Wife left him, bad investments. He thinks I'm a lifeline."

Jack shrugged. "What are you gonna do?"

Brian cracked a smile. "Wrong man, bad plan. But I'll show them better than I can tell them."

INT. PRECIOUS'S HOUSE – LATER THAT DAY

Precious paced while on the phone with Brian.

"I have the keys. She moved out. But listen, I think Paris has been drinking. She's in the bathroom throwing up."

Brian's voice came through, calm but serious. "You sure?"

"I been there. I can smell it. Milan had to drive her home. But I didn't say anything yet. I think she's just embarrassed."

"I'll be there in an hour," Brian said.

The midday heat clung to their skin like wet cotton as Brian and Jack stood in the backyard, eyes locked on the dirt. Brian's shovel dug with the weight of memory until it hit something solid. He knelt, wiped sweat from his brow, and uncovered a buried box. A moment later, he opened it and grinned, pulling out a thick plastic bag.

"This here's some 1990s money, man," he said, holding it up like a trophy. "But can't lie, wish I knew about compound interest back then – would've been triple."

INT. BRIAN'S HOUSE - DAY

That grin didn't last long. Brian cut open the bag and unzipped the smaller bundles inside. The smell hit him first—damp, old, sour. He peeled back the rubber bands, revealing bills eaten by time, mildew, and decay. Some crumbled in his hands.

"FUCK!!! This is crazy! This can't be happening." His voice cracked—part rage, part heartbreak.

INT. AL'S WORKSPOT - DAY

Meanwhile, Al and Bo fed crisp bills through a money counter, the steady *whirr-click* humming like applause.

"We just ran through 150 bricks in one week," Al said. "We gotta be extra careful—the streets are talking. Wish Ross was here. We'd really be strong-arming the city."

Bo nodded. "Yeah, Ross had Dill Ave on lock. My dawg's definitely missed."

Al leaned back, reflecting. "Can't lie, Brian said something deep the other night. Been replaying it in my head. He said every day a new script is being written for us in the streets. I never looked at it like that before, but it's true. Look what happened to BMF, Deck, Danny Boy, Fat Steve, Buck Frank... and the list keeps going."

EXT. CEMETERY - DAY

Balloons floated upward as friends and family let go. The grief hung thick, but quiet. Off to the side, Terri and Toni walked together, their voices hushed but sharp.

"Bro, Lil Eazy and Lil B's names keep coming up in the streets," Terri muttered. "They're moving a lot of work. That true?"

Toni nodded. "Yep, sis. They're having a mean run—Al put them on."

Terri's eyes narrowed. "I'll see about that. Gotta avenge our daddy's name. Plus, I heard Brian's home. It's time to make them feel our pain."

INT. LIL B'S TRAP HOUSE - DAY

The front door never closed long. Customers came and went. Cam and Mike Mike made exchanges with focus while Lil Eazy and Lil B watched, sipping out of red cups.

"My girl thinks she is pregnant," Lil Eazy said.

Lil B raised an eyebrow. "Which one?"

"What do you mean, 'which one?' Hannah!"

Lil B laughed. "Man, you love all your bitches. Just had to ask."

"You do too. But I only go raw with like… four of them."

INT. BRIAN'S HOUSE - DAY

Stacks of damaged bills sat in piles—some salvageable, most not. Brian looked defeated, rubbing his temples. Jack stood over the mess.

"I buried over a million and a half," Brian said. "Only about 600K and some change is good—this just fucked up my whole game plan."

Jack exhaled slowly. "You know our saying: take the good with the bad. Could always be worse."

Brian nodded, heavy. "Yeah… but damn, I had high hopes."

INT. RESTAURANT - NIGHT

Cory and Precious sat in a booth, mostly quiet, forks tapping plates.

"You good, Precious?" Cory asked. "You seem distant."

"Yeah," she said, stirring her drink. "Just thinking about a deal that didn't close. Hate missing opportunities."

"We can't win them all."

CHAPTER 27

The day had a heat to it—one of those sticky southern waves that seemed to slow time down. But in Atlanta, business didn't stop because of the weather. Especially not for the ones playing behind the scenes.

INT. STONE'S HOUSE - NIGHT

Blu stood in the bathroom, phone pressed to her ear.

"Look," she whispered. "We're about to go to the movies. Code is 1678, the money's in the dryer, and the keys in my gas tank."

"Okay," Apple replied. "We're down the street. Erase all our messages. No fumbles."

In the den, Stone poured himself a drink, blunt hanging from his lips.

"You ready?" he asked. "Movie starts in 30. Have a drink."

Blu walked out, smiling. "Why not? Cheers to me and my new boo thang."

INT. STONE'S HOUSE - LATER

Apple and Blu slipped in through the back. Quiet. Efficient. Apple grabbed the cash from the dryer while Blu trashed the living room—flipping chairs, scattering paperwork. Outside, Amy hurled a brick through a window, setting off the alarm.

Back in the car, Apple grinned. "He'll think it was a break-in."

Blu smirked. "Smooth as butter."

The bar glowed with low neon light, casting shadows across the small table where Lil B and Felicia sat, shoulder to shoulder. The table was piled high—trays of smoked oysters, buttery crab legs cracked open and dripping with sauce. Lime wedges littered the side of the plates. Shot glasses, slick with condensation, stood in a half-circle like little soldiers around a near-empty bottle of top-shelf tequila.

Felicia leaned in close, licking a bit of juice from her thumb, her voice warm and tipsy.

FELICIA "Something about you... I love how you are so in control, always in the moment."

Lil B smiled, cracked an oyster, and slurped it smooth like a pro.

LIL B "My dad always told me—stay in the present, and know what you want."

Felicia bit her lip, her eyes lingering on his face.

FELICIA "These shots and oysters got me feelin' you… You better watch yourself."

Lil B tilted his shot glass toward her with a smirk.

LIL B "The night is young. I ain't never scared."

Felicia's eyes sparkled mischievously. She reached into her purse, pulling out a small foil pack. She tore it open with her nails, revealing a pale, pressed pill.

FELICIA "Ever pop X?"

Lil B raised an eyebrow.

LIL B "Hell nah—and don't plan on it."

Felicia smiled seductively, popped the pill into her mouth, cracked it in half with her teeth, and leaned in. Her lips pressed against his, soft and electric, passing the half into his mouth in a slow, deliberate kiss. He didn't resist.

FELICIA (whispering) "Just half. Let me take you to this place. I only go with that special one."

They knocked back three more shots, the burn hitting harder now, chasing the pill with lime and adrenaline. Laughing, feeling invincible, they stood, left a generous stack of bills on the table, and headed toward the night—toward wherever Felicia's secret place would take them.

The city pulsed outside, unaware of the intoxicated chemistry walking its sidewalks. In that moment, it wasn't about right or wrong. It wasn't about the streets, the past, or the deals waiting at sunrise. It was just two souls chasing a high—emotional, physical, and forbidden.

Whatever happened next? It wouldn't be forgotten. Not in a place like this. Not with her. Not tonight.

INT. BAR – NIGHT

Neon lights painted the walls. Shots hit the bar like clockwork. Leah and Lil Eazy leaned in close, laughing, drinking, flirting.

LEAH "Russell, where do you see yourself in five years?"

LIL EAZY "Rich. Able to do what I want, when I want—with you on my side."

LEAH "You gotta be more detailed if you really want a better life. You know you can't sell drugs forever, right?"

LIL EAZY (rolls his eyes) "You sound like my mom now."

LEAH "It's a saying: if you fail to plan, you plan to fail, Russell."

LIL EAZY (grinning) "I hear you... but for now? Let's take more shots—see where the alcohol takes us."

LEAH (laughs) "Oh, you trying to get me drunk so you can get some? Let me tell you a secret—I'm at my best when I'm sober."

The door creaked as the two stepped inside the dim-lit swingers club. Heavy bass thumped low in the walls, while moans and the scent of sweat and sex hung thick in the air. Bodies passed like shadows, draped only in towels. Some clung loosely. Others—barely covered anything.

Lil B walked in behind Felicia, his eyes darting from side to side, unsure where to look. Around them, men were talking wild, boasting about how they were "beating the pussy down." The closer they got to the back rooms, the louder it became. Couples were going at it everywhere—against walls, on sofas, even on the floor. One woman had her legs hanging off the arm of a chair as a man dove between them. In another corner, a man leaned back, groaning with his head thrown as a stranger pleasured him on her knees.

A group of men stood in line behind a mattress, hyped like hyenas ready to pounce. Each of them looked sweaty, shirtless, and eager.

FELICIA "Looks like a good spot for us... are you not nervous?"

LIL B "What the hell is this? This shit wild—they fuckin' everywhere."

The sounds got louder. Screams, grunts, beds creaking. One woman was clearly in the middle of an orgasm as she begged not to stop. Felicia laughed and pulled Lil B deeper inside.

FELICIA (smirking) "Told you not to get me takin' shots... them pills kickin' in now."

INT. HOTEL ROOM – the AM

Leah stepped out of the bathroom, her towel wrapped tight, hair damp. Lil Eazy sat on the edge of the bed, scrolling his phone.

"Sorry I fell asleep earlier," she said, rubbing her temple. "Wasn't feeling good. Thanks for being gentle."

"No problem," he replied.

"My dad's throwing a meet-and-greet at the golf range next week. You should come meet the family."

"Sounds cool. What's the dress code?"

"Clean and casual. Golf courses are where the real deals go down."

"I'm there. Just let me know."

After Hours

The air in the room was thick with smoke, sweat, and the soundtrack of temptation. Lil B gripped Felicia's waist, her body arched against the velvet sofa as he hit her from behind with steady, punishing strokes. Her moans echoed off the walls, uninhibited and raw, as she came back to back, her body trembling beneath his.

People lingered nearby—some voyeuristic, some pretending not to look. But no one interrupted. This was a space with no rules, only indulgence.

Lil B slowed his strokes as he came, his breath ragged, muscles tense.

LIL B "That pill and these shots got me on one... I busted twice and am still ready—like Freddy."

Still catching his breath, his eyes flicked to movement across the room. Two women approached, both dripping with exotic allure. One was a curvy white girl with a London accent, hips like a Black girl, confidence like a queen. The other—an Asian and Black mix—radiated sleek beauty, sharp eyes, and a dangerous smile.

JADA (the mixed beauty) "Bravo... Now that was a movie. Still got some juice in the tank for a tag team?"

Lil B barely blinked. He looked them up and down like a lion sizing up fresh meat, lust rising again like a wave.

Felicia, sprawled on the plush rug, wiped sweat from her brow and grinned, lips swollen, eyes wild.

FELICIA "Sounds good to me. One can eat me... while he punishes the other. Which one do you want first, baby?"

SANDY (the London vixen) "I need to be punished."

Lil B didn't need to answer. He simply reached out, grabbing Sandy by the wrist with authority. She dropped to her knees like she belonged there, eager and unashamed. Felicia leaned back, legs parted, while Jada descended between them, her tongue tracing slow fire along Felicia's thighs.

Around them, the room swelled with attention. A crowd circled, eyes gleaming in the low light, waiting for what came next. Some filmed. Some just watched. But no one dared interrupt.

This was no longer just a wild night—it was a legend in the making.

The lines had vanished—between pleasure and performance, fantasy and reality. It wasn't about sex anymore. It was about dominance, release, power, and exhibition. It was about being free in a world that chained so many.

And in that room, Lil B was king. The night had no rules. And the ghetto... it echoed louder than ever.

The lights inside the private swinger club glowed low, casting a seductive haze across the plush, towel-clad crowd. Lil B and Felicia sat at the bar, steam still rising from their coffee mugs, their towels damp from the heated encounters of the night.

Felicia took a pull from her blunt, her eyes playful but piercing.

"You better not come here without me," she teased, exhaling a soft cloud.

Lil B chuckled, leaned back, and took a long sip of coffee. "I never thought I could bust that many times in one night," he admitted, smirking with disbelief.

"That's 'cause you never had me before," she said, locking eyes with him.

His phone vibrated on the bar. He glanced at the screen, then flipped it back down without answering.

"She's been calling for the last hour," Felicia said casually, still watching him. "Go ahead, answer it. I won't blow your spot. She ain't got much longer anyway… Felicia has officially claimed her stake."

INT. DRIVE-IN MOVIE - NIGHT

Blu had Stone's full attention. Her head bobbed in his lap when his phone rang.

"Hello?"

"Hi, this is ADT. Can I have your password?"

"Linda G."

"Seems like a break-in occurred at 3242 Creek Lane. Shall we send the police?"

Stone cursed under his breath. "No, I'm a few minutes away."

INT. STONE'S HOUSE - NIGHT

Stone stood in front of the dryer, fists clenched. Clothes scattered. Blu watched TV, calm.

"You got a lot going on," she said. "I'll just leave."

Stone stared at her down. "Nah. Go chill out in my room. Something's not adding up."

Blu's phone buzzed. It was Apple. She declined the call and deleted the message.

Some wins come dirty. Some losses come clean. Brian's money rotted in the ground while a new generation rose, bold and reckless. The city's chessboard had flipped—power was shifting, quietly and quickly. And in this world, where every favor had a cost and every smile hid a threat, only the most calculated would survive the next storm.

CHAPTER 28

LIL B'S HOUSE – BATHROOM – NIGHT

Aaliyah paced in the hallway, her voice rising as she spoke through the door. Lil B had just cut the shower off and stepped out, towel around his waist.

"Brian, you just don't respect me. Out 'til morning, not answering your phone. Got me worried."

He dried off in silence, letting her words hang in the air.

JOYCE'S HOUSE – NIGHT

The mood was soft, seductive—R&B playing low, candles flickering, and bodies tangled in silk sheets. Joyce and Brian moved together, the rhythm slow, the air heavy with heat and release.

Later, in the stillness, they lay in the afterglow.

APPLE'S CAR – NIGHT

Amy and Apple sat outside Stone's house, parked in the shadows. Their eyes were sharp, locked onto the house as they sipped from iced coffees, keeping the energy low but the focus tight.

Three men entered. One exited minutes later with a duffel bag.

"Something's not right. We gotta get our girl outta there," Apple said, squinting.

BEDROOM – NIGHT

Joyce rested on her side, tracing a finger over Brian's chest as he stared at the ceiling.

"When can you travel?" she asked.

"Gotta get permission from my PO."

"I'd love to take you somewhere by the water. Treat you."

"Can't lie—I got too much on my plate. Too many moves to make. Been on one long vacation already."

She handed him a folder.

"Here's the list of houses you asked for. They need work, but once livable, they'll flip clean. My LLC has good credit—whatever you need, I got you."

TARA'S HOUSE – NIGHT

Al and Tara lay in bed, sheets kicked off, a laptop open between them.

"Babe, it's time we start investing heavier. I'm thinking daycare... maybe more duplexes," Tara said.

"Great minds," Al smirked.

"One more thing—I'm giving my brother 30%. His money started all this. It's only right."

OUTSIDE STONE'S HOUSE – NIGHT

Amy and Apple sat tense, pistols in their laps, eyes locked on the dark shadows moving inside.

"Bad vibes. Too long without a word. What Legs say we hit for?" Amy asked.

"$135,000. Clean," Apple answered.

AL'S WORK SPOT – DAY

Stacks of cash flipped through the counter. Al and Bo stood over it, counting brick by brick.

"Ms. Vickie said that was the last 150 till Santiago gets back. The drought's on," Al said.

"People I ain't heard from in years blowing up my phone. What's the play?" Bo asked.

"I'm checking around. We'll keep moving, but prices are gonna shoot. We gotta be ready."

STUDIO – DAY

Cam was in the booth, punching in bars, flowing with ease. Wiz manned the boards. Kiara and Dana danced in the back, thick smoke in the air.

"Bro killin' it! This might be the single right here," Mike Mike said.

"That track was made for him. He riding it like it owes him money," Midnight Black added.

"In pocket. Whole vibe is crazy. Midnight, you laced it," Wiz said.

FBI HEADQUARTERS – DAY

Agents surrounded a whiteboard.

"Only one WIC store bites on stamps. The others shut it down," Miller reported.

"That's our focus then. Start there. He'll give us the rest," Schwartz said.

"Buy's enough to get a wiretap. Let's move," Cap Hill added.

BRIAN'S LOUNGE – NIGHT

Brian sat alone, staring at an empty glass before him.

Brian (V.O.): If it's not one thing, it's another. What are the gods doing—testing me? Maybe I can sneak in, make a quick million, and vanish again. But nah... gotta trust the process. I preach patience—I need to live it. That 900K hit? That stung deep.

His phone buzzed.

"Yo yo," Brian answered.

"Big bro, life treating you good?" Von said over the phone.

"Hard, but I'm pushing. Still stacking pieces."

"Hate to bring bad news... spots got hit. Fifteen phones, twelve cartons gone."

"Nobody caught?"

"Nope. All ghosts."

"We'll bounce back. Sis will re-up another pack."

Just as he hung up, Cowboy and Julio walked in.

"Brian, my friend, why do you treat me like a stepchild? Been waiting for you to pull up to my bar," Julio said.

"Been busy trying to build my own," Brian laughed.

"I'll come straight with it—I want us back in business. It's a drought, man. Just like last time."

"Last time, your work didn't lock. You vanished. I had to hold that. You came back clean, I'll give you that—but I ain't running again."

"I need someone to take over. I trust you."

"Not now. I'm free, and I wanna stay that way."

"Fair enough. But for the record... the streets talking 26 to 28. For you? I'd do 23."

They walked outside. From a parked car, flashbulbs clicked—feds snapping shots from the shadows.

IKE'S HOUSE – NIGHT

Terri and Ike played tonk at the table, money stacked and drinks poured.

Terri read a message. Her face changed.

"We have a problem. Blu's still at Stone's house. No word. More companies pulled up."

She typed back quickly: "I'll be free in 30."

"That sounds like a setup. How'd they know about the dryer?" Ike asked.

Stone (V.O.): Someone broke the window, climbed in. Alarm triggered. They went right to the dryer.

"I'll be there in 30," Ike said, standing and grabbing his keys.

Terri poured another drink.

"Just when I was about to win back my money... and my pussy was getting warm. Shame."

"Don't trip. We'll pick up where we left off."

The game never sleeps. While Brian rebuilds and tries to walk a clean line, temptation pulls at every edge of his world. Feds close in. Enemies plot in silence. Alliances are fragile. And trust—rare as loyalty. In a city where love mixes with larceny and sex masks strategy, every night holds a new twist. Tomorrow's war could start with tonight's drink. And when the drought dries up every brick and dollar, the true players show their hand.

CHAPTER 29

THE EDGE OF EXPOSURE

INT. TASHA'S HOUSE – NIGHT

Smoke curled up toward the ceiling. Cards slapped the table. Liquor was flowing, and so was the shit-talking. Tasha, Black Rick, Vanessa, and Ellen played Spades with serious intent. Tara and Shan lounged on the couch, sipping drinks. The vibe was gritty and grown.

VANESSA

"Girl, last night I found my match. That man went rounds one, two, three, four—and five! I tapped out!"

ELLEN (laughing)

"Girl, he was on Viagra! When Stan takes one, he has my stuff tender for days."

BLACK RICK

"Hell, Tasha knows what y'all talkin' about—I beat that thing down plenty of nights on the blue pill."

TASHA (laughing, smacking her cards)

"Boy, shut your damn mouth."

The table roared in laughter.

TARA (serious now)

"Girl, if AL cheating on me, I'm takin' his ass to the cleaners. I been too damn down for him."

SHAN

"He ain't that stupid. Didn't you say he got a new plug flooding him with work?"

INT. BRE'S BEDROOM – NIGHT

Low light. Deep conversation. Jessica and Bre sat on the bed, passing a blunt between sips of wine.

JESSICA (softly)

"I think I'm falling for you."

Bre leaned in slow, brushing her lips over Jessica's. A kiss turned to more. Her hand slid over Jessica's breast, massaging gently. They melted into each other until Jessica paused.

JESSICA (breathless)

"I didn't know you were gay?"

BRE (calm, eyes locked)

"I didn't either… but you get my pussy wet. Been tryin' to hide how I feel."

INT. KK'S HOUSE – BEDROOM – NIGHT

KK sat on the edge of the bed, naked, her eyes locked on AL, who stood across the room in nothing but his boxers, his phone in hand. He read the text from Tara, smirking slightly.

TARA (TEXT MESSAGE)

"Been drinking, feeling some type of way. How long before you get home? I'm over at my sister's house."

AL typed back, quick and confident.

AL (TEXT MESSAGE RESPONSE)

"Perfect timing. I'll beat you there."

A moment later, Tara sent back a running emoji.

KK shifted, eyeing him.

KK

"Like that? Got me soaking wet, and you're about to dip over a damn emoji. She got you handpicked, nigga?"

AL chuckled and pulled on his pants.

AL

"You know the rules. Just keep that sweet box tight—I'll see you in the morning."

He smacked her ass playfully and walked out, leaving KK fuming, but quiet.

INT. TASHA'S HOUSE – LIVING ROOM – NIGHT

Tara gathered her things, clearly moving with purpose.

TARA

"Girl, time for me to go. AL's on his way home. Sis, I'll see y'all later."

TASHA

"That must be a dick call—you don't move this fast for anything else."

TARA

"Vanessa right, mind your business."

BLACK RICK

"Don't worry, she'll be out y'all business soon. Some might eat her out for an hour tonight—how I'm feelin'."

The room gave off an awkward pause before breaking into laughter. The night rolled on.

INT. LOUNGE – NIGHT

Brian stood surrounded by six sharp-eyed hustlers, his energy centered, voice calm but firm.

BRIAN

"Spread the word. People can place bets up here. I'll pay the next day. Poker games four days a week. Ten racks to sit at the table. Free meal. Two drinks on the house."

TROUP

"You 'bout to take over again, B. Most bookies make folks wait—day-one payout? I'll definitely get the word out."

BRIAN

"I got an app coming. Load your money, pick your games, pull up to collect. I'll have slots to—make it a full experience."

BURGER

"Just make sure the food is on fire. Nothing like good eats."

TROUP

"That's all you think about—food."

They laughed, but the energy was shifting. Brian was building something again.

INT. JULIO'S CAFE – NIGHT

Julio leaned in close to Cowboy, the low light reflecting off his anxious eyes.

JULIO

"We gotta get Brian back in the game. I haven't had anyone even close to his numbers. We just need to find his weakness."

COWBOY

"He'll come around. Jack said he had $1.5 million buried—only $700K was still good. Rest turned to mildew. That'll pull him back."

He stood and walked off.

EXT. JULIO'S CAFE – NIGHT

DEA agents sat in an unmarked vehicle, snapping photos of Jack walking out the café doors while Julio stood casually outside.

DEA AGENT

"Let's head back to the office. Show the captain what we got. This ties in nicely."

INT. TERRI'S CONDO – NIGHT

Terri paced, phone tight in hand.

TERRI

"Waiting on bro and Charlie Mo. We riding over there. I was with Ike when Stone called him."

AMY

"We're gonna set it off. If there's one scratch on Blu, they can't get there fast enough. I need a hit."

Amy bent and snorted a line of coke.

APPLE

"I texted Big John. No response yet. There's no way they can link Blu. We broke the window ourselves—made it look like a regular break-in."

TERRI

"How'd Blu even get y'all a key?"

APPLE

"Girl, Blu slick. Played drunk and sleepy, got the alarm code. The night we shot pool, she held his keys. Had our locksmith homegirl pull up and make copies."

TERRI

"So that's why she was in the bathroom so long. That girl always finds a way."

INT. FBI HEADQUARTERS – DAY

Agents Miller and Schwartz sat in front of a cluttered table filled with files and surveillance shots.

MILLER

"The store belongs to Imani Peterson. Married to Jamie Peterson—he's done federal time. If we get a pull-over and search warrant, we'll likely find a gun. That'll put pressure on him."

SCHWARTZ

"I like that. Let me talk to Cap—get the ball rolling."

MILLER

"We hit the other stores, sent in someone, but no luck. They didn't bite."

SCHWARTZ

"Forget 'em. We're going all in on Jamie. He's our ticket."

EXT. PARK – DAY

Cory, JP, and TA leaned against their cars, watching families and kids file out from practice.

CORY

"We win these next three—we're bowl bound. Frank Ski game. Big platform."

TA

"Only one I'm worried about is Ben Hill. They are loaded."

CORY

"Can't sleep on Atlanta Vikings or Dekalb Gold either."

JP

"Everything is steady on my end. Looking for a new spot though."

CORY

"Make sure no new faces get involved. I had two funny types come into the store. Didn't even know how to ask about selling stamps."

TA

"I'm keeping my eyes out. And about those houses?"

CORY

"Down payment is ready. Just waiting on the LLC to come back. Then we rocking."

EXT. GOLF RANGE – DAY

Sunlight hit the green as waiters moved between tents, serving wine and hors d'oeuvres. Power vibrated through the air—old money and new ideas.

LEAH

"You see that couple? Own the biggest Black Chevy dealership in Atlanta. And him? He owns Radio One with his momma—Hot 107.9."

LIL EAZY

"A lot of money and influence here."

LEAH

"My dad says it best—'It's not what you know. It's who you know.' So smile. Rub the right elbows."

A waitress passed. Lil Eazy grabbed a glass of wine.

LIL EAZY

"I'll drink to that. You not drinking?"

LEAH

"No."

Every hustler, every player, every dreamer standing at the crossroads of the game faces the same question: stay in the lane you're in—or pivot, evolve, and play a bigger one. But when the streets start drying up and the feds begin circling, some choices come faster than comfort allows. The whispers are growing louder, the heat is rising, and the weak won't survive the burn.

CHAPTER 30

In a world stitched together by secrets, droughts, and double plays, moves were made behind closed doors while other plays unraveled under park skies and golf course champagne. The grind never slept, and neither did the whispers. Trust was thin, supply was tighter, and every player—from trap boys to power brokers—was calculating their next checkmate.

Lil B sat on a bench at the park, watching Felicia's son play while his mind danced between pressure and potential. Felicia, always observant, caught the weight in his silence.

"Are you good?" Felicia asked. "Seems like something's on your mind. Are you in trouble at the house?"

"I'm good, just thinking about my next move," Lil B replied. "This drought is messing me up—and my birthday is coming up."

"Yeah, it's ugly," Felicia said. "I can get you ten or twenty. My mom always keeps a stash. We always work during a drought."

Lil B's eyes lit up like birthday candles. "Don't be playing with me. AL said it's over with for two weeks."

"Yeah, with what Santiago left for her to give AL—but we have work. Numbers a little higher."

"You're music to my ears. When? Let me know."

"When I get back. How old are you turning?"

"The big 21."

Later, at the golf range, Leah introduced Lil Eazy to her brother.

"Russell, this is my brother, Lenny. Lenny, this is Russell."

They shook hands firmly, measuring each other.

"Okay, Leah, I see you switching up. He's not your normal prototype," Lenny said with a laugh, though his eyes were sharp.

"What do you mean by that?" Lil Eazy asked, tension layered in his voice.

"No offense to you. I'm actually giving you props. Sis normally brings squares or lames around—like Carlton from Fresh Prince."

"Lenny, you always think you know me," Leah said.

"I'm definitely a long way from that," Lil Eazy added.

Later, in Lil Eazy's car, smoke curled through the cabin as Lenny passed the blunt.

"So many fakes out there. All they really want is city contracts. They lick your balls for them," Lenny said.

"That's a good thing for your dad, right?" Lil Eazy asked.

"I guess, but it gets tricky. Piss the wrong person off, and they're telling about behind-door deals."

Lenny pointed out people on the golf course. "See him? Blue sweater, yellow shirt—married, kids, million-dollar company—loves tricking with strippers. Pastor Short? Likes young boys. That white lady in the white hat? Ms. Rose. Made millions off insurance fraud—owns three stores at the airport."

He turned to Lil Eazy. "Two reasons I told you all this: One—it's not what you do, it's how you do it. Two—you find people's weakness, you find their pockets."

At Felicia's house, Lil B was watching TV when Felicia walked in.

"You can get 15. Everything was counted for, but my mom loves your daddy," Felicia said.

"Thanks. Sure appreciate it. What's the number?"

"Twenty-seven. You can pay upfront, or get on your face card."

"I'll pay for half now, and the rest in three days."

Ms. Vickie walked in, spandex tight and eyes sharp.

"You can thank your dad. During the drought, I only rock with my day ones."

"Thanks so much."

"No problem. You thank your dad."

"See, Lil B—we make a good team," Felicia said. "And have plenty of fun while we're getting plenty of money."

At the DEA office, Captain Spencer leaned over photos.

"Brian Jordan back on the streets? He's the reason I was promoted. Is he back in business?"

"Not as of yet. But Julio's trying to pull him back in," Agent Cox said.

"Now the plot thickens. Keep me posted. Any location?"

"Off Cascade—by that beautiful restaurant he's trying to flip into a lounge."

At Terri's condo, tension filled the air. Cocaine lines. Loaded clips.

"We are ready. Load up. We park down the street till morning. If Blu is not out—we are going in. I texted Ike, no answer."

"Been a minute since I spilled blood. Overdue," Charlie Mo said.

"Yeah, sis. Me and Mo putting something together. I'm dealing with one of Lil Easy's folks. We are about to MJG his ass—lay it down," Toni added.

"Let me know if y'all need backup," Terri said.

At Brian's lounge, Jeff leaned over spreadsheets while Bre looked uneasy.

"We did badly on that GE option trade," Brian said.

"I read it wrong—bad earnings. But I'll make it up," Jeff said.

"So if it doesn't hit by the strike date, we lose it all?"

"So yeah, we pretty much take a gamble on the stock moving to such a target by a date and if it doesn't, you lose your money. High risk. High reward."

"But with investing in regular stocks, as long as you don't sell, you have a chance of getting your money back."

"Correct. If anything, buy the dip. Hold tight if you know it's a strong company."

"10-4."

"I saw all the red. Got scared. Thought I messed up," Bre said.

"Nah, you're doing good. Just never let fear lead. Sometimes we are wrong. Sometimes the market's crazy. In the words of Warren Buffett—when they panic, we buy."

In the drought, survival wasn't just about product—it was about position, relationships, and the weight of history. As old money stirred and new connections formed, pressure mounted across the board. From federal agents to corner dealers, golf ranges to backroom poker games, the line between success and set-up blurred. The game wasn't just about staying afloat anymore—it was about who could swim when the tide finally pulled out. And the water was already getting cold.

CHAPTER 31

PRESSURE BURSTS PIPES, BUT DIAMONDS SHINE

The drought had turned the streets into a chessboard—every move calculated, every hustle sharpened. Loyalty was up for sale, and the only ones surviving were those who could adapt. But in the heart of this chaos, the game wasn't just about bricks and bags anymore—it was about legacy, leverage, and learning how to win while smiling through the losses.

Lil B, Mike Mike, and Cam sat around a table in the trap house, stacks of money spread out like war trophies.

"So you telling me Ms. Vickie's daughter put the play together? You got one—she down as hell," Mike Mike said.

"I need her other daughter if they are doing like that," Cam added.

Lil B nodded. "She set the play, but it was my dad's face card that made Ms. Vickie pull the trigger. She only deals with day ones. My pop needs to make a comeback—we'd have the streets in a headlock."

"Not too many moves like Unk. We are about to kill the streets with this work," Mike Mike said.

Outside, Lil Eazy stood near a car talking to Leah.

"Look, I gotta go. I'll call you later on," he said.

"OK. Be safe. And my brother? He's taken a liking to you—that's half the battle. Dinner's later this week with my dad. Don't flake," she replied.

They kissed. Lil Eazy hopped in the car and pulled off.

At Brian's house, he was on the phone while Joyce stirred a pot in the kitchen.

"The Mexicans got it hot on the compound—meth and fetty have it hotter than 4th July. Been four shakedowns this week," Joe said through the phone.

"Hard drugs are bad for business. That's why I told Von—no drugs. Phones and cigs hit different. Quiet money," Brian responded.

"Right. DC car and South Carolina car are still fueling someone getting stabbed every day. Have you connected with Lou and them yet?"

"In a few days. My lounge is coming together. And what I had buried? Don't even wanna talk about it. Still piecing it all back," Brian said.

That night in the trap house, Lil Eazy dropped a money bag on the table.

"Went to the park playing step dad—came back with 15 bricks. This is my half."

"Say less. You know I don't play," Lil B said.

They high-fived.

"Streets bone-dry. We 'bout to run through these. You tell Al?" Lil Eazy asked.

"Not yet. Wasn't sure if I should."

"He might get salty. I was around some elite folks—deep pockets, real legit. We gotta stack and get a seat at that table."

At Al's work spot, Al and Bo spoke with frustration.

"Nobody is moving. Streets dry as bones," Al said.

"I'm down to scraps. Tyrone gon' stretch my last ones. Till the re-up..."

"Ike might know something, but he is dealing with his own situation."

"Something always breaks. Just gotta stay tight."

"Hit Ms. Vickie—see how she looking," Al said.

Later, in the trap house, Lil B was on the phone grinning. Cam and Mike Mike handed off bags, cash coming fast.

"Zip a thousand," Lil Eazy said, entering with G-Mack.

"Need 25. You are right on time," G-Mack replied.

"Fire jumpin', in the water."

They sealed the deal. G-Mack left.

"We moved 250 zips. Stack a piece. Drought is real," Cam said.

"Hope it lasts. My dad and Brian made their best runs during droughts. And we are not even cutting," Lil Eazy added.

"We separate the boys from the men," Mike Mike said.

"What are you doing for the big 21?" Lil Eazy asked Lil B.

"Throw a fool party. Hit a beach. Need that."

At Ms. Vickie's house, she sat with LB, Felicia, Dominique, Clay, and Slim.

"I talked to Santiago. Might be back soon. If not, Hector got someone," Ms. Vickie said.

"They thirsty gotta move streets dry dry," LB said.

"LB is hot with you over those bricks you sold Lil B," Ms. Vickie said to Felicia.

"He'll live. I needed a new outlet. Plus he was somewhat grandfathered in," Felicia said.

"He is already eating with Al. He is not leaving blood," LB said.

"We'll see. Don't underestimate me," Felicia replied.

"Clay got something to say," Dominique said.

"Thinking expansion. Need more work next run," Clay said.

"No problem," Ms. Vickie answered.

"Clay, I like how you move," LB said.

That night, Lil B and Lil Eazy sat in the trap house, drained.

"Long day. I'm laying low—some shady moves in the city," Lil B said.

"Today was solid. We'll pay 'em off tomorrow," Lil Eazy replied.

"Studio time," Cam said.

"Got a hot one waiting," Mike Mike added.

At Brian's house, he played Monopoly with his daughters.

"Key to a good life? Passive income. Money works while you sleep, travel, or do nothing," Brian said.

"Daddy, that's my property! You owe me $1,000!" Malin shouted.

Laughter erupted. Pairs rolled.

"How much do I owe you?" Pairs asked.

"$950. I'm winning tonight!" Malin said.

The phone rang. Brian walked off.

"Lou?" he answered.

"Uncle ready to meet," Lou said.

"Send time and location. I'll be early," Brian replied.

At Lil Eazy's house, he entered to find Hannah on the couch.

"Found us flights and beach rooms," Hannah said.

"Where do you see yourself in 5 years?" Lil Eazy asked.

"More babies. Marry you. Travel. Stay home," she said.

"Gotta think bigger. A lot can change in 5."

"As long as we are together, I'm good."

"Yeah but two is always better than one. You need to think of a plan for a business or something."

"I hear you," Hannah said.

At the gas station that night, Terri, Apple, Amy, Toni, and Charlie Mo sat in a car.

"We are going in at dawn. Ike is gone. Time to strike," Terri said.

"We need to hit 3 AM. Cold still in their eyes," Charlie Mo replied.

"Nah. Ike texted—wants to see me. I played along," Terri said.

"Say anything about Blu?" Amy asked.

"Nah. Just wanted pussy pics. I sent him legs, pretty pussy," Terri replied.

"Blu better be good. If not? It's war," Apple said.

That night, Brian and his girls curled up watching TV.

"Daddy, what was it like in there? Did you drop the soap?" Pairs asked.

Brian laughed. "It's what you make it. Hardest part? Missing y'all."

"Was the food gross?" Malin asked.

"Had folks cooking for me. Never touched chow hall food."

"We missed you. Cried nights. Daddy dances. Everything," Pairs said.

"I cried too. Never again," Brian replied.

"What's passive income again?" Malin asked.

Brian smiled. "Google it. Teach me tomorrow."

The drought brought clarity. Everyone wanted a slice, but few had the vision to bake the cake. In the shadows, new kings were learning the weight of a crown. The money was stacking, but so was the tension. Brian saw the next storm brewing, and Lil Eazy? He was learning fast—being at the table required more than bricks and brawn. It needed strategy, poise, and sacrifice. Because in this game, only the sharp survive. And Blood will either bind or spill.

CHAPTER 32

CLOSE CALLS AND CRACKED LOYALTIES

In the game they played, time and trust were always in short supply. Pressure made people slip, lust clouded logic, and even day ones could become liabilities. As the drought kept tightening its grip, every move became a test of discipline and every silence screamed betrayal. Lines between love and loyalty blurred, and the ones who survived were those who listened close, moved quiet, and kept a bullet for the unexpected.

Stone sat on edge, voice low, half paranoia, half clarity. "At this point, I don't know what to think. You think Down by Law had something to do with this?"

"Hard to say. Fifty-fifty. Streets are too quiet right now. We just gotta keep our ears to the ground," JE replied. "What about ol' girl in there—you letting her go?"

Stone exhaled, rubbing the back of his neck. "Maybe I'm overthinking it. She got some good pussy, but damn... they timed it perfectly. Just glad they missed the half a mill."

Behind the cracked bedroom door, Blu listened. Her face soured. She'd played her role too well—only to be reduced to a body and a suspicion.

In the dark outside of Stone's place, Terri and Apple sat posted in a car, heater in arms and tension in the air.

"We are about to surprise attack their ass," Apple said.

"One-two punch," Terri agreed. "Let's just hope we are not too late."

Brian leaned back in a pedicure chair beside Malin and Pairs at a nail shop. Their toes soaked while the conversation deepened.

"So Malin, what college are you eyeing?" Brian asked.

"Howard. Like Mommy," Malin answered with a smile.

"What about you, Pairs?"

"Duke or LSU. Me and my boyfriend are thinking about 'em. That's where he wants to play ball."

"Hold up—Malin, you got a boyfriend?"

"No, Daddy."

They laughed. The moment was light but the undertones heavy— Brian quietly clocking how fast his girls were growing.

Precious wiped sweat from her neck in the gym, her tone casual but her mind clearly elsewhere.

"Girl, I almost called Brian for a booty call the other night. I was out with Cory... but I was thinking about Brian."

"You already know how I feel," Roxy replied. "Y'all been tied to the soul. He's your rhythm."

"He's different now. Grounded. Something about his energy... it sticks."

Later that night, Stone dropped his jeans, tossing them near the bed.

"Get naked, on all four," he ordered.

Blu obeyed. Stone hit her with a grudge from the back like he knew this would be his last time. Afterwards, silent and mechanical, he tossed her phone back without looking her in the eye.

"You can leave. I'll call you later."

As Blu stepped out of the house moments later, Terri, Apple, Toni, and Charlie Mo crouched across the street.

"Me and Charlie take front. You and Toni hit the back," Terri instructed.

The door creaked open. Blu walked to her car like she hadn't just been under fire.

In a restaurant across town, Brian, Lil B, Malin, and Pairs shared a meal—laughing, joking, bridging gaps.

"Bro, thanks for the Jordans," Pairs said. "Me and sis were the first to rock 'em at school. Everyone was asking how we got them early."

"Y'all already know," Lil B smiled. "Got a bigger surprise coming too. Stay tuned."

"Have you talked to your mom lately?" Brian asked.

"I was over there with Doc. She walked in, we talked for a minute. But you know Meke... always about money."

Brian's mind drifted as his voice crept in.

It's my job to give them the tools. I can't get back the time I lost, but I gotta make this time count. My son? He moving like I did. And my girls? Sharp, but still green. There's still time... I just have to reach them.

"I got it, Dad. My treat," Lil B said, grabbing the check.

"Thank you. Just remember—know thyself. Trust yourself. Everything that glitters ain't gold. Life's about decisions... some you live with forever."

At the pool hall, Lil Eazy, Mike Mike, Bo, and Al tossed back drinks while chalking cues.

"Where is Lil B at?" Al asked.

"With his pops," Lil Eazy replied.

"Good. Family time—keep the soul fed. These streets don't refill you."

"Real talk," Bo nodded. "Gotta cherish that time."

"Y'all my family for real," Lil Eazy said. "Pop gone. Me and Mom are not on the best terms. Y'all it for me."

"When Santiago land, he double me up. Strap your cleats on," Al said.

At Terri's condo, Blu sat on the couch—drinking, smoking, trying to forget.

"Girl, I'm glad to be back. I started thinking the worst," Blu admitted.

"We were on the way with choppers. Me and Charlie Mo were 'bout to bring the storm," Terri said.

"Charlie Mo pulled up? Oh yeah—it was really up."

"We hit $135K," Apple added.

Blu paused. "That doesn't sound right. Stone said $150K. Who counted?"

"Legs. She went back alone. You sure?" Terri asked.

"Positive. Told y'all... she's suspect."

"Don't worry—I got a trick for her. She reaches for that cookie jar again? We are breaking fingers."

Pressure breeds movement—and not all of it in the right direction. People plotting, people watching, people slipping. One minute it's love and laughter. The next, it's whispers, weight, and war. Trust is bleeding out. And the ones who think they're ahead? Might already be in someone's crosshairs.

CHAPTER 33

THE DOOR SWINGS BOTH WAYS

Every move had weight now. The drought wasn't just drying up the streets—it was drying up patience, loyalty, and even morality. Money moved fast. But so did whispers. And when the game heats up, the smart either diversify, disappear, or play quiet long enough to flip the board. Brian was planting flags. The feds were pulling strings. And beneath the surface, people who once moved with trust started moving with caution.

Brian pulled up to his newly renovated sports bar with his daughters, Pairs and Malin. Jack stood inside with a crew putting up lighting, testing audio systems, and setting tables.

"Girls, this is my business. I'm about to open it up," Brian said.

"Daddy, we wanna work here when it opens!" the girls chimed.

"I'll find something for y'all to do."

He smiled, proud and grounded. Jack walked over as Brian kissed his daughters on their heads and walked off with him.

"Coming together is really nice," Jack said. "Hey, Ashley came by my spot—left her number. Wants you to call."

"Damn. Haven't heard from her in many moons. How is she looking?"

Jack grinned. "Damn good."

Terri walked in on Blu soaking in a bubble bath, candles lit, a glass of wine nearby.

"You good-good?" Terri asked.

"Yeah. Just mad we moved too fast—missed out on half a million. And Stone actually bragged about taking that hit. Call it chump change."

"Girl, that must've been what one of them walked out with in that duffle. Damn, we snoozed. I'm putting together a vacation. Water is so clear you forget your problems."

Lil B walked in with Felicia. Al, Bo, and Lil Easy were finishing a game.

"Right on time. Strip club tonight. Been a minute," Al said.

"Word around town is Stone got touched for a few hundred grand," Bo added.

"Damn. That gotta sting," Lil Eazy said.

"Just a lil'. Boy got cash, though. He'll eat the loss. Y'all ready?"

Strobe lights hit the floor. Terri and her crew were already inside, making it rain, bottles popping, dancers on them. Charlie Mo and Toni nearby. Walk in, AL, Lil Eazy, Lil B, and their crew strolled in.

"Ladies, some real ballers just walked in! AL and his crew in the building!" the DJ boomed.

The club erupted as "Ballin'" by Jill Jones dropped. Terri and Toni cut cold looks across the club—eyes locking with Lil Eazy and Lil B as tension sparkled under the bass.

Brian and Jack sat across from three Asian men in a backroom steam room.

"I can have your app built in three months. I need half up front," Lee said.

Brian handed him three thick envelopes. "Appreciate you doing business with me."

"No, thank you. You looked out for Lou inside. He said you were like a big brother. He's small, timid. But smart."

"He's solid."

"Let me return the favor. It's our tradition. You both get a hot bath, massage... and a happy ending."

Brian and Jack exchanged smirks as two girls stepped into the hallway, motioning them down.

Both crews were throwing money, dancers everywhere. Mike Mike stepped out of the restroom and bumped into Legs.

"My bad," Mike Mike said, catching her eyes and admiring her short skirt.

"No problem, handsome," Legs replied.

They locked into small talk, exchanged numbers with subtle smiles.

Jack and Brian walked out glowing.

"One thing we didn't cover—the app's upkeep. $25K a year. If you're growing, it means you're winning. We're making millions. You can too—if you run it right," Lee said.

JP sat in his car, blue lights flashing behind him. He groaned as two agents, Miller and Moore, approached.

"What now?" JP muttered.

"Mr. JP, this paper gives us permission to search your vehicle," Miller said.

"For what? I haven't done anything!"

"Step out, sir."

JP got out reluctantly. "There's a gun in the glove box. It's my wife's. Her car, not mine."

Moore retrieved the gun.

"JP, you're a felon. Doesn't matter whose gun. You're coming with us."

Boston and Mal played video games. Ashley dug through Mal's backpack—and froze when she pulled out half-eaten food and puzzles.

"Mal… why do you have this stuff in your bag?"

Mal looked down, embarrassed, and ran into the bathroom.

Precious sat beside Cory. A smooth playlist filled the space. He puffed a cigar.

"We're close. Just waiting on the bank to accept the offer," Precious said.

"We play this right, we get two more stores and a few more houses, we'll be legacy living," Cory replied.

"Roxy and I have been thinking about opening a WIC store together. She needs a break."

"That's a boss move. Black wealth. Let's make it happen."

JP sat sweating under bright lights. A red record light blinked on the camera in the corner.

"Before I say anything—I want my lawyer. That gun? My wife's. She left it," JP said.

Miller chuckled darkly. "Gun's half your problem. What about the WIC store?"

JP leaned forward, now serious. "What about it? It's a legit business."

"It would be. But cash-for-stamps? That's a federal offense. We could lock your wife up... unless you help us," Moore said.

"Help y'all? Naw. That's all on me."

The street lights don't shine on secrets for long. Everyone's making plays—some loud, some quiet, some just desperate. While Brian builds legit, the feds tighten ropes, and love is beginning to look like leverage. And just when things feel stable, the truth usually walks in without knocking.

CHAPTER 34

THE COST OF KEEPING QUIET

In a city where secrets pay and silence is currency, the loudest moves are the ones no one sees coming. While the streets stay parched and pockets scream for relief, the game doesn't slow—it adapts. Some hustle for survival. Others for legacy. But everyone knows: one misstep, one whisper too loud, and everything collapses. And still, the money flows—quietly, dangerously, relentlessly.

Ashley's condo was quiet except for the faint hum of the TV. Mal stepped out of the bathroom, eyes low, body language timid. Ashley sat on the edge of the couch, her expression soft but concerned.

"Mal, you're not in trouble," she said gently. "I just wanted to understand why everything you ate was wrapped up and half-eaten."

Mal hesitated. "Ms. Ashley… I bring food back for my little brother and sister. My mommy sells her food stamps for drugs. There isn't any food in the house."

Ashley sat back, stunned—no words, just silence and swelling emotion. She walked over, pulled him into a hug that lingered, protective.

"We're going grocery shopping," she said. "Whatever y'all eat, we'll get it. But this here? Been sitting out too long—might make them sick."

Mal's shoulders shook, fighting tears as she held him tighter.

In the park, Brian jogged along the paved path, his breaths steady, his mind sharper than ever.

You can be Black, Brown—but don't be broke, he thought. *That's the real racism in America: finance. Smart decisions, smart timing. One mistake can set you back years. Making money is one thing. Keeping it? That's the real test.*

He slowed near a bench and pulled out his phone as it rang.

"Hello?"

"Hey," Joyce said through the speaker. "Our closing date's set—December 15. That work?"

"Perfect. What are you doing tonight?"

"Showing a couple houses. Then I'm in for the night."

"Cool. I'll grab us something to eat. Slide through."

"Can't wait."

Tasha parked in a busy lot and stepped out just as Ms. White pulled up beside her. With a quick exchange of cash and two bags, they nodded, shared a few words, and parted like clockwork.

Inside Ms. Vickie's back office, the energy was low and tense. She sat across from LB.

"Hector's about to pull up," she said.

"Is he still moving with his people?" LB asked.

"I told him we want to grab a hundred—maybe two."

"Santiago?"

"Still saying anytime. I'm not waiting on anybody."

At Leah's house, Lil Easy lounged in her room. As he stepped into the hallway, he caught a glimpse inside Lenny's room—four men locked into laptops, screens flashing.

"Russell, slide in," Lenny called.

They dapped up.

"You got some of that fire on you?" Lenny asked. "Just told my boys about it."

"Only a little," Lil Easy replied. "Got more back home."

"Bet. This is my partner, Pierre."

They shook hands.

"What y'all on?" Lil Easy asked.

Lenny grinned. "Millions. But I'll break it down to you later."

At Terri's condo, the girls lounged on the couch, watching the news.

"Turn that up!" Apple said. "Ain't that them white boys from the PJ party?"

Amy smirked. "That's the one who ate my pussy… then asked for fingers. Freaky ass!"

They cracked up.

"Dan said we needed to be at that table," Terri added. "But didn't mention they were billionaire tech heads. We hit a goldmine. We throwing another party. Soon."

The anchor on TV continued, "A $2 billion company is moving to Atlanta, bringing with it 200 jobs."

"Then we definitely put on something," Terri said. "Bigger. Better."

Julio's business was low-lit but steady. Hector and JP walked in with LB. Julio and his crew were mid-meal, calm and casual.

"Hector, my brother," Julio said, standing.

"Julio, my brother. This is LB. He wants to do business."

Julio eyed LB carefully, then gave a subtle nod to his friends. They returned it.

"I thought Ms. Vickie wanted to meet," Julio said.

"This is her man. Partner, too," Hector replied.

Across the street, inside an unmarked car, DEA agents Sanders and Cox watched with interest.

"You recognize the two that went in?" Sanders asked.

Cox snapped photos. "Nah, but I got good shots."

Back inside, Julio leaned back in his chair, tone now firm.

"So, what's on your mind?" he asked.

"Looking to purchase 200," LB said. "If the numbers are right."

"Only one running the city right now," Julio said. "My number is 25K. Non-negotiable."

LB nodded. "We'll take 100. Ready now."

They shook hands, sealing a deal that would ripple fast and wide.

While the drought starved the streets, silent deals whispered new tides. Loyalty began folding under opportunity. Trust shifted into transactions. And just like that, the game tilted again.

The question wasn't who had work—it was who had leverage.

In a city this thirsty, even half-truths could buy a full seat at the table.

CHAPTER 35

POWER PLAYS & PRESSURE POINTS

In a world where every move costs something, love and loyalty aren't just feelings—they're leverage. From penthouse suites to trap house streets, the players are leveling up. But behind every smile, there's strategy. Behind every deal, a deeper motive. And when the feds are circling, every moment counts. This is the part where the masks fall off… and the stakes explode.

The suite at the Ritz-Carlton was dipped in soft sunlight and indulgent silence. Felicia lounged in a silk robe on the edge of the bed, while Lil B lay back in boxers, sipping from a flute of champagne.

"Lil early birthday gift," Felicia said. "Sometimes, just relaxing, good food, and great sex refresh the mind."

"Thanks. You really are one of a kind," Lil B replied.

"I want us to be a power couple," she said. "Your hustle. My reach. We'd be unstoppable."

"You know me and Lil Eazy—ride-or-die. Ain't nothing coming between us."

"I respect that. I'm not saying split. Just… think about getting straight from us instead of through Al. Save you a few racks. Growth, baby—that's the game."

Lil B grinned. "You said we are here to relax. All this talk? Bend over. Let me think about it while I stroke."

Felicia licked her lips. Lil B grabbed her gently, flipped her over and pulled her dress up, giving her what she came for.

At the DEA office, photos of Julio, his crew, JB, and Hector filled a corkboard. Seven agents gathered around the table while Agent Sanders led the session. Spencer sat in the back—silent, calculating.

"Julio's been slippery for five years," Sanders said. "Won't talk on the phone. The two CIs we had? Ended up dead."

"These two people met with him today," Cox added. "Hour-long meeting. We ran the tag—waiting on deeper intel."

"Drought's got the city dry," Sanders continued. "Julio's still working. We need to find his stash house. Start pulling over his clients. Apply pressure."

Finally, Spencer spoke. "Julio plays chess, not checkers. I believe he's got an insider. Brian Jordan was our closest link. But he wouldn't flip. Let's identify those two men. They might be our best shot."

At her son's school, Tara kneeled next to a table of crayons and finger paint, smiling as Allen played.

"So glad you came to help," his teacher said. "The kids adore you."

"I almost became a teacher after college," Tara said. "It was my first love."

"What changed?"

"Entrepreneur bug bit me."

"Wish I was that brave."

Allen ran up. "Mommy, can we get ice cream after school?"

"Yes, baby. Now clean up—bell's about to ring."

Outside the mall, Al strolled with KK, bags in both hands.

"Thanks for my gifts, Daddy," she said.

"You know I got you. What does Marques' daddy say?"

"Said he'll talk to his girl this week about letting Marques move in."

Al's phone rang. He answered, "Tell me something good."

"Tomorrow, first thing. Price is 30 ball—but I can only get 10," Ike said on the line.

"Say less," Al replied.

"That call made you happy," KK said, smirking.

"Baby, I ain't worked in a minute."

At JP's house, Imani stepped out of the shower. JP sat on the bed, hunched.

"You've been off the last few days," she said. "What's going on?"

"Feds pulled me over. Searched the car. Found a gun."

"We are legit now. Forget them."

"They're threatening you. And the kids. They want me to help bring down Cory and TA."

"Are you serious?"

"Somebody in the store sold it to an undercover. I can't let you go down."

His phone rang. "Yo."

"Our toys are in. We pick up tomorrow," Cory said.

"What time?"

"Noon. See you there."

At Ms. Vickie's house, she stood behind her desk while LB paced.

"You agreed to this deal without me?"

"We can flip 'em for 28, 30 easy."

"Still… don't ever move without me. I would've talked Julio down and bought the whole load. You gotta think like a boss—not a worker. Now come make me happy."

Ms. Vickie laid back. LB slid between her legs, kissing her thighs. She moaned low, dangerous.

At a bar and grill, Mike Mike sat across from Legs. Two drinks deep, chemistry lit.

"So what are you into?"

"Spontaneity. Surprises."

"You got kids?"

"Nope. Selfish with my time. Maybe at 30."

He rubbed her leg. "Long legs. You hoop?"

"Nah. Volleyball. Got a scholarship to Clark. That's how I ended up in Atlanta."

They took shots. In Mike Mike's truck, she gave him head. He busted in eight minutes, shocked.

"Wow," he said, embarrassed.

Legs wiped her mouth, looked at him, grabbed his hand and placed it between her legs—soaking wet.

"That was just an appetizer. Wait till the full meal."

She stepped out, walked to her car, leaving him stunned.

As power shifts hands and alliances test their weight, the silence before the storm gets louder. Feds are watching. Relationships are colliding. And the game—forever ruthless—tightens its grip. Every move now has consequences. And in a city like this, only the sharp survive.

CHAPTER 36

POWER PLAYS & PRESSURE POINTS

Every move in the streets was like a chess piece—timing, angles, and sacrifices. And in the middle of droughts, when emotions ran high and money got tight, loyalty became negotiable. Everyone wanted leverage. Everyone had secrets. And the ones who smiled the most usually held the deadliest cards.

Julio sat in his back office, eyes locked on Hector.

"When will LB be ready?" Julio asked.

"He said in three hours," Hector replied.

Julio nodded. "I need people like Ms. Vickie on my team. Hosa, take Hector out the back door. You know the feds are across the street as usual. Now's the time to elude them."

"Okay, boss. Take him to the spot with me?" Hosa asked.

"Yep. Put an extra fifty on top of the hundred. Show Ms. Vickie I appreciate her business. She can pay me on the back end. Let her know, Hector, I want to meet with her in person next time."

"I will do that. Thanks for everything."

Hosa and Hector exited through the back. Julio stepped out the front with a friend, slipping into a pickup. The DEA, parked discreetly across the street, waited a beat before tailing him down the block.

Felicia tossed a burner on the bed, already grabbing her bag.

"Just received a text. We are about to be back on. You want in?"

"What kind of question is that, babe? Hell yeah," Lil B said.

"Not sure what the count is, but if possible, I'll try to get you twenty, as long as her boyfriend doesn't hate."

"That'd be real good."

"The number might have changed. Hate to break the trip, but we need to leave if you want to get in on the party."

"You can't get dressed fast enough," Lil B smirked.

Terri crouched, tying her shoe, but her eyes tracked Al entering the building with a heavy duffle.

What the hell Al doing here with a bag? she thought. This Ike's work spot. This nigga just slipped. Have to put a plan together fast.

She spotted another man walking out with a bag. Instinct kicked in—fast. She texted Toni.

TERRI (text message): How long can you and Charlie Mo be at Glenwood Rd? Have something sweet but need to move fast.

TONI (text response): 30 top.

TERRI: Get here.

Inside the apartment, Lee counted a thick stack of hundreds. Ike leaned back, cool but calculating.

"Main reason I'm letting you get in—I want the same favor. I had to leave a few of my people out."

"I appreciate you," Al said. "I haven't worked in a week. I'll take anything to make a dollar or two. Wish you could sell me more."

"Stone will kill me. He is the last person I'm waiting on, and I'm out. Only was only able to get fifty."

"Thanks again. Here, three hundred. How is it doing in water?"

"Great."

"Good. I'm re-rocking this deal—bring extra six back. Only deal with my out-of-towners; they won't complain."

At Lil B's trap house, Lil Eazy tossed a duffle on the floor. Mike Mike counted.

"Man, ol' girl showing out. Boy, she saved the day," Lil Eazy said.

"That's what happens when you lay that wood right. She wants us to get on their team—said we save a couple thousand on each brick and give us more on facecard," Lil B responded.

"That sound 'bout right. It's not personal, it's business."

"Yeah, but Al been good, and he has a family now. If Lil B gets her pregnant or married, that changes some things."

"I'm gonna talk to my dad, see what he says. 'Cause we know the grass is not always greener on the other side."

"Think we need to let Al know this time. Maybe Ms. Vickie will sell him something."

"I agree, but don't know if she will. Felicia had to fight for these ten."

Inside Ike's apartment, Terri sat on the edge of the bed, tapping away on her phone as Ike counted stacks.

"Man, we ran through them fifty quick. Here, take this eight hundred K—clear my tab with Hosa. See if it is more."

"Okay, I'll be back," Lee replied.

Outside the apartment, Lee stepped out with a briefcase and got into his car. Toni and Charlie Mo sat nearby, watching.

"Damn, looks like he is leaving with a nice chunk of change. We might need to follow him—clip his ass," Toni said.

"Naw, let's stick with the strip," Charlie Mo replied.

Ike entered the bedroom. Terri, in nothing but panties and a blunt, looked up.

"A day like this has me feeling some type of way. You look all sexy," Ike said.

"Nothing like a real go-getter. Love me a boss! You need to take a shower, fresher up, so I can suck you dry and swallow your baby—ride you till you cum all in me."

"Damn, you're getting me hard. Let me jump in the shower. I've been going hard since last night."

Terri texted:

TERRI (text message): Door gonna be unlocked. Come in three minutes—we will be in the shower.

She joined Ike under the hot stream. Lips met, steam rising, bodies connecting—until—

SHOWER DOOR OPENS

Charlie Mo and Toni stepped in with cold steel in hand.

"Get out. Now."

In the game, betrayal didn't come with warning labels. It came in steam and silence—right before the muzzle flashes. And when loyalty's up for negotiation, you better make sure your exit plan ain't just wishful thinking.

CHAPTER 37

The streets were buzzing louder than ever, but underneath the flash of G-Wagons and open mics was a storm brewing—one stitched together by loyalty, betrayal, and the whispers of old codes being rewritten. The city was alive, and the players were moving fast. Too fast. The question wasn't who was winning—it was who would survive the next move.

Cory, Precious, TA, Tammy, JP, and Imani stood outside the owner's office at a car lot, anticipation written all over their faces. The sunlight bounced off the chrome G-Wagons parked behind them like trophies waiting for kings and queens.

"Can't lie, y'all—just showed out. His and hers G-Wagons? We stunned harder than the D-Boys," Tammy said.

"Only one way to do this—we make statements. Loud ones," TA replied.

"This is just the beginning," Cory said. "We are locking in generational wealth for our kids' kids. Breaking cycles, one asset at a time."

"Just waiting on the bank to accept our offer on the houses. Plus, I have another list of gems. We are not slowing down," Precious added.

As two Black men stepped in and out of the office, the group remained locked in—eyes focused, hearts steady. The owner soon emerged, smiling, handing over a bundle of keys.

Across the street, behind tinted windows, the FBI's camera shutters clicked like clockwork. Six G-Wagons lined up like armored soldiers—chrome, matte black, white, red—each gleaming with promise. Cory and the crew looked directly into the lens, unbothered. They knew eyes were watching. Let them watch.

Inside an apartment, Ike lay motionless, blood beginning to cake at the corner of his mouth. The air was cold. Final.

"Make it look like a break-in gone bad," Terri ordered. "Take this phone—get rid of it. I want y'all to kick the door in. I'm jumping out the window just wearing a bra and panties, and running to the neighbor's in panic!"

"You sure about this plan, cuz?" Charlie Mo asked.

"Only one that will work. Lee knows I can't go MIA. We missed the big bag, but it still feels like a few hundred thousand," Terri said.

"Told Charlie we should've clipped him!" Toni chimed in.

"Alright, y'all. Two minutes. Pull it off clean," Terri said.

In an unmarked car across from the car lot, Miller and Moore sipped coffee. The air was thick with tension.

"They ballin' on the government dime. We're gonna seize every asset and tag them with big fines," Miller said.

"Six G-Wagons. Ain't no frontin' now. Wonder how deep this really goes," Moore replied.

"We have names. We got faces. Now it's time to build the web."

Cory's crew pulled off in formation—hazard lights blinking like a siren call.

Later that night, Ike's apartment was wrapped in yellow tape and flashing lights. A crime scene.

Terri, wrapped in a sheet, held her arm as she spoke to officers and neighbors.

"I had just gotten out of the shower. The door kicked in. Ike was still washing up. Two masked men stormed in. I jumped out the window—barely made it," she told the officer.

"You get a good look? Faces, size, race, clothes?"

"Black males. Average size. All black everything."

"We'll need your info. You'll need to come to the precinct too. Need a hospital?"

"No. Just cut from the glass. My number—504-788-2368."

Across the street, Lee drove by slowly... but never stopped.

At the Sweatbox Sports Bar, Brian and Jack chopped it up. Lil Eazy and Lil B walked in, surprised to see them.

"Russell, you look more like your pops every day," Jack said. "I spoke with Penny—she said she ain't heard from you."

"I was mad at how she handled things," Lil Eazy replied. "I was 16 when she kicked me out. Said I couldn't live under her roof and be in the streets. So I left. Now 23, and knee-deep in the game. Time flew."

"She's been through a lot. The Feds tried to take everything. She just didn't want you ending up like your father."

"She started drinkin'. Poppin pills too. Still love her—but she left me cold. Brian and Precious took me in. That's real."

Elsewhere, Stone and Lee sat close, nerves exposed.

"Ike died," Lee said. "Girl said somebody kicked the door in while he was showering. She jumped out the window half-naked."

"First me... now Ike. And in both cases, the same crew is around. Same girls. Patterns don't lie," Stone replied.

"Feels real familiar."

"Time to press them. No more playing cool."

At Terri's condo, the money was stacked. The team was high. Celebration in motion.

"$165K even. Nice hit," Apple said.

"But not the whole pie. We missed a million-dollar bag by seconds," Terri replied.

"I saw him walk out with the bag. Should've followed my instinct," Toni said.

"You sure nobody comin' for you?" Charlie Mo asked.

"They better not. Or they'll regret it."

Glasses clinked. Laughter rolled through smoke.

"This my early Christmas, sis," Toni said. "Bout to go grab that car I've been eyein'. Thank you for hitting us up."

Back at Brian's lounge:

"Y'all need an LLC," Brian said. "Start a legit trail. Bank account. EIN. Get a real paper trail."

"We're thinking of launching a label. Cam got real heat," Lil B said.

"I'll get Joyce to file it once y'all tell me the name. But remember—the music business is a dirty game. Study the business. Learn the lingo. It's called show business for a reason."

"Been talking to Ms. Vickie's daughter. She is pushing for me to work with her team," Lil B added.

Brian and Jack locked eyes.

"She's been hustling since she came outta her mom womb," Brian said. "But listen—every man Ms. Vickie or her daughter's date ends up dead or in jail. Not saying it's their fault. But that's the trend."

"So what would you do—stay with Al or switch teams for better prices?" Lil Eazy asked.

"Loyalty over numbers. If Al is solid, why flip? I stayed with Eazy when Miami Boys offered me double and better numbers. But... I also know you might outgrow him. Just move smart."

AL was frustrated.

"Ike's gone. Just left there, man. Something off bad!"

"What about Lil B getting work from Ms. Vickie's daughter?" Bo asked.

"I'm hollerin' at Santiago first. He fuckin' Felicia and Ms. Vickie loves his daddy. Not sure why she didn't let me get in."

"Weird energy. But Lil B did come clean by telling us."

"Yeah. One monkey doesn't stop, no show."

At FBI headquarters:

"This ain't small time. They pull millions yearly. Family structure. Old-school game with new-school faces," Miller said.

"I'll get you six more agents on the case," Hill replied.

"Appreciate it. They are flashing too loud now. Buying homes, G-Wagons. Gonna pull all their accounts. We are about to crack this wide open."

At a bar, Cory, Precious, TA, and Tammy sat sipping drinks. Calm before the next storm.

Brian sat in silence at the Sweatbox.

"I worry about my boys. They like me and Eazy... too much. But this generation plays fair."

"Jealousy. Greed. And no rules. We gotta steer them out before it's too late," Jack said.

"Streets placing bids on my legacy. Gotta protect the name. The bloodline."

In the club, Cam rocked the open mic stage, Mike Mike hyping behind him. The bar was lit. Energy thick. A moment of triumph in a city at war with itself.

The game was expanding, alliances shifting, power consolidating—but the cost? It hadn't fully revealed itself yet. Not everyone would make it to the end. And the ones who did? They'd never be the same.

CHAPTER 38

Money in motion. Streets whispering louder. Loyalty being tested. And power moves being made in the shadows. In this game, one bad decision doesn't just cost money—it costs lives. The fire's back lit. Everyone's hungry. And the clock's ticking.

The trap house smelled like raw hustle. In the thick air of Lil B's spot, stacks of hundreds lay across the table like trophies. The smoke curled upward, wrapping the room in a gritty haze.

"Bro, we just ran through 30 bricks in less than a week. We are marching!" Lil B said, his voice a mix of awe and adrenaline.

Lil Eazy kicked back, exhaling smoke. "So glad Santiago is back in pocket. Mike Mike and Cam need to hurry back with them hot wings, a nigga hungry."

They laughed—deep, chesty laughs only men winning the street war could afford.

Across town, Sweatbox Sport Bar hummed with renovation energy. Tables were stacked, screens being mounted, floors polished. But tucked in a corner booth, Brian and Jack spoke in low, calculated tones.

"I'm about 300,000 short from doing everything I want to do," Brian admitted, the weight of his dreams written in the crease of his brow. "I'll talk with Precious, see if she'll loan me half a mil. I left her 1.5. Business looks good on her. I still want to get three box trucks, put more money in stocks, flip houses."

Jack nodded slowly. "I'll get my wife to refinance two of our houses. You know I can't let you carry this load alone."

Brian let out a breath. "Man, that money turning to dust crushed me... I had it all worked out in my mind."

"Nothing comes easy for men like us," Jack said, firm. "But that's what makes us dangerous. We don't fold."

Meanwhile, at the spa, Apple, Terri, and Blu laid out on warm tables, getting their bodies waxed and their minds set.

"I'm so ready for this trip," Apple moaned.

"Clear water, blue skies..." Terri grinned. "Legs got Mike Mike on the hook—we are about to cook his ass."

"She was on the phone with him all night," Apple laughed. "That boy is hooked."

Blu raised a brow. "Speaking of hooks... Stone wants to see me before I leave. Says he got something for me."

Terri gave her a side-eye. "Girl, he's plotting. You know he feels some type of way about Ike. Shady vibes."

Blu smirked. "Only thing that beats a double cross is a triple cross."

"Amen to that," Terri chuckled.

At the wing spot, Cam and Mike Mike waited.

"You been smiling since we got in the car," Cam grinned.

"Bruh... her head game was so fire. That long-legged stallion got me stuck. Pussy was wet wet," Mike Mike said, shaking his head. "She might be the one."

They grabbed their wings and dipped.

Elsewhere, Tara and Tasha toured a potential property.

"Sis, I'm giving Bro 30% of all the investments I make," Tara said. "In two years, I want a $2 to $5 million net worth."

"Have you talked with him?" Tasha asked.

"Not yet. I'll call. This house would make a great daycare."

"Yeah, it's perfect," Tasha nodded. "And you heard about Brian's sports bar? Fly and sexy."

"I'm really out of the loop," Tara sighed.

Back at KK's house, AL reclined with a drink, watching KK drop to her knees.

"Bae, I found the daycare house," Tara said over the phone.

"That was fast."

"Are you coming to see it?"

"I'll call you back," AL said, keeping his tone even as KK slid closer.

After the call, he looked down.

"Understand something—nothing separates me from Tara. Play your role, you'll be happy."

"Yes, Daddy," KK purred. "Now give me that dick."

Back at the precinct, Detective Small laid out photos.

"This guy's AL. That's Bo. Young ones? No names yet."

"Intel?" Lt. Jackson asked.

"Can't rule them out. But they're definitely in the streets. Dealing."

"Remember the Roosevelt case? Family missing stuff?"

"White City Rd. Sounds like a pattern. Female lure, drugged drink, then boom. Might be a female killer crew. Let's pull cold case files."

The streets never sleep. The game doesn't pause. And the players? Some winning, some slipping. But one thing's for sure—ain't nobody safe when the fire's lit.

CHAPTER 39

SECRETS NEVER STAY BURIED

Secrets never stay buried forever—not in the streets, and definitely not in blood. While the crew chased bricks and the women stacked bodies and dollars, life came back for Brian in the one place he thought he had under control: his past. The trap was still booming. But so were the truths.

INT. LIL EAZY'S TRAP HOUSE – DAY

Empty chicken boxes littered the floor like fallen trophies from a war zone. A thick cloud of kush hovered in the air, barely moving, only adding to the murky glow of LED lights bouncing off a pile of rubber-banded stacks spread across a chipped wooden table. Pistols and semi-autos rested within arm's reach—quiet insurance in a loud world.

Lil Eazy paced back and forth, chest out, adrenaline pumping.

"Man, these twins had me goin' ham," he bragged. "Hit both at the same damn time!"

Mike Mike, slouched back on the worn-out sectional, grinned while thumbing his phone. His eyes were lit like he just hit the lottery.

Lil B leaned in, laughing, the gold in his smile catching light.

"Damn, cuz. Give her a break—let her miss you some."

The room cracked up, the trap house echoing with unfiltered laughs and braggadocio.

"We sextin', cuz!" Mike Mike held up his phone like a trophy.

Lil B smirked. "Cuz, your nose is already wide open. Gonna be scary when you finally get between them legs."

Cam, lost in a cloud of smoke, nodded in agreement. The trap was alive. Money, energy, and danger swirling like a storm yet to touch ground.

INT. BRIAN'S LOUNGE – DAY

Brian sat at the polished bar, the lights dimmed low, sipping slowly from a tumbler of dark liquor. The room was still under renovation, but it was coming together—bricks, mortar, and vision.

Behind him, the door opened with a soft chime.

"Hey, stranger."

Brian turned. His posture straightened instantly as Ashley stepped in, confidence wrapped in a fitted dress. Her smile was soft, but her presence? Sharp.

They hugged tight—a long, loaded embrace.

"Must say... you look damn good," Brian said.

"Father Time has been kind to you, too," Ashley replied, smirking.

After a few minutes of conversation, Ashley reached into her purse and pulled out a folded photo. She slid it across the counter.

Brian looked at it.

A boy—tight fade, serious eyes. A spitting image of Lil B as a baby.

"Why didn't you tell me?" Brian asked, voice low.

"I found out right before your sentencing. Didn't want to cause more chaos. He's eight now. His name's Boston."

Brian nodded slowly, heart pounding behind a still face.

"I gotta meet him."

"You can," Ashley said. "Football practice tonight."

INT. PRECIOUS WIC STORE – DAY

Business buzzed. EBT cards swiped. Kids tugged on moms. The hum of the city pulsed through the space.

Behind the counter, Precious moved like a boss, handing off baby formula and cereal boxes. Cory stood beside her, organizing receipts and managing the flow.

"This card got a thousand on it," a customer said.

Cory swiped, then handed her five crisp hundreds. "Thanks, Ms. Betty. Next!"

The customer smiled and exited. Precious dipped into her own purse to help a young mother short on change.

"Are we meeting up after football practice?" Cory asked.

"Nah. Girl night," Precious replied, smiling.

"Cool. I'm headed there now. Told you—government money's the sweetest kind."

He kissed her cheek and dipped.

INT. SWEATBOX – EVENING

The lights were low. A jazz playlist hummed from speakers. Jack walked in to find Brian alone, staring at the same photo Ashley gave him.

"What's on your mind?" Jack asked.

Brian pushed the photo forward.

"Ashley told me I got a son. Eight years old."

Jack studied the picture.

"No DNA test needed. He's yours. I always liked Ashley."

Brian nodded, eyes distant. "Hope I ain't got no more surprises."

INT. TERRI'S CONDO – NIGHT

The condo was alive. Bass rattled the walls. The scent of hookah, loud, and champagne filled the air.

Terri, Apple, Legs, Amy, Blu—a trap queen summit in full effect.

Terri raised her glass, standing tall in red bottoms and lingerie.

"A toast... to the Power of the P."

Apple made her rounds, handing out rubber-banded stacks.

"We did good. Big fish on the hook."

Money flew. Bodies moved. The condo turned into a strip club for the night. Sisterhood and savagery. Champagne and conquest.

EXT. PARK – EVENING

Football practice field. Kids ran drills. Coaches shouted. Parents sat bundled up in hoodies and lawn chairs.

Brian sat alone on the bench, watching #9—Boston. The kid juked two defenders, broke into a sprint, and scored.

Ashley clapped hard from the sideline.

Brian exhaled deeply. He wasn't used to watching from the sidelines.

After practice, Boston approached slowly, ball in hand.

"Good run," Brian said.

"Mom... is this my daddy?" the boy asked.

Ashley nodded.

"Yes, baby. This is your daddy, Brian."

Boston dropped his football and ran into Brian's arms. The hug hit hard.

Brian held him tight, emotion flooding his chest.

Cory approached, clipboard in hand.

"Remember, snacks on Saturday," he said to Ashley.

"Under control, Coach," she replied, smirking.

"Coach!" Boston yelled. "This is my daddy! He's coming to my game!"

Cory extended a hand.

"Good to meet you, bro."

Brian shook it, controlled.

But when Ashley and Boston walked to the car, she paused.

"Brian... I take it you don't know?"

"Know what?"

She hesitated.

"Coach Cory... he's dating your ex-wife, Precious."

Brian's face changed. Quiet thunder behind the eyes.

In the streets, betrayal came in gunshots and setups. But this? This was personal. Bloodline drama. A new son. A new rival. And a past that wasn't as buried as he thought.

The fire was far from out.

CHAPTER 40

Money in motion. Streets whispering louder. Loyalty being tested. And power moves being made in the shadows. In this game, one bad decision doesn't just cost money—it costs lives. The fire's back lit. Everyone's hungry. And the clock's ticking.

Lil B's Trap House – Day The air was thick with smoke and ambition. Lil B, Lil Eazy, Cam, and Mike Mike were deep in grind mode. Stacks of cash sat like bricks across the table, paper bands clinging to each bundle. The aroma of kush and fried wings from earlier takeout hung in the room like part of the hustle.

"My party 'bout to be lit-lit this weekend. Big 21," Lil B announced, breaking the silence with a grin.

"Where you having it?" Cam asked.

"Underground Atlanta. Whole city invited," Lil B replied.

"I'm performing," Cam said. "I'ma rock the crowd."

A knock at the door. Lil Eazy cracked it open to see G-Mack standing there with confidence in his posture and purpose in his eyes.

"G-Mack, what's good?" Lil Eazy greeted.

"Cash rules everything around me. Dollar, dollar bill," G-Mack smirked, tossing a rubber-banded stack on the table. "Here's the 30 I owe. I got 60 more to spend."

"You buying two?" Lil Eazy said, nodding in approval. "I'm fronting you two. Like how you are moving."

"Only way I know. Got a little one on the way."

"Congrats," Lil B added. "Come out for my bra party this Saturday. Underground. You know it's going down."

JB's Work Spot – Day The room smelled loud and ambitious. LB, Nard Jay, and Nia passed a blunt lazily, eyes halfway open as they discussed numbers. A large duffle bag rested on the table like a centerpiece.

Hosa entered, another bag slung across his back.

"That your money?" LB asked, nodding toward the table. "You sure Hector ain't in our business?"

"He doesn't know anything," Hosa said quickly. "My friend Julio's glad you're doing business with him."

"Keep it low and we rockin'. I need to spread my wings."

They shook on it. Hosa stepped back out, slid behind the wheel of his ride, and peeled off. A block later, red-and-blue lights lit up behind him. Two DEA agents stepped out. No guns drawn, but the weight of law hung in the air. They took the bag, asked a few questions, then let him ride.

Stone's Room – Day Stone sat around a table with a few of his tightest partners. His speakerphone was on. Blu's voice echoed through the room. Terri and Apple were with her, all on the line.

"So, when I'm seeing you?" Stone asked.

"Hope before I leave for my trip," Blu replied.

"Say no more. We locked in. What time you thinking?"

"Two."

"Say less."

Al's Work Spot – Day Al and Bo were mid-move. The counters buzzed, the air stale with cash dust and tension.

"We just ran through 150 quick," Al said. "Santiago got 150 more, then he's a ghost for a week or two."

"Need to re-rock 'em," Bo nodded. "Only Lil B and them gettin' pure dope."

"Tara's on some investment plays too. Timing feels right."

"Can't go wrong with her. April needs to find a lane."

"Still thinking about Ike," Al muttered. "Stone said Terri was over there when it happened."

"That girl? She's with the BULLSHIT. Ike didn't know her M.O."

Lil Eazy's House – Night The house was dim, the air tense. Hannah stood with her arms crossed. Lil Eazy leaned on the doorframe.

"Lil Eazy, who are you cheating on me with?" she asked.

"There you go again. I'm out risking my life for us."

"Your whole vibe changed. Just be real."

"You stressing yourself and the baby. Don't forget, you'll always be good."

"I remember flipping my tax money for you. I was there before the come-up."

"Okay. You said what you had to say. Let me watch my show."

She slammed the bedroom door.

Lil Eazy looked at his phone.

Text from Leah: "WYD?"

Hosa's House – Day Hosa paced. Jorge sat nearby, sipping slowly.

"This is bad," Hosa muttered. "They took the money. Asked about Julio."

"You tell Julio?"

"Hell no. He finds out, I'm dead. I'm giving them JB. Maybe he gives 'em Ms. Vickie."

"Smart play. But you gotta come clean sometime."

"Three hundred bands gone," Hosa said. "I'll cover it. Buys me time. Still hurts."

Homicide Department – Day The lieutenant sat at his desk, a man tired but sharp. A young officer stood by.

"You run Terri Miller's calls and texts?"

"Yes, sir. Waiting for the full report."

The sergeant from narcotics walked in, holding a thick folder.

"Lieutenant, Ross, Ike, Al, Bo—all in this. Ross and Ike were heavy before they dropped."

"Any links?"

"Maybe through Al. But what if women are robbing and killing them?"

"That would be a twist. Run it."

"Already pulling cold case files."

"Small, run Terri's name. Let's see what floats."

"On it, LT."

The board just shifted again. Quiet moves echo loudest when no one's listening. And in a game where loyalty fades fast, the next hit could come from the smile across the table.

CHAPTER 41

THE TORCH

Underground Atlanta pulsed with life. The bass from the speakers shook the foundation, echoing down brick walls slick with condensation and decades of secrets. Fog machines spilled haze across the room, catching the strobe lights as they danced through the crowd. The scent of hookah, loud weed, and high-end liquor wove through the air like incense at a sacred ritual. This wasn't just a party. It was an ascension.

Lil B's twenty-first birthday had transformed into a coronation.

INT. UNDERGROUND ATLANTA CLUB - VIP SECTION - NIGHT

The VIP area sat like a throne above the dancefloor—roped off, packed with ballers, hustlers, and old heads who remembered when Lil B was running errands for his pops. Now they were toasting to him. Bottles popped. Women moved with intention. Quiet meetings happened in shadowed corners while the beat pounded like a war drum.

Lil Eazy leaned in close to Lil B, scanning the crowd like a general surveying his empire.

"You brought the city out tonight," he said, raising his drink. "Look around, my brother. Some who's-who in here. All your side pieces too. Felicia coming?"

Lil B grinned. "They don't call me Lil B for nothing. She sliding through."

Across the VIP, AL and Bo were deep in conversation. Their faces didn't match the mood.

"They still haven't found Stone," AL muttered. "Been seventy-two hours. Vanished."

"Weird as hell," Bo replied. "Gotta watch our backs. I bet them bitches had something to do with it."

The atmosphere shifted as Julio entered, flanked by Cowboy and Hosa. Dressed in designer suits, they moved like ghosts with money and muscle. Behind them, DEA agents Cox and Sanders slipped into bar stools, acting like regulars but scanning every detail.

Julio approached Brian, handing over a sealed envelope.

"Give this to your son," he said, "with my blessing."

Cox discreetly lifted his phone and snapped a photo.

Brian nodded, cool as ever. "Thanks."

"The game misses you," Hosa added.

Brian raised an eyebrow. "The game never lacks players."

"True," Julio said with a smirk. "But not many MVPs."

Cowboy chuckled. "Golden time, my friend."

Brian sipped his drink. "Yeah... until somebody gets pulled over and doesn't say anything. Trust me, I've heard what happens behind them walls. So-called homies playing foul."

Hosa nearly choked on his drink.

Back near the bar, Lil B and Lil Eazy were turning up with Hannah and Aaliyah when the room stilled. Felicia entered like a storm in heels, followed by Ms. Vickie, LB, Slim, Clay, and Dominique. Their arrival had the gravity of a cartel.

"Another drink?" Lil Eazy asked.

"Hell yeah," Lil B replied, eyes still on Felicia.

Meke, Lil B's mother, strolled in with a drink and a glow.

"Happy birthday, baby. But I ain't saying it officially 'til 11:35 PM," she winked. "That's when you were born."

"Aaliyah, you look beautiful," she added. "Brian—where's your daddy at? Think I look good enough to catch him tonight? Might put these lock jaws on him. I know his weakness."

Lil B groaned. "Mama, come on now."

"Boy, please. Y'all more freaky than we ever were."

INT. DANCE FLOOR - NIGHT

The DJ dropped "The Wobble," and the floor turned electric. Meke tried grinding on Brian, who dodged her hips like Mayweather. Joyce doubled over laughing from across the room.

Precious entered with Roxy, Tammy, and Imani. Their eyes swept the club like seasoned queens assessing the court.

"Your son's holding the torch well," Ms. Vickie told Brian.

"Not my choice," he replied.

Ms. Vickie smiled. "You know the cloth... No matter how we cut it, trim it, or dye it—it's the same thread. It's how we wear it that changes things."

"Maybe. But sometimes, the system needs burning," Brian said.

"Maybe so," she murmured. "Who knows? We might end up grandparents to the same child. You're the only man close to my age I'd've handed the whole operation to."

"Is that right?" Brian said, sipping slowly.

LB approached with drinks.

"This is Brian," Ms. Vickie said. "Brian, meet LB."

"Heard great things," LB said. "Your son? A real go-getter."

"Nice to meet you," Brian replied, reading him quickly.

Precious approached, giving Lil B a warm hug.

"Big 2-1. How are you feeling?"

"Good, Mom. You should've brought my sisters."

"They wanted to come. Come by and get your gift."

"You always got the best gifts," he said, grinning.

Across the floor, Black Rick jumped up.

"That's my song! Y'all don't know nothing about this!"

He started Yeeking, dragging younger girls onto the floor. Laughter broke out.

Felicia slid up to Lil B.

"Running from me? Can't talk to girls in front of your girl?"

"Not like that. Been getting pulled everywhere."

"Got a penthouse at the Four Seasons. Don't be lame."

She walked off, hips swaying. Lil B turned to find Aaliyah staring, hurt in her eyes.

Julio leaned toward Ms. Vickie.

"This a real big three. We could take over the Southeast. Say the word."

"Sounds interesting," she replied. "Too bad our boy got cold feet. Maybe he'll pull a MJ. bring out the 23."

"Every man ain't fit for the job," Julio said.

"Good to know y'all thinking of me," Brian said. "Funny, though. No one asked if I already had the new blueprint to clean up all this dirty money."

The table went quiet. DEA agents across the club leaned in.

"Are you getting good pictures?" Sanders whispered.

"Crystal," Cox replied. "Spencer's gonna love this. Everybody's here. We need to brief Hosa ASAP."

The club thumped on, lights swirling. Laughter, cheers, and flirtation filled the space. But beneath the surface, shadows moved. Loyalty bent. Plots brewed. And in the crosshairs of it all stood Lil B—crowned, celebrated, and surrounded.

He held the torch now. But in this city? The fire always burns both ways.

The energy in Underground Atlanta pulsed like electricity. Neon lights bathed the walls in streaks of red and blue, bouncing off glass bottles and diamond chains. Hookah smoke curled through the air, mixing with the heavy scent of top-shelf liquor, designer perfume, and loud weed. It wasn't just a club—it was a city within a city. And tonight, it belonged to Lil B.

His twenty-first birthday had become more than a party. It was a coronation.

INT. UNDERGROUND ATLANTA CLUB – NIGHT

Cam stepped up to the DJ booth with boldness in his stride, microphone in hand, face lit with swagger. The music cut. The crowd, thick with anticipation, quieted just enough to hear his voice.

"First," Cam shouted, his voice booming over the sound system, "I want everybody in here to hold their drinks up—my big cuz just turned 21! Sagittarius season in full effect! On the count of three, we all wish Lil B a happy birthday! 1...2...3!"

CROWD

"Happy Birthday!!"

The entire section exploded with energy—drinks raised high, clinks of glasses echoing, cheers erupting from every corner. The DJ dropped the beat again, and the walls shook with bass.

Cam took center stage, holding the mic like it owed him respect.

"One time for 9th Inning Records—that's our new label," he called out. "Lil B and Lil Easy believed in me. I'm the first artist on the roster, and this my debut right here."

The beat shifted. He began performing. Instantly, the crowd locked in. Heads nodded. Bodies swayed. Kiara and her friend broke into dance near the stage, while Black Rick ran up front, losing his mind like a day-one fan.

Tasha stood near the bar, pointing toward the stage with pride. "That's my son—you get it, boy! He came outta me!"

Bre and her crew shouted lyrics word-for-word, rapping along with the chorus. In the VIP booth, Brian leaned closer to Lil B, watching it all unfold.

"He's damn good," Brian said. "I like his energy, vibe, and style."

Lil B grinned. "Yeah, Dad, we've been listening. This is our first business. We pushed the button on Cam."

"Alright," Brian said, nodding. "Just get y'all paperwork straight. You gotta start somewhere. What's the name of the label again?"

"Ninth Inning," Lil B replied. "'Cause we believe it's all or nothing. Bottom of the 9th, bases loaded."

Brian raised his drink in approval. "I feel that. Here." He reached into his jacket and handed over a thick envelope. "This from Julio."

INT. KICKBACK PARTY – NIGHT

In a cozy apartment across town, Paris and Milan chilled with friends. Music played low. Drinks in hand. Jenga blocks stacked high. A soft vibe.

Pairs leaned toward Milan. "Me and Pac-Man 'bout to leave."

Milan smiled. "OK, where y'all going?"

"To his place." Pairs raised a brow. "You need to have a drink or smoke something—it'll loosen you up."

Milan laughed. "I'm good. I feel great. Having a cool time."

INT. SUV – NIGHT

Terri leaned against the back seat window, sipping champagne. Apple sat up front, while Blu rolled a blunt behind her shades.

"I'm so ready for this trip," Terri said, stretching her legs. "I heard it's a nude beach there."

Blu sighed. "Been a long week and I need to forget. Police questioned me about Stone going missing. That drained me."

Apple shook her head. "Time we change it up. Too much heat. Focus on Billy and his rich-ass white friends."

Terri smirked. "Once Legs get Mike Mike, we flip the page. We played this hand well."

INT. CLUB – LATER THAT NIGHT

Near the back, Brian leaned over to Precious.

"You should swing by the sports bar," he said. "Check it out. I need to talk with you."

"I'll come. Wanna see your progress," Precious replied. "I'll text you." She paused, eyes playful. "I saw your baby mama all over you. What's up with that—trying to rekindle?"

Brian chuckled. "Meke's a hot mess. Just glad she clean now."

"Definitely was a rough time," Precious said. She glanced toward the dance floor. "Wow. Lil Brian's 21? Time flies."

All around them, people danced, sang happy birthday, toasted, laughed. Bottles poured. The night raged on.

EXT. CLUB PARKING LOT – NIGHT

Outside, the parking lot buzzed with excitement. Engines revved. Laughter rang out. Hosa and LB walked toward a line of SUVs.

"This week," Hosa said.

"Yep," LB replied, hopping into a blacked-out Suburban where Ms. Vickie waited in the driver's seat.

"What is he talking about?" she asked, backing out smoothly.

"Just wondering when we shopping again," LB said.

Ms. Vickie's voice sharpened. "Watch your mouth. Don't discuss business with them. I got a trick for Julio. He gon' give us his whole load. Remember—chess, not checkers."

A few rows away, Hosa approached Julio's Cadillac. The door opened. Hosa leaned in.

"He said this week."

Julio's jaw tightened. "He's in the way. Dealing behind Ms. Vickie's back. I want her—not her flunky boyfriend. He is here today, gone tomorrow."

INT. HOTEL ROOM – NIGHT

Inside a high-rise suite overlooking downtown, Lil B laid back on the velvet couch. Hookah smoke spiraled toward the ceiling. Felicia and two women in lingerie moved gracefully around the room. Drinks clinked. Music hummed from a wireless speaker.

Felicia leaned in, rolling another blunt. "It's not the party—it's the after-party that counts," she purred. "Y'all wanna pop another pill?"

The women nodded. Felicia smiled, then gently placed pills on their tongues. Lil B's phone lit up on the table: *AALIYAH: WHERE THE FUCK YOU AT!!!*

He didn't respond. He flipped the phone face-down and reached for his drink.

INT. DEA OFFICE – DAY

The white walls hummed under buzzing fluorescent lights. Hosa sat at the metal table, sweating, eyes darting.

Cox stood across from him, flipping through a file.

"Where Brian fit into all this?" Cox asked.

"He's not a player," Hosa said quickly.

Cox raised a brow. "His son is one, right? Is he dealing?"

"Yes," Hosa admitted.

"Ever dealt with him directly?"

"No. He works with LB. Think he's dating his stepdaughter."

"Ms. Vickie?"

"Never dealt with her. LB's her middleman."

Cox leaned forward. "So if we get LB, we get Ms. Vickie and company?"

"Exactly," Hosa said.

"When's the deal?"

Hosa swallowed. "LB said this week."

In the haze of celebration, the trap of ambition tightened. Lil B may have turned 21, but the candles lit more than cake—they lit a fuse. Behind the scenes, allegiances twisted. Feds tightened the noose. And everybody in the room wanted to be king.

But in this city?

Kings fall quickly—and legends are made in the bottom of the 9th.

CHAPTER 42

"LET THE DEVIL DANCE"

The air in Atlanta was thick—not with heat, but tension. The streets moved with a silent rhythm, always one breath away from eruption.

G Mack's house is alive , G Mack making good money. The faint buzz of a late-night talk show played in the background, barely enough to drown the quiet dread settling over the room. He'd just seen off two people, his hustle never stopping. But as the door clicked shut behind them, it creaked open again.

Toni and Charlie Mo stepped in like shadows.

"Man…" G-Mack said, offering a weary smile, "today has been one of those days." He patted his pocket and gave a small nod. "I got that nine for you though."

Toni exhaled, relief in his voice. "You a lifesaver, G. I need it bad."

But before G mack could turn down the hallway to get the goods, everything changed.

Charlie Mo lunged forward, grabbing G mack's girlfriend and jamming a gun to her head. Her scream cut through the house like a blade.

"Don't move," Toni said, his own piece drawn and pointed. "Get everything. If you wanna live—all the drugs. All the money."

G mack froze, hands slowly rising. "OK… OK, man, just—don't kill us, bro. We went to school together. And my girl… she's pregnant, man."

Charlie Mo snarled. "Shut your mouth. Do what you told."

Shaking, G Mack moved to a hidden drawer beneath the TV stand, pulling out a shoebox packed with cash and plastic-wrapped bricks. He laid it on the table like an offering. His girl was trembling, barely upright. Tears poured down her face.

Toni calmly opened a gym bag, loading the contents like groceries.

Then came the silence. Cold. Heavy. Like death itself had paused for a breath.

"Lay down," Charlie Mo ordered.

G mack and his girl shared one last look. Fear. Love. Regret. Then they obeyed—face down on the hardwood.

Two shots. Loud. Final.

Blood seeped into the floorboards, and the only sound left was the buzzing TV.

Toni and Charlie Mo vanished out the door, gym bag in hand, like ghosts slipping into the night.

The house sat still, the energy gone from the walls. Flies buzzed. The TV flickered.

A knock at the door. Then another.

"G mack?" Ms. Elaine's voice was soft, Southern, concerned. "I you ok I thought I heard something "

The door creaked open. She stepped inside—and froze.

 Her scream filled the night.

By the time detectives arrived, the house was swarmed. Yellow tape stretched across the porch. Blue and red lights bounced off neighbors' windows. The crowd outside whispered behind camera phones. The block knew something big had happened.

Detective Harrison leaned against the wall, tired eyes scanning the scene.

"Two shots. Execution style. No struggle. No forced entry," Rivera, the rookie officer beside him, noted.

"They trusted whoever came in," Harrison muttered.

Rivera nodded, grim.

Local news went live within the hour. A polished reporter stood outside the house, microphone in hand, solemn tone cutting through the noise.

"Tragic news tonight in this Eastside neighborhood. Two young adults—one reportedly pregnant—were found shot to death in what police are calling a targeted home invasion."

Back in her robe, Ms. Elaine was being interviewed, still trembling beneath a blanket.

"He was a sweet boy… Never have any trouble. I just saw him..." She wiped a tear. "His lady was pregnant…"

And down the street, a teenager spoke to a different news crew, shaking his head.

"I ain't surprised. G had people in and out of that house all day. Jealousy is real when folks know you eatin'."

At a trap house across town, the same news broadcast flickered on a dusty TV. Smoke clouded the air. A blunt burned between Mike Mike's fingers while Cam stacked bills.

"Bro… folks dyin' left and right shit crazy ," Mike Mike said.

Cam didn't look up. "ATL news is like watching a hood movie. Bodies droppin left and right '. Gotta be more careful "

"I'm hittin' up ol' girl later."

"Who—Legs?"

Back at Terri's condo, silence hung in the room as the report played.

"That G mack was one of Lil Eazy and Lil B's boys," Toni said quietly. "They are next. One by one. We huntin' 'em."

Legs walked out in nothing but a silk robe, cocaine on a plate in her hand. She sauntered over to Toni, sat on his lap, and passed him the plate like a ritual.

"I got Mike Mike in the blender," she grinned. "Eating out my hands. With this head game "

Charlie Mo chuckled, cold. "Get his ass. Uncle Silk gonna love how we payin' back his enemies."

Blu leaned on the wall, watching it all unfold.

"Just remember—it's about the money. Stick to the plan."

"That comes with it anyway," Toni replied, licking powder from his finger.

Legs leaned in, wild-eyed. "Let's hit the strip club."

Later that night, the club exploded with energy. Bass thumped like a heartbeat. Red and purple strobes sliced through the smoke. Girls spun on poles. Money floated through the air like confetti.

Charlie Mo, Toni, Legs, and Blu reigned over VIP like gods.

Legs poured champagne down a dancer's chest. Toni tossed a stack in the air. Blu sparked a blunt with a hundred-dollar bill. The dancers swarmed like moths to flame.

"This is free money!" Toni shouted over the music. "Let it circulate!"

Legs winked at a stripper. "That's war money, baby! Every dollar got blood on it—taste it!"

A dancer licked her lips and went lower. Charlie Mo sipped dark liquor, eyes scanning the room. "Let 'em watch," he muttered. "Let 'em wonder if they next."

The celebration roared on, but in the corner, a few street guys whispered and texted, eyes locked on the crew.

Blu leaned in, voice serious. "They watchin' us too."

"They can plot in silence," Toni said, waving his hand. "We already two moves ahead."

Charlie Mo's stare cut through the fog of lights and laughter. His finger tapped the pistol under the table. He could feel it—energy shifting.

"You feel that?" he asked.

"What?" Toni replied, still pouring.

"Energy. It's gon' come knockin' soon. But until then…"

Charlie Mo stood, pulled out another stack, and let it rain.

"Let the devil dance."

The night pulsed like a heartbeat. Money moved faster than loyalty. Blood soaked deeper than fame. In the streets of Atlanta, one thing was always true—every victory dance came with a price. And every celebration whispered the same warning: your time might be next

CHAPTER 43

The weight of betrayal always lands with blood.

In a city where loyalty is currency and silence is survival, one bad play can make you a memory. Some alliances are bound in fear, others by greed—but all of them come with an expiration date. And in this game? That date arrives in silence, with a blade.

The restaurant was quiet, tucked away from the noise of the city. A booth in the far back held two men, both of them too seasoned for small talk. Hosa and LB sat across from each other, tension disguised beneath casual gestures. Two black bags sat between them—one for each. Wordless, they slid the bags across the table like clockwork.

"When Julio gonna start matching what I'm buying?" LB asked, eyes sharp.

"He said next time," Hosa replied.

The conversation was clipped, calculated. Neither said more than necessary. They understood the rules: silence protects.

Julio's bar had the kind of lighting that made secrets feel safe. Behind the counter, Julio dried a highball glass with surgical precision. Cowboy, Hector, and Jorge nursed drinks at the bar. Laughter floated between them, masking the undertone of tension. Cowboy reached for a small bag and stood.

"Look, I'm outta here. Thanks again, Julio. I'll call you—tell you how it works out," he said, tipping his hat before heading out.

Julio gave a small nod, then turned back. Jorge's face had shifted—serious, heavy.

"Julio, I've been debating something... heavy on my mind."

Julio set the glass down slowly.

"Tell me what's up."

Jorge didn't flinch. **"Straight to the point—Hosa got pulled over a while back. They took the money from the deal. That time he met Hector's people... Ms. Vickie's boyfriend."**

Julio's expression didn't change, but the atmosphere did.

"Tell me more."

"He doesn't plan on setting you up. He's scared—for his family. But the boyfriend... he's on the cross."

Julio said nothing. His silence was volcanic. It didn't erupt—it seethed, quietly.

The parking lot stretched wide like a trap laid open. LB dropped a bag into the trunk of a black sedan. Hosa sat in a separate vehicle nearby, engine humming. He gave a nod.

Then—
Tires screeched. Red and blue lights flooded the lot. Multiple DEA vehicles boxed them in. Agents leapt out, weapons drawn.

Orders barked. Chaos followed.

Inside Sweatbox Sport Bar, Brian sat in a corner booth, phone to his   ear.
As he hung up, Lil Eazy and Lil B walked in. He motioned them over.

"Glad y'all could pull up on me. First thing—Joyce filed y'all LLC. Name: 9th Inning Records. It may take a few weeks, but we are moving."

"Thanks, Dad," Lil B said.

"**Thanks, Unk,**" echoed Lil Eazy.

Brian nodded. "**It's my duty. But now let me walk y'all through something deeper. How the Feds work. I'm a believer—you do better when you know better.**"

He leaned in.

"**Let's say someone gets caught. Small time. Five bricks. No record. That's five years, max. But a mean DA? He adds enhancements—leadership role, drug premises, scales, a press machine. Suddenly that five becomes twenty.**"

A waitress slid up beside them.

"**Brian, want the cook to come back?**"

"**Hell yeah. He's fire. Tell him I want him cooking Friday—I got someone special coming. And ask about crab cakes.**"

"**You got it.**"

Lil B smirked. "**Mom must be coming over. She loves crab cakes. What y'all trying to do?**"

Brian's face hardened. "**It's business. We move on. But like I was saying—add a gun charge? You're done. Throw away the key.**"

The table went quiet. Reality was sinking in.

Outside the restaurant, LB sat on the pavement, head hung.

DEA Agents Cox and Sanders towered over him.

"**Looks like we caught you with your pants down. How old are you?**" Cox asked.

"**Thirty-two, sir.**"

"**You're facing thirty years. But I told my people we should let you go.**"

Sanders snapped, **"Hell no! He's not helping us. Why let him go?"**

"I'll help. I'll call Hosa right now," LB said quickly.

Cox laughed darkly.

"The joke's on you. You're Hosa's 'get outta jail' card. We need another fall guy. Welcome to the show."

Down the road, Cowboy leaned against his car like a man with nothing to fear.

DEA agents turned his vehicle inside out. One grabbed the bag he'd left with and tore it open.

Fruit spilled out.

The agent grabbed another—same result. More fruit.

"What the hell!?" the agent barked, storming toward him.

"You think you're slick? I'll find something. Even if I gotta plant it myself."

Cowboy didn't flinch. **"Y'all have been planting shit on us since day one. I can afford a good lawyer. Do your worst."**

Back inside Julio's bar, the lights were low and the danger high.

Hosa entered with a fake smile and a bag of money.

Julio sat at a corner table with four stone-faced men. He didn't move.

"Here you go. He said he'll be ready in a few days," Hosa offered, placing the bag down.

Julio didn't touch it.

"Hosa... how long have we known each other?"

The other men adjusted in their seats. The room tightened.

"Long time," Hosa said. **"Why?"**

"What's the golden rule?"

"Loyalty. My brother's keeper."

Julio's stare cut deep. **"Have you been to that?"**

Hosa's body failed before his mouth could.

His hands trembled. Knees buckled. He dropped down.

"Please. They had me by the balls. I was gonna send them Ms. Vickie. That's who they really want!"

One of Julio's men stepped forward, blade already drawn.

The slice was clean.

The silence—colder than steel.

Blood kissed the floor. The bag of money remained untouched.

And so the circle tightens.

In this world, mercy is weakness. Hosa made his move—and paid his price. The Feds keep fishing. Julio stays ten steps ahead. But pressure? Pressure makes some fold… and others explode.

Chapter by chapter.

Move by move.

The game continues.

And the reaper stays watching… from the shadows.

CHAPTER 44

Some warnings don't come with sirens.

They come dressed in smiles, slipped through text messages, whispered across late-night meetings and quiet deals. The ones who hear them… live. The ones who don't? Well, the news runs their name by morning.

The aroma of garlic butter and seasoned crab filled the air like a promise.
 Inside Ms. Vickie's South Side mansion, the chef moved with precision—plating each dish like he was back-of-house at a five-star restaurant instead of a private home. Wine glasses clinked. Felicia's laughter danced through the kitchen. Slim rolled up late, wearing that usual sleepy grin.

Ms. Vickie barely acknowledged the joy in the room. Her phone buzzed. One message froze her expression.

TEXT FROM HECTOR: "We need to talk ASAP. Only me and you."

Her reply came without emotion. Just cold precision.

TEXT RESPONSE: "Meet me at our usual in an hour."

LB stepped through the doorway like a lion returning to his den, sniffing the air.

"Sure smells good in here," he said, smirking. **"I'm ready to eat. Look at my beautiful queen."**

He kissed Ms. Vickie, greeted Felicia and Slim. But the energy he carried didn't match the smiles. He seemed... off.

Felicia tilted her head. **"Damn, someone usually happy. You know something we don't?"**

AL'S WORKHOUSE – NIGHT

Tension sat heavy like smoke that wouldn't clear. Al, Bo, Big John, and JE gathered around a dim table, only a low-hanging bulb keeping the dark at bay. Every man looked on edge.

"Man, Stone just disappeared," AL muttered, his eyes darting. **"Weird as hell."**

JE leaned in. **"Terri and Blu had something to do with it. Stone was setting Blu up. We were gonna snatch her... hold her till she cracked."**

Al's face darkened. **"Yeah. Terri and them? Definitely capable. Especially with Charlie Mo in the mix."**

Bo's jaw flexed. **"We might just need to knock them all off. Before someone else disappears... or ends up dead. She recoups females, sic 'em on us."**

AL rubbed his temples like a man losing sleep. **"Yeah... we might just have to do that."**

LIL EAZY'S TRAP HOUSE – NIGHT

The TV sat on mute. The smoke hovered. Nobody moved.

"Man... they just found G-MACK and his girl dead," LIL EAZY said, flat and cold.

The silence that followed cracked the air.

"Execution style," he added. **"Back of the head. Both of 'em."**

Lil B stared at the floor. **"Whoa... that's cold."**

"G-MACK was just about his money," Cam added quietly. **"We saw that on the news."**

Lil Eazy let out a slow breath. **"Yeah. His girl was pregnant... and he owed us sixty bands."**

Mike Mike sat up, his tone tightening. **"Been a lot of shady things happening. Ross. Ike. Stone's missing. And G-MACK? Someone is cleaning house."**

PARKING LOT – DAY

Two cars sat across from one another, a quiet standoff wrapped in sunlight.
 Ms. Vickie glanced down at her buzzing phone.

TEXT FROM LB: "Just gonna leave me without saying anything? I'm hard hard."
 TEXT BACK: "Stay hard and ready. Be back in 20." *[Playful. Deadly.]*

She slid into Hector's car like a queen with steel in her veins.

"Make this quick," she said.

Hector didn't waste a second. **"Your boyfriend's been dealing with Hosa behind our back. Hosa got pulled by the DEA. He's working with them—to get to your boyfriend... to get to you."**

Her eyes didn't flinch. **"How far along is this going on?"**

"Don't know. That's why I hit you with a 911. Julio's already planning to deal with Hosa—he is about to disappear."

"So you don't know if they've gotten to LB yet?"

"No."

She took one last glance at her phone. **"Thanks."** Then drove off. No questions. No goodbye.

SWEATBOX SPORTS BAR – NIGHT

Cowboy, Jack, and Brian sat in the corner of the bar like they had a reservation with fate. A round of fresh drinks sweated between them.

"**Man, I'm just happy I didn't have any work,**" Cowboy said, smirking. "**They gotta be watching Julio's spot.**"

"**Told you. Game's over,**" Jack muttered. "**You've been out too long.**"

Brian looked over. "**Did they ask you anything?**"

"**Yeah, about Julio. But they really thought they had me. They were hot when they found fruit instead of bricks.**"

Brian leaned in, voice quiet.

"**Two things are true—either Julio already knows, or he's working with them. Feds pulling cars is how they wave goodbye.**"

Cowboy shook his head. "**I don't even want to be near that man with a ten-foot pole.**"

Brian smiled. "**Smartest thing you've said in ten years.**"

HOTEL ROOM – NIGHT

Lil Eazy lay shirtless on the bed, tension in his muscles. Leah massaged his back, her touch tender. The room was still, weed smoke curling above them like ghosts.

"**Babe... so much going on out here. I just lost a close friend. Sixty thousand gone, and his lady was pregnant,**" he admitted.

Leah paused, kissed his shoulder.

"**Maybe it's time you think about doing something else.**"

He sighed. "**I gotta make a million before I walk away. It's always been my plan.**"

"**Russell,**" she whispered, "**you can't take it with you. It's no good if you're in prison... or gone.**"

"**I hear you. But I gotta roll the dice. Play the hand I was dealt.**"

PARKED CAR – NIGHT

Felicia leaned against the passenger door. Lil B sat behind the wheel, smoke slipping from his lips.

"Just took a sixty-thousand-dollar loss," he said. **"And lost a friend."**

Felicia stayed calm. **"Losses come with the game. Better to lose the money than lose your life. You'll get that back. Tenfold."**

Lil B smiled, tired but genuine. He passed her the blunt.

"Didn't look at it like that. But you're right. That's why I love talking to you."

Felicia grinned. **"Told you. You'll never find another me."**

In the underworld of silent wars and quiet setups,

Sometimes the loudest noise is the one you never hear—the bullet, the betrayal, the breath before it all falls apart.

Everyone was smiling.

But in the corners of Atlanta, eyes were shifting. Guns were loading.

And the game… was tightening its grip.

who's left standing when the smoke clears

CHAPTER 45

Some moments start quiet… calm… the kind you sip slowly with a drink in hand. But in the underworld, quiet is the camouflage before the kill. And sometimes, even love comes laced with intention.

Brian's lounge had that grown vibe—warm lighting dancing over polished wood, candles flickering on low tables, and the scent of crab cakes and roasted vegetables floating in the air. Precious sat next to him, her smile soft as she looked down at her plate.

"You still remember my favorite," she said, eyeing the crab cakes. "These look delicious."

Brian grinned, taking a sip of his drink. "I remember everything about you. Like the back of my hand."

She blushed, trying to play it off. The glow in her cheeks gave her away.

"This place is really coming together," she said, glancing around. "I see the vision."

"One day at a time." He leaned in a bit. "But I do need a favor."

She raised her brow. "And what might that be?"

"I need a loan. If you can—'bout half a million."

She paused. Watched him for a second.

"Brian, you know you are good for it. I can wire it, but if you need it in cash, I'll need about a week." Her voice dropped to a softer tone. "This ain't really a loan though... it's part of your buyout. You ain't gotta pay me back."

Brian smirked. "You're really on your A-game. I'm impressed. Trying to get me out your hair, huh?"

She laughed. "I was taught by one of the best, thank you. Real estate has been good to us. And your girl got her hand in a few cookie jars now."

"Like what?" he asked. "Your college sweetheart is putting you on game now?"

She leaned in, eyes sharp, shining with quiet confidence.

Outside Lil B's trap house, the crew was posted up by their cars—Lil Eazy, Lil B, Mike Mike, and Cam. Summer heat wrapped around them like stress in the air.

"This week's been crazy," Lil Eazy said, rubbing the back of his neck. "I'm tired. 'Bout to go rub Hannah's belly and crash—if she doesn't trip."

Lil B let out a breath. "Yeah... slick and tired myself. Aaliyah has barely even spoken to me lately."

Mike Mike laughed. "I got a hot date with Legs."

Lil B turned to him. "Oh shit. This man 'bout to find out what the hype is really about."

They cracked up. Cam stretched, popping his back.

"I'm hittin' the gym in the morning before I link with y'all."

One by one, they dapped up and pulled off.

At Amy's house, it was nothing but heels and hustle. Legs stood in the mirror, blending blush across her cheekbone, rocking just a bra and G-string. Amy was laid back nearby, sipping a wine cooler with a grin.

"Are you making your move tonight?" Amy asked.

Legs smirked. "Got him eating out of my hands."

Amy laughed. "Terri said get it done before they get back in town."

"Oh, we're on it. He'll be here in an hour. Me and you—tag team."

Stacks of money covered Tara's bed. She flipped through bills like she was counting future property lines. Al sat nearby, watching her like she was the most beautiful thing in the room.

"We put down eighty on the daycare property," she said. "Needs about fifty in repairs. The house cost two eighty. All in, it's three-thirty—but once we flip it, it'll be worth half a mil and make us double the money."

Al smirked. "Talkin' like that gets my dick hard."

He slid over $150K. Tara grinned. Clothes fell. Passion followed.

"Boss up like that," she said in a whisper, "keep this pussy wet. Now come make Allen a brother or sister."

Later that night, back at the lounge, Brian and Precious were sipping drinks, the air thicker with game than smoke.

"We hustlin' food stamps," Precious said. "People come in, sell their stamps half off, and we cash 'em out. Then the government reimburses us for the full price."

Brian looked at her, eyebrows up. "You makin' fifty percent profit? Insane. And here I was thinking your man was just tryna spend your money."

He started clapping slowly.

"We can toast to that," he said. "Just be careful. Don't catch no fraud cases."

She raised her glass. "You know I don't cross no lines."

Their eyes locked. No more words. Just silent respect.

Mike Mike knocked at Legs' apartment. She opened the door in a silk robe, wide open, revealing just enough.

"You ain't ready," he said, grinning.

"Change of plans. I'm cookin'. Me and my girl. What you drinkin'?"

"Tequila."

He stepped inside. Amy stood at the stove, barefoot in boy shorts and a bra top, frying chicken.

Mike Mike blinked. "Didn't think white girls could fry like that."

They laughed. Legs handed him a drink and a perfectly rolled blunt.

"A woman who cooks, rolls blunts, and looks like this?" he said, shaking his head. "I'm in love."

The girls danced, giggling, half-naked, teasing. Mike Mike relaxed, sipped slowly.

Then the room tilted.

His body started melting into the seat. Eyes drooping. He tried to rise. Couldn't. The glass slipped from his hand.

Legs stepped forward, her whole face changed. Cold now. Focused.

Amy stood behind her. "Just like that, you in our spider web."

Some victories come dressed in silk and soft voices. But in this world, trust is a loaded weapon—and Mike Mike just handed it over. Too late. The trap had sprung. And the queens were calling checkmate.

Brian sat at his usual corner in Sweatbox, elbows on the table where he'd made more plays than most. But this time it wasn't business running through his head. It was blood. His son.

It's really a small world, he thought. *The guy dating my ex-wife is also coaching and teaching my son? Crazy how paths cross. It's like he's here to replace me... if I'm not careful.*

His phone buzzed.

"Tara?" he answered.

"I'm good," she said. "Really excited. Can we meet up?"

"I'll be at the lounge all day. Just pull up—I'll text you the address."

At the DEA office, the walls were covered in photos, pins, and scribbled notes. Cox, Sanders, and Spencer stood over the board like it held answers they didn't want to find.

"Hosa went into Julio's bar," Cox said. "Never came back out."

"We need a search warrant," Sanders added. "Two cars still watching."

Spencer nodded. "Hosa made the deal with LB. We caught LB with fifty suspected keys—said he got it from Hosa. Hosa made it to Julio's... but after that? Poof. No Hosa. No money."

"LB's working with us now," Cox said. "He's gonna help us get Ms. Vickie."

Spencer grabbed a folder. "We file that warrant, we lock Julio up. JB confirmed it. Said that's where the coke came from."

At Ms. Vickie's, steam clung to the bathroom air as she stepped out the shower glowing. LB was stretched across the bed, chest bare, eyes calm but alert.

"Are you ready for the big leagues?" she asked.

"I was born ready, baby."

"You goin' to Mexico. Santiago got a big shipment. I need that connection solid."

"I'm takin' money? Who's holdin' it down while I'm gone?"

"Felicia and Dominique. It's on autopilot. Runs itself."

LB nodded, proud. "Glad you trust me with next-level moves. Now come let me taste that sweetness."

She smiled, playful but firm. "You earned this position, LB. Julio's crew showed me you ready to run it. But tonight... I'm thinkin' power moves, not sex."

Cam's studio was thick with smoke. He stepped out of the booth like he just dropped a classic.

"That hook was crazy," Wiz said.

Cam nodded. "Me and that beat got the same heartbeat. Let's line up the mix CD—I bought a chalkboard."

"Say less."

Applause circled the room. Drinks in hand. Girls nodding. Midnight Black gave a cool nod from the back.

"You up next," he said.

In the woods, Legs and Amy moved fast.

"You sure we burnin' his car?" Amy asked. "You sure we keepin' that money? Terri was good to us. We always broke bread."

Legs tossed the duffel in the trunk. "Terri ain't thinkin' about us. She thinkin' about blood. We got what she wanted—Mike Mike. Let's take this as our Christmas bonus and bounce."

Tires screeched. They were gone.

At Precious' house, Pairs stared at the pregnancy test. Frozen. Everything around her was silent.

"Girl, you been in there forever!" Milan called from the other room. "We playin' or what?"

"Just gimme a few minutes..." Pairs said, voice low.

Lil B and Lil Eazy sat in silence, car windows fogged with weed smoke.

"Bro," Lil B said. "I ain't gon' lie. I got a bad feeling about Mike Mike."

"I've been thinkin' on it all day," Lil Eazy said.

"Autie called three times. Still no sign of him."

"Ain't adding up. Lenny wanna hit a party tonight. Come through—maybe clear our heads. Mike Mike'll show up tomorrow."

Back at Brian's bar, Joyce slid keys across the table.

"Your duplex—done. Needs about thirty to forty in rehab, but it's yours. Passive income. Just like you wanted."

"Couldn't have done it without you," Brian said. Then paused. "But... there's something I need to tell you."

"Talk to me."

"I have an eight-year-old son. Just found out."

Joyce blinked. "Damn... Right before you left?"

"Yeah. Good kid. His name's Boston."

There's a ticking clock in every street story. Sometimes you hear it ticking loud. Sometimes it's quiet... until it explodes. With the feds circling, alliances shifting, and blood heating up, every step feels like the last. In a city where love, loyalty, and legacy all cost something—the question ain't who's next. It's who's left standing when the smoke clears.

CHAPTER 46

The walls are closing in. Everyone can feel it—the weight, the paranoia, the pressure. The holiday lights outside barely cut through the dark cloud rising in Atlanta's underworld. In the heart of betrayal, vengeance, and dirty money, lines are being drawn in blood. Some move for power. Others, just to stay alive. But no one walks away clean.

Legs' apartment smelled like incense and bad decisions. Terri, Blu, and Apple stepped inside, eyes scanning every detail. Legs stood near the kitchen, a sly grin curling on her face. Amy stood behind her, quiet and loyal.

"Christmas came early for you," Legs said. "Your gifts in there."

Terri raised a brow and led the way into the back bedroom. When she opened the door, she stopped cold.

Mike Mike was zip-tied, stripped to his boxers, head hanging. His chest moved slowly—breathing but barely. His pride was gone, stripped along with his clothes.

Terri's eyes lit up. "Silk must be smiling down on me. Time to make Brian and Eazy pay."

"Damn," Blu whispered. "He is packing—and not even hard."

Apple shook her head. "Girl, your head is always in the gutter."

"I'm just saying," Blu smirked. "The print doesn't lie. Hope Legs got a taste before she tripped him."

Legs laughed. "Heard you—and nope. He didn't get any pussy. Just some fire head."

They all laughed, but beneath it—pure venom.

At the strip club, neon lights blinked like heart monitors. Bass hit like gunshots. Lenny, Pierre, and their clique rained money from VIP. Strippers bent low, grinding slow, the air thick with sweat and liquor.

Lil B and Lil Eazy sat to the side, drinks in hand, eyes scanning the room like hawks.

"You good?" Lenny asked Eazy. "Why are you not partying with us?"

"I'm chillin'. Long story," Eazy said, barely looking up. "Y'all enjoy. You got the whole club jumping."

"It's my partner's birthday," Lenny said. "Think about it—two days before Christmas, and we are out here paying for kids' gifts like we're the ones sliding down chimneys."

He laughed and walked off. Lil B leaned closer.

"Yo… Leah's brother in fraud," he said.

"You crazy?" Eazy frowned. "You forget her daddy's the mayor?"

"Trust me. Only three types throw money like that—dealers, rappers, or fraud kings. He not in no studio and he ain't selling work. Plus, he posted with Haitians. Don't be slow."

Lil Eazy nodded. "You right. Them and the Africans… they got that swipe magic."

Across town, Cory and Precious stepped out of the car looking like royalty. Suits, diamonds, confidence. Across the street, two unmarked cars watched silently. Cameras clicked without flash.

Inside the unmarked vehicle, Agent Miller adjusted his earpiece.

"JP says he's the leader," Miller muttered. "Said Cory, the one who put 'em all on—WIC stores."

Moore flipped through a tablet. "What about the female?"

"Precious… she is clean-ish. Still digging. Got a few stores in her name. Made a couple mil off real estate flips a few years back. We'll know more once those other store records hit."

"They live like legends," Moore said under his breath, watching as TA, Tammy, JP, and Imani followed Cory and Precious inside.

A table full of power—and federal suspicion.

At JB's spot, dim lights glowed through a haze of smoke. JB kicked back on a loveseat, a joint between his fingers. Nia curled beside him, legs tangled over his lap.

"Baby, I'm about to make my move on Ms. Vickie," JB said, voice low. "Me and you—call it the heist of the year."

Nia smiled. "Do your thing, baby. I can't wait."

"Once it hits, we leave Atlanta. Find some coast. I want water, fresh air, no more duckin' or dirty money."

"Ooh, I like that. ATL burnt out anyway."

JB's phone buzzed—text from Cox.

TEXT FROM COX: *Where are you? We need to talk.*

He started typing. **RESPONSE:** *Tell me where. I'll be there in an hour. Got something you'll wanna hear.*

He kissed Nia's neck, fire in his eyes.

"Let's do a quickie before I go."

Clothes hit the floor.

At Julio's bar, it was standing room only. Laughter, domino slaps, drinks flowing. A normal night—until it wasn't.

The doors flew open.

"Move to one side! Show me your hands!" one agent shouted.

Chaos erupted as DEA agents swarmed in, a search warrant in one's grip. Julio stood frozen behind the bar. He didn't ask why. He already knew.

At Tara's house, she paced like her feet were on fire. Al leaned back on the couch, watching her.

"I think something happened to my nephew," Tara said.

"Lil B said he met a girl at the strip club. Had his nose wide open."

"Nobody knows her. All we got is a name—Legs."

Al nodded. "I'll get with B in the morning."

"I'm pulling up on Brian in an hour," she said, grabbing her keys. "He needs to know."

Back at Legs' apartment, the air had changed. The laughter was gone. Now it felt like a knife waiting to drop.

"I wanna cut off every finger and toe," Terri said, eyes locked on Mike Mike. "Mail 'em weekly. Like Paid in Full."

Blu crossed her arms. "Girl, you're getting personal. Let's just get the money."

"She's right," Apple added. "It's about the Benjamins."

"You can bounce if you want to," Terri said, not blinking. "I'm calling my brother and Charlie Mo. Mike Mike's about to be touched."

Apple grabbed a seat. "When Amy gets back with the drinks and that dust, I need both. It's gonna be a long one."

The tables were shifting. Alliances turning toxic

Everyone wanted the crown, but the empire was cracked—and blood was soaking the bricks.

A storm was brewing.

And in this world, even your wins came with a body count.

CHAPTER 47

In the heart of the city where silence never sleeps and loyalty is just a word until tested, tension drips from every corner like condensation on a barroom bottle. Everyone feels it. The streets are whispering. Names are being passed from one mouth to another like loaded guns—Mike Mike, Julio, Hosa. Some vanish in the night. Others make deals with devils. And some... are walking time bombs, ticking toward betrayal.

Blue and red lights flickered faintly in the distance. The crime scene sat quiet, but the air was thick. Miller stood still, arms crossed, eyes scanning every inch of cracked pavement like it owed him something.

"Nothing," he said, jaw clenched. "No sign of Hosa or Julio. We need the lab team to check for blood residue."

An agent responded over the radio, "I'll call the team out now."

Moore stepped forward, holding a folder. "What did LB say?"

"He said Ms. Vickie's about to plug him in with her supplier. Wants a written deal—no jail time and a new identity."

Miller's tone turned colder. "Let's sit him down. Get more names. See if we can get him to wear a wire before we start making promises."

At The Sweatbox, Brian's sports bar hummed with low conversation, poker chips clinking, and old-school soul sliding through the speakers. A high-stakes poker game was underway. A few hustlers, one woman, and two waitresses moved through the room like they belonged to the smoke.

Jack leaned in, voice low. "Just talked with Cowboy. They raided Julio's bar. I'm glad you stuck to your word and stayed away. Cowboy's shaking in his boots."

Brian rubbed his chin. "Told Cowboy everything that glitters ain't gold. Hope he didn't move reckless."

"I don't think he did," Jack said. "But these days? Who really knows."

Brian nodded slowly. "My spirit's been uneasy. Something ain't sitting right. I've been thinking about Lil B and them heavily."

One of the waitresses stepped up, nervous.

"Money wants another line of credit. Twenty-five thousand."

Brian glanced toward the table. Calm, but firm, he walked over.

"Money, the limit's fifty. You've reached that. You need to clean your face."

Money pleaded. "Brian, you know I'm good for it."

Troup leaned in. "I'll loan him fifteen. Keep the game going."

"Thanks," Money replied. "My lady's on her way now with more."

Brian nodded. "Cool. I know you're loaded, but I gotta stick with the house rules."

He walked back to Jack, who was sipping slowly on a glass of Hennessy.

"How are the games going?" Jack asked.

"Good," Brian replied. "Now I see why you pushed Easy about just having gambling houses."

Jack smiled. "It's all about the company you keep."

"Between Troup and Big Will, they got all the D-boys, rappers, and ballplayers coming through."

That's when Tara stepped in with Shan. Warm hugs passed between them.

"First," Tara asked, "have you talked with Tasha?"

"Yeah. She told me to stop by. Said she needed to tell me something."

Tara frowned. "Bro… Mike Mike's been missing almost forty-eight hours."

Brian sat up straighter. "Damn. She should've told me. That's a 911."

"Lil B and them think he's just laid up with some girl. But he is not answering any calls or texts."

"I'll hit them up."

Tara leaned in. "I'm making real moves now—daycare and real estate. You want thirty percent on everything, or just a lump sum?"

"Thirty percent," Brian said. "I believe in money while I sleep. Passive income. That's the American way."

"I close on the house slash daycare first of the year."

"What area?"

"Southside. Off 138 Highway."

Tasha's house was dim, smoky. Shadows danced on the wall from the flickering TV. Black Rick and Tasha sat low, nerves raw.

"Don't worry, baby," Rick said, rubbing her leg. "Mike Mike gon' be home in one piece. I'm sure he just laid up with a girl."

Tasha's voice cracked. "I'm about to lose my mind. I think I could use a line right now."

Rick shook his head. "No, baby. We are not going back down that road. We have been clean for too long." He reached into his pocket. "Here. Take this pill. It'll relax you."

She took it and swallowed it dry.

Under a flickering streetlight, Lil Eazy, Lenny, Lil B, and Pierre stood posted beside a black car.

"That was a good time," Pierre said. "That weed hit differently."

"I'm dropping that QP off to Lenny tomorrow," Lil Eazy added.

Pierre pulled out a fat stack of hundreds and handed it over. "Make it a pound. I'm partying through New Year's."

Lil B and Eazy exchanged glances as Pierre peeled off.

"Thanks for hanging with us," Lenny said before hopping in the car. "You know the Westside gets wild. I'll hit you tomorrow."

Once they pulled off, silence set in.

"I feel sick as hell," Lil B said. " cuz out there somewhere."

"Let's pull up on Al and Bo," Lil Eazy replied.

The streets were shifting. The silence was starting to scream.

Too many names floating in too many mouths.

Too many calls left to read.

The ones who used to run Atlanta smooth and quiet were now moving sloppy, chasing shadows and paranoia.

Some chased paper.

Some chased peace.

But the countdown kept ticking.

And not everybody was gonna make it to the ball drop.

CHAPTER 48

Pictures, Chips, and Ghosts in the Smoke

Some nights expose more than the daylight ever could. Beneath the flashing walls of DEA offices, across smoky poker tables, and behind the cold smiles at a repass, power shifts quietly. Secrets inch toward daylight while grudges stretch across generations. It's a delicate dance of silence, surveillance, and suspicion—and no one is moving without leaving a shadow.

DEA Office – Night

Pictures from the Underground Atlanta party lined the wall like a rogue's gallery. Spencer stood in front of them, eyes slicing through each face like a case file. Her tone was calm, but laced with fire.

"Amazing how a twenty-one-year-old can get us in the room with all these major players," she said. "Truthfully, I was wondering how Ms. Vickie was aging. We haven't had updated photos of her in over ten years."

Miller leaned against the wall. "Hosa told us Lil B's dating her daughter."

Spencer turned. "Which one?"

"He didn't say. We'll check with LB to get everything."

Spencer nodded slowly. "This case is getting more interesting by the minute. Could be career-changing if we move right. I want names to match every face. Backgrounds, connections—everything."

Miller pulled out his phone. "On it. I'll have LB ID them."

"No," Spencer said. "Bring him in. I want to proffer him myself."

Al's Work Spot – Day

Money slid across the table like playing cards in a casino. Tyrone pocketed fifteen thousand like it was light work.

"You weren't playing about locking down Myrtle Beach," he said. "I got dudes driving three hours just to buy."

Bo nodded. "Still just the beginning. Be safe. Text when you make it."

Tyrone and a woman were excited. Al and Bo sat back. The silence felt heavy.

"Man, can't lie," Al muttered. "This Mike Mike situation… bad timing for us. Hope he good."

"Me too. Mike Mike was solid. Real fam."

The door opened. Lil Eazy and Lil B stepped in. Daps were exchanged.

"No news?" Al asked.

"Hell naw," Lil B muttered. "Shit driving me crazy."

Lil Eazy exhaled. "Tomorrow we gotta go to G-Mack's funeral and repass. Killed him and lady Execution style. Same shit. Holidays always bring pain."

"Too many people close to us," Al said. "Got me thinking. Like we've been targets ever since Ross."

"We were just talking about that," Lil B nodded.

Bo leaned forward. "Now that y'all say that… Terri and them were at the strip club that night."

Lil B's face shifted. "You're right. Man, if she's behind this, her whole family is gonna die."

Lil Eazy nodded slowly. "Long-standing beef between the families. This second-generation shit runs deep."

Sweat Box Sports Bar – Night

Poker chips clacked like bones. Tension sat low over the room like cigar smoke. A tall 6'8" player shoved his chips forward and stood up.

"I'm out of this hand. 'Bout to eat."

He moved to the bar. Brian turned as a woman approached.

"Money said give you this," she said, sliding a stack over. "His fifty… plus twenty-five more."

Money followed behind her. "Brian, my word and my money always good. Bring me more chips. All a man got is his word and face card."

Brian held his stance. "Just house rules. Nothing personal. If MJ's here, the line stays fifty."

"I hear you, Mr. BusinessMan."

Across the table, tension cracked.

Troup tossed his cards. "I need my fifteen back. Lost three straight."

Big Will laughed. "They're going down the rabbit hole, Brian. It's Christmas time—they want more chips."

Brian nodded toward the waitress.

"Damn, these lamb chops are good as hell," the 6'8" player said from the bar. "I'm coming here just to eat next time I'm in town."

Troup grinned. "Keep hoopin' like that, you gon' be here more often. I told you—Black Mabam shoots over a thousand shots a day."

Repass – Day

The smell of collards and sorrow filled the house. Soul food dulled the pain, but the grief still pulsed in the air. Everyone dressed in black. Soft embraces passed from hand to hand.

A large photo of G-Mack holding his son, Lil Easy, watched from the mantle like a ghost in the room.

Outside, Lil B rolled a blunt beside G-Mack's cousin. Lil Eazy stood nearby, eyes low.

G-Mack's mother stepped forward.

"Thank you for helping with both funerals," she said. "Keep in touch. Don't forget about us."

"Don't worry, Ms. Yates," Lil Eazy said. "I'll be around. I got Lil Man."

She nodded and went back inside.

"Damn," G-Mack's cousin said. "Cuz was just bragging about how you were really helping him get money."

"G-Mack was about his business," Lil Eazy replied. "Anybody you think he might've been dealing with?"

"Not really. Only person I saw over there who seemed off was Twin."

Lil B looked up. "Toni and Terri's Twin?"

"Yep. Him and his cousin, Charlie Mo. I asked Cuz about 'em. He said he'd been serving Twin since high school."

Lil B passed the blunt.

Lil Eazy looked up at the sky. "How all the smoke keep pointing to them these past few weeks?"

Lil B nodded. "Yeah. I'm convinced they are involved. Mike Mike's still missing."

Precious' House – Day

The tension in the room wasn't loud—but it was thick.

Brian sat on the edge of the couch, eyes serious. "First, thanks for the wire."

"No problem," Precious said. "Actually… just keep the money. Put it toward the buyout."

Brian narrowed his eyes. "You really want me out of the business. You must be thinking about marrying Coach Cory."

She froze.

"How do you know him as Coach Cory? You've been spying on me?"

Brian chuckled. "Nah. Reason I'm here is 'cause I found out I got an eight-year-old son… and Coach Cory coaches him."

Precious blinked, then rolled her eyes.

"I already knew. I said Lil Boston reminded me of you—and Lil Brian? Wow. Thought that trick looked familiar."

"Sorry, Precious. I just found out. But I never got mad when you wanted the divorce. Truth is… I know I ain't right by you."

She looked at him with pain simmering.

"Can't lie. Feels like you stabbed me with a dagger. If we stayed married, you would've done the one thing I begged you never to do—bring home another child. God works in mysterious ways."

The lines are drawn. The heat is rising. Every move made is being watched or whispered about. From poker tables to funeral homes, loyalty is on trial. The feds are circling. Feuds are resurfacing. And the past is burning a hole into the present.

What's done in the dark?

It's sprinting toward the light.

And the next play… could change everything.

CHAPTER 49

The Masks We Wear

In a world where loyalty is tested, money makes the rules, and trust is a luxury few can afford, Atlanta felt like it was holding its breath. Christmas hovered just days away, but the air pulsed with unspoken tension. Friends were looking sideways. Partners questioned each other's motives. Families prayed for peace that felt further away by the hour. Everyone wore a mask. And only a few knew how the story would end.

At Santiago's warehouse, Al stood across from the man whose name alone kept people cautious. Santiago leaned back in his chair, a leather jacket hugging his broad shoulders, tinted glasses hiding unreadable eyes.

"Sorry for being so slow with the package," Al said, keeping his voice steady. "I have real issues. My nephew—he's missing. Works with me. It's thrown everything off."

Santiago didn't flinch. "Sorry to hear that. But my business has to keep moving. Trucks come. Money goes back. I fall behind, and my people start looking at me sideways."

"I understand," Al said. "I'll have your money in a few days."

"If you can't handle the loads," Santiago replied, his tone sharpening, "I'll give more to my other crews. They'd be more than happy."

Al nodded quickly. "Nah. I got you. Just give me those few days."

"You got three," Santiago said. "After that, I make changes."

Outside Precious's house, Pairs sat in a parked car, nervously tapping her foot. Malika watched her, puzzled.

"Why aren't we going in?" Malika asked.

"My dad's in there," Pairs muttered. "I can't face him. He sees through me... like he got some kind of power."

Malika's voice softened. "So when are you getting an abortion?"

"I don't know. Pac-Man wants to keep the baby. I'm torn. You and him are the only ones that know."

"You gonna tell your sister?"

"Tonight. I have to. She'll help me figure it out. Never thought I'd be pregnant in twelfth grade. Such a big disappointment."

In Legs' apartment, tension choked the room. Amy, Blu, and Terri sat on the couch, all too quiet until Amy finally broke the silence.

"Terri, me and Legs ditched Mike Mike's car. But before we did, we found fifty bands in the trunk. She cuffed it. Didn't tell anybody."

Terri's face twisted in anger. "She is greedy. I made plenty of plays on the low and still broke bread. She just crossed the line. Let her and Apple keep playing—she gon' meet her end."

Blu leaned forward. "Told y'all she wasn't right. Had that junkie vibe since day one. Y'all thought I was hating 'cause she from New Orleans and on that dog food."

In a black DEA SUV parked off Peachtree, Miller and Moore flipped through photos and bank records spread across the dash.

"Hosa and Julio just vanished," Miller said.

Moore glanced up. "You think they skipped back to Mexico?"

"Doubt it. Julio hasn't touched the bar's accounts. It's like they're plotting something."

"LB is still doing the proffer?"

"In two days. Says Ms. Vickie's keeping him close. Said there's a big deal brewing."

Moore chuckled. "She's pushing sixty. He's thirty-two. Wild."

Miller didn't laugh. "She likes them young. Easier to control. Easier to throw under the bus."

Legs and Apple stood outside a food cart near Edgewood, hissing words between sips of sweet tea.

"I hope Terri stops being in her feelings and puts a price tag on Mike Mike already," Legs whispered.

Apple didn't blink. "Relax. It's always about the bag."

"Don't feel that energy lately."

Apple's eyes narrowed. "Play your part. When we met you, you were strung out, homeless in the Bluff. We cleaned you up. Don't forget who gave you the game."

Legs sucked her teeth. "Damn, Apple. You cut deep."

"Just a friendly reminder."

Brian and young Boston moved through the mall like a unit, arms full of bags, eyes scanning holiday sales. Later, in the car, the boy looked up from his phone.

"What do you wanna be when you grow up?" Brian asked.

"Football player."

"You can be anything, as long as you have focus and heart."

"Coach says the same thing."

Brian nodded. "Smart man. How are your grades?"

"A's and B's… one C."

Brian smirked. "You got a girlfriend?"

Boston grinned. "I got two, Daddy."

Brian laughed. "You definitely are my son."

His phone buzzed. A text from Tasha appeared on the dash screen: *I'm up and worried. Please come by. We really need to talk.*

 He replied: *Dropping your nephew off. Be there soon.*

At the gym, Precious and Roxy wiped sweat from their foreheads between sets.

"Weird hearing Brian got an eight-year-old," Precious said.

Roxy looked sideways. "Do you still love him?"

"Always did. Still do. Cory's a good man, but... Brian makes my body react. Cory doesn't."

"Damn," Roxy murmured. "That's deep. Are you cooking for Christmas?"

"Yeah. But the girls with their dad."

Tasha sat at her kitchen table wringing her hands while Tara paced nearby.

"Should I call the police?" Tasha asked.

"Not yet."

"We'd have gotten a ransom by now," Tasha whispered. "I'm thinking the worst."

"God still works miracles," Tara said.

"Brian's on the way. I'm losing my mind."

Cam and Bre stepped inside. They hugged everyone, but the heaviness in the room never lifted.

At a quiet two-story on the Westside, Slim, Dominique, and Felicia were knee-deep in cash. Stacks covered the table. In the living room, LB and Clay watched highlights on a muted TV.

"You weren't lying," LB said. "You really needed more work."

Clay nodded. "I'm locking down Douglas, Cobb, Villa Rica, Carlton. My guys are all local, popular, and clean. We push slaps to bricks."

"Outskirts got money," LB replied. "I like it."

His phone buzzed again. Miller.

My boss mad you didn't show.

LB responded, *Trust me. You'll love what I'm about to bring.* Then he took a photo of the cash pile and sent it.

Clay raised an eyebrow.

LB got up and walked over. "Don't worry. I make sure you get everything you need. Ms. Vickie gave me full control."

That night at Santiago's warehouse, Ms. Vickie sat across from him, eyes clear and voice flat.

"Al hit a bump," Santiago said. "Might need you to move his product."

"That's why I came. We have a problem. LB might be hot. He did some dirt on his own. Deal went bad. I don't know who's watching now."

Santiago shrugged. "By the time you know for sure, it's already too late."

"Exactly," she said. "That's why I told him—he needs to fly to Mexico. Meet y'all. Get the drift?"

Santiago leaned back in his chair. "Yeah… he won't see America again."

Brian sat parked outside Tasha's house, hands on the wheel. The city buzzed beyond the glass—sirens, laughter, bass from someone's trunk. But inside the SUV, it was quiet.

Life comes at you fast, he thought. You don't get to rehearse it. You just respond. And how you respond... that's what defines you.

He stared out through the windshield. These streets... They don't sleep. And they damn sure don't care. Everyone out here got a role. A mask. And a hustle.

His jaw tightened. Sometimes I wonder if we're all just characters in a never-ending loop. A new scene. A new victim. Same damn script.

He exhaled, slow and long. But me? I'm rewriting mine.

He opened the door and stepped into the night, truth and consequence trailing him like shadows that had finally come home.

CHAPTER 50

Blood in the Gutter

The pressure was rising like a kettle left on high. Betrayals were catching up, and the smell of vengeance thickened the air. Loyalty had a cost, and everyone was about to learn its price.

Terri paced the living room inside Legs' apartment, her voice sharp as she barked into the phone.

"Yeah, bro. Get over to Legs' house now," she said. "I got a Christmas present for you. Make sure Charlie Mo is with you."

Blu entered from the hallway and stopped at the edge of the room where Apple leaned against the wall. She could feel the weight in the air.

"What's the play?" Blu asked.

Terri didn't hesitate. "First thing—that bitch Legs must die. She really was on some backstabbing shit. I can't trust her. Should've left her ass in the Bluff."

Blu raised her hands slightly. "Look, Terri. We gotta keep this about business. Can't make it too personal. That's how people slip. That's how mistakes happen."

Terri shook her head. "We gon' get a fat bag regardless. I'm sure Brian and Al can come up with it."

At Tasha's house, her eyes were red and wet, tears sliding silently down her face. She stood with her arms limp at her sides. Brian watched her closely, the pain on her face hitting him like a gut punch.

"I just don't know, Brian," she whispered. "I told and begged Mike Mike, Cam, and Lil B to leave them streets alone. That life has no retirement plan."

Brian stepped closer. "Sis, just know—we are about to put all hands on deck. I'm reaching deep into the Rolodex on this one. Ain't no half-steppin'."

Back at Legs' apartment, Toni and Charlie Mo stood by the window. Their eyes were lit up—not with concern, but with hunger. The kind of hunger only money could feed.

"Sis," Toni said, "we need to ask for a mill ticket."

"I was thinking somewhere in that ballpark," Terri replied, her tone cold, calculating.

At Lil B's trap house, the room was thick with tension and smoke. Lil B's voice cracked from stress and lack of sleep.

"Man, we gotta find Cuz," he said. "My dad is on the way. I got the streets lookin' high and low for Legs—if that's even her real name."

"Yeah," Lil Eazy added, "we put a twenty-five K reward out. Streets should tell us something soon."

"I got people working it from my side too," Al said.

Bo nodded. "Hell yeah, word's out. The vultures gon' talk."

At the police station, Detective Small stepped into the lieutenant's office, concerned all over his face.

"Word on the streets is that one of Al's boys got snatched," he said. "They think a female might be behind it."

"Anyone file a missing persons report?" the lieutenant asked.

"Nah," Small replied. "You know the streets. They handle their own."

"Get somebody on it. Pull in all our CIs. We might be able to kill two birds—take down a drug op and find our killer. I'm looping in the drug task force."

Lil B's phone rang, slicing through the tension like a blade. Everyone froze. He answered quickly.

"Hello?"

"Cuz..." Mike Mike's voice came through the line, shaky but alive. "They want a million dollars in forty-eight hours or I'm dead."

"Mike Mike?! You okay?"

"Yeah—" The call suddenly shifted. A different voice, low and unbothered, came on the line.

"You heard him. Now play with it. We'll be in touch."

The line went dead.

"They want a million dollars..." Lil B said slowly, staring down at the phone.

"Damn," Al muttered. "They really shot high."

Brian and Jack entered the room as the others caught them up.

"Let me ask y'all something," Brian said. "How much can we pull together?"

"I'll put up two-fifty," Al said without pause.

"Me and Eazy can do one-fifty," Lil B added.

"I got a hundred," Bo said.

"Fifty from me," Cam threw in.

Brian nodded, calculating. "That's a little over half a mil. Y'all said he met her at Blaze Night Club, right?"

"Yep," Lil Eazy confirmed.

"Alright. We got forty-eight hours. Let's shake some trees. And while we're at it, see if we can find fake money—real on top, fake on bottom. Might save us if they don't look too hard."

Detective Small stood beside an unmarked cruiser on the south end, talking to two street informants. Both looked twitchy but eager to trade knowledge for clearance.

"What can y'all tell me about Mike Mike?" he asked. "What's his real name? Who he run with?"

Chad scratched his beard. "Used to sling rocks. Heard he moves weight now. Last I saw, he was in a black Charger. Don't know his last name."

"Who did he run with?"

"Lil B and Lil Eazy."

"You know someone named Al?"

Chad shook his head. "Not really. Oh—heard there's a twenty-five thousand dollar reward floatin'. That got people talkin'."

Inside Blaze Strip Club, the back office smelled like cheap bourbon and history. Brian and Bill sat across from an old white man who ran security. He looked like he hadn't missed a night in thirty years.

"How many days back?" the man asked.

"Few weeks," Brian said. "Friday night. Around eleven to two."

"Only doing this 'cause we go way back," the old man muttered. "You always spent good money here. Normally I stay outta people's business."

They scrubbed through footage. Rewind. Zoom. Frame by frame. Then—there he was.

Mike Mike. Laughing. Clear as day. Handing his phone to a woman, exchanging numbers.

Brian leaned in. "That's our lead. Let's find out who she is."

The game was tightening. The clock was ticking. Every move felt louder now, every step riskier. People were scrambling to come up with answers—or bury their secrets before they surfaced. What had started as a celebration now had blood on its hands. And the holiday spirit? Nowhere to be found.

In a world where loyalty could get you killed, and betrayal bought you time, every step forward came with a price. And someone, somewhere... was always watching.

CHAPTER 51

A Christmas Ransom

The season was supposed to be filled with warmth, family, and peace. But in the shadows of blinking lights and fake smiles, real pain was boiling over. Loyalty had been shattered, and blood ties were being tested in ways no one expected. While the world shopped and sang carols, they were preparing to trade hostages—not gifts.

Tasha sat curled up on the couch, her eyes swollen and red. Her hands twitched slightly, like her body was trying to shake the weight of her worry.

"Sis," she whispered, voice thin and cracking. "I'm about to have a nervous breakdown. I almost smoked some laced weed."

Tara slid beside her, wrapping an arm around her shoulders. She rubbed her back the same way she did when they were kids, when nightmares were simpler.

"Stay strong," she said. "Nephew's going to be alright. They're on it."

Tasha shook her head slowly. "I know… but this all reminds me of when Precious got kidnapped. It's like the same nightmare all over again. But I still have hope."

"They'll pay whatever it takes to get him back," Tara said firmly. "I made it clear to Al—family comes first."

Around them, family members sat in silence, the air thick with unspoken prayers and heavy faces. No one had the right words. Just quiet faith and deep fear.

Inside Legs' apartment, the walls echoed with anxiety.

"There's a $25,000 reward out on Legs' head," Charlie Mo said, arms crossed. "Streets talking, but nobody knows who she is for real."

Terri smirked. "Good. That means our move was tight. They better be stacking up what we asked for. Look, go in there and do something to him—so they know we are not playing."

Apple shifted uncomfortably against the wall. "I don't like this. Too many eyes watching. Too many mouths talking."

Terri didn't blink. "The only person of interest is that bitch in there—which makes her perfect."

From the back room came muffled cries and a dull thump. Apple flinched. Charlie Mo lit a cigarette and stared at nothing.

Al paced inside the trap house, phone pressed tight to his ear. Santiago's voice buzzed through the line like a warning siren.

"Trust me, Santiago. Just give me a few more days," Al pleaded. "It's a family emergency."

"If you're not ready by Wednesday, Al, someone else gets your order. No exceptions," Santiago replied coldly.

Al sighed, ending the call. "Santiago is ready to pass our load off if I don't show by Wednesday."

"We need that," Lil B said. "Especially if we gotta cough up ransom for Cuz."

"Who you telling?" Lil Eazy added, shaking his head.

A knock at the door cut through the tension. Bo peeked out the window before letting Brian and Jack in.

"I need y'all to see something," Brian said. "Think we just found a face to go with the name. Y'all got a VCR?"

The room went quiet.

"I can go grab one from my house," Bo said. "Better yet, I'll get my wife to drop it off."

In the back room of Legs' apartment, Terri stepped in slowly. Legs was tied to a chair, her face battered and bruised. Mike Mike sat nearby, his face swollen, but his eyes burning with defiance.

"Terri, why y'all doing this to me?" Legs croaked. "I'm on your side."

Terri stepped closer, jaw tight. "Are you so trifling? You've been stealing and backstabbing from day one. I let it slide 'cause you were a junkie and I felt bad. But now? We know you took that fifty grand out the trunk. Ain't no coming back from that."

Back at the trap house, Brian pressed play on the tape. The footage rolled in silence as everyone crowded around.

"Wow," Lil B muttered. "Terri really put a female on Cuz."

Brian leaned back. "Terri—as in Silk's daughter? The twin?"

"Yeah," Lil B confirmed.

Brian's mind spun, putting the pieces together. "It's deeper than we thought. Now we gotta play chess. We gon' go by Silk's mama's house… kidnap everyone in there. Offer an exchange. Or they gon' be wearin' black just like us."

Lil Eazy nodded. "That MOB shit, Unk. Might as well hit her right hand too—Apple. And snatch her mama up. I know the address."

Brian looked around the room. "Always remember—it's not what you know. It's who you know. Let's move fast."

Outside Terri G's mama's house, a van eased up to the curb. Two men stepped out wearing red Santa hats and holding boxes of chocolates and flowers. They looked like delivery men, festive and harmless.

They rang the bell.

A sweet-looking older woman opened the door, smiling.

Seconds later, the scene exploded. Screams pierced the air. The men forced their way in.

Moments later, they emerged with three women—blindfolded, bound, and silent.

Inside the house garage, the van backed in. Brian, Lil Easy, Lil B, Cam, Al, Jack, and Bo stood waiting. The air felt colder than it should have.

Brian exhaled slowly, looking around the dim space. "Damn. This is the first Christmas I've been home in years. I didn't expect this. I should be drinking eggnog, not doing shit that could get me twenty years. My daughters are waiting on me."

Lil B gave a faint smile. "Yeah, Dad… but sometimes, you gotta let people know how gangster you are."

Brian didn't reply. He just looked down at his boots, then back at the blindfolded women in the van.

The holidays weren't supposed to go like this. But in this world, peace was a luxury—and war was a tradition passed down like family recipes. The cost of loyalty came wrapped in duct tape and desperation. And for every silent prayer whispered under Christmas lights, there was someone out there sharpening their knives.

The next move was already on the board.

No one knew who'd be left standing after the game was over.

CHAPTER 52

Blood for Blood

When the lines between family and revenge blur, everything becomes fair game. This wasn't about money anymore. This was about the code—the unwritten rules of the streets where betrayal meant blood, and disrespect was only erased with death. They had played a dirty hand, and now, they were staring down the consequences. The streets had flipped the script. The wolves weren't just watching—they had bitten back.

Inside Legs' apartment, Amy, Toni, Charlie Mo, and Blu sat around the kitchen table, red cups in hand and a plate of cocaine laid out like a holiday spread. The mood was dark but electric—laughter mixed with madness.

"I can't lie," Toni said, grinning. "I've been waiting so long for this moment. I know our dad is smiling."

"Yeah," Charlie Mo agreed. "Unk was the realest. We're about to get a mill and kill their ass—two birds with one stone. Bet they running around like chickens with their heads cut off tryna get the money up."

Amy leaned back and yelled toward the hallway, "Terri! Apple! Get in here! We are about to toast to Silk and a million-dollar hit."

Terri and Apple walked in, both grinning like it was New Year's. They raised their cups as the others did the same.

"To Silk," they all echoed.

They drank.

None of them knew the high was about to crash—hard.

At the precinct, tension buzzed like a faulty wire.

"The streets are looking for this girl Legs, but nobody even knows her real name," the lieutenant said, rubbing his forehead. "We need to find Mike Mike's last known address. Let's speak to his mother."

Small nodded. "According to my CI, there's talk of blood being spilled. Somehow, this all loops back to G-Mack."

"This is getting outta control. Bet money Ross is connected somehow. Pull all hands on deck. Now."

Back at Brian's house, Pairs sat beside her younger sister Malin on the living room couch, knees pulled to her chest. She stared out the window, lost in her thoughts.

"Dad's been gone a long time," she said.

Malin glanced at her. "How do you feel about our new little brother?"

"He's cool. Smart. Look like Lil B."

"Do you think Mom and Dad will ever get back together?"

Pairs shrugged. "Don't look like it."

The late-night celebration at Legs' spot had turned into a hangover in the making. They were still buzzing, running their mouths, already spending money they hadn't touched. Talk of new houses, investments, club ownership—they were building empires on blood.

Then Terri's phone vibrated.

She glanced at the screen. Her smile dropped instantly.

Across the room, Apple's phone buzzed too. She checked it. Her hand trembled.

Both women stared at the same message.

ON SCREEN TEXT (BOTH PHONES):

"IF MIKE MIKE DON'T BE RETURNED ASAP, WE ALL GONNA BE WEARING BLACK. FUNERAL TIME."

"No, no, no…" Apple muttered, her voice cracking. "We messed up. They have my mommy."

Terri swallowed hard. "They got our mommy… our G-mommy… and lil sis. Bro—it's over."

Toni snatched the phone from her. "What? Let me see that."

His jaw clenched as his eyes scanned the screen.

Outside a modest home, LT and Small knocked on the door. A man answered.

"Yeah? How can I help y'all?" he asked.

"We're looking for Mike Mike's mom or Mike Mike himself," Small said.

The man shook his head. "Nobody lives here by those names."

"Do you know anything about them?"

"Nope. We've been living here for two years. Don't know who was here before."

"You rent or own?"

"Rent."

"Can you give us the landlord's info?"

Back at the apartment, the mood had shifted entirely. Gone was the joy. Now it was fear, anxiety, and quiet rage.

"Bro, calm down," Terri said to Toni. "Lil Eazy and them hold all the cards now. Let's do what they say—live to fight another day."

"But how the hell did they find out we were behind the kidnapping?" Apple asked, shaking her head. "That's what's really bothering me."

Terri sighed. "Right now, I can't even think straight. We just need to comply."

"This hurt me to my core," Toni growled. "They snatched up Granny?! They gotta pay."

"Hell yeah," Charlie Mo snapped. "Only blood and dead bodies from here on out. F*** the money."

"I hear you," Terri said, her voice quieter now. "But for now… we drop Mike Mike off like they said. We ain't got no choice."

At a bus stop in the early daylight, Mike Mike sat alone, stripped to his underwear, shivering. A thin stream of blood ran from his temple, his face swollen but his spirit somehow still intact.

A black car pulled up fast. The back door swung open as Lil B jumped out.

"Cuz! Damn, we're glad to see you," he said, crouching down. "You okay? Do you need the hospital?"

Mike Mike shook his head. "Naw… just take me to my mommy's house. Thank y'all. For real. Whatever y'all did—I owe you."

Lil Eazy helped him into the car, silent, eyes hard with thoughts he didn't say out loud.

The cost of war was always paid in blood. And sometimes, the ones who started the fire never expected the flames to find their doorstep.

Terri and her crew thought they had the upper hand. Thought pain was power. But they forgot one thing—blood protects blood.

This wasn't just about Mike Mike. It was about every move that came before. Every disrespect. Every name whispered in the dark.

The board had been flipped.

Now, it was time to checkmate.

CHAPTER 53

The Price of Peace

Sometimes, survival ain't about who's the toughest—it's about who can think five moves ahead when everything is crumbling around them. The streets are unpredictable. Loyalty is tested. Family gets caught in the crossfire. And when silence falls, it's the echoes of your decisions that speak the loudest. What started as a million-dollar play had now become a game of legacy—who'll last, who'll fall, and who'll walk away whole.

Detective Small stormed into the lieutenant's office with urgency written all over him.

"A female body's been found in the woods," he said, barely catching his breath. "My CI says it's Legs, but we're not a hundred percent sure."

The lieutenant didn't hesitate. "Grab your coat. Let's get over there now. Fast-turning events. Where's Mike Mike?"

Small exhaled. "That's the million-dollar question."

Terri stood in her condo, inches from her mother. Her eyes bounced between worry and rage. Her mother, visibly shaken but unharmed, lowered herself into a chair.

"Mom, are you okay? Did they hurt you?" Terri asked.

"No, baby," her mother replied gently. "They were really nice. I told you to let the past be the past. Too many old bones. Brian and Jack are like the mob; they're in everybody's pockets."

Toni stood nearby, his voice clipped and full of fire. "Mom, we can't let this ride. They've really violated."

Her mother's tone shifted.

"Boy, you're going to get us all killed. You haven't heard a thing I've said."

That evening, the front door creaked open at Tasha's house. Mike Mike stepped in, battered but alive.

Tasha dropped to her knees, clinging to him, tears soaking into his hoodie. "Son… God answered my prayers. I fasted and prayed the whole time. You almost made me start back smoking crack."

Tara joined, wrapping them both in her arms.

"Now sit down," Tasha said, pulling him to the couch. "Let me get my baby well."

In the den, the circle had regrouped. Brian, Jack, Lil Eazy, and Lil B sat together, the tension melting slowly into strategy.

"Y'all, things really could've gone south," Brian said. "You've got to pay attention to the signs. I got a proposition. How about y'all come join me?"

Lil B leaned forward. "Dad, what are you really doing besides opening a sports bar?"

Brian's tone dropped low. Measured. Seriously.

"I'm about to have one of the biggest betting sportsbooks in Atlanta. I'm also investing in stocks, buying houses to flip and rent, and I got box trucks moving. It's all about compound interest. In five to ten years, Heirlooms Enterprise LLC will be worth ten to twenty million—no prison, no paranoia."

Lil Eazy rubbed his jaw. "I don't understand all that, Unk… but I believe in you. I'll keep it real—I gotta make my own million first. Then I'm in."

Lil B nodded. "We're this close. Mike Mike's situation was a fluke—wrong girl. But I do think about going legit… someday. Just not today."

Brian looked at them both, love and warning filling his gaze.

"I love y'all with all my heart. Trust me, if it was easy to walk away and live clean, more of us would've done it. The streets write a new script every day. Yesterday it was Mike Mike. Tomorrow… it's somebody else. Just know—my offer always stands."

At the FBI's regional headquarters, agents gathered around a wall plastered with mugshots and surveillance photos. At the top was Cory. Below him, six faces aligned—including Precious.

Agent Hill tapped the board.

"Cory. TA. JP. Tammy. Imani. And who is her?"

Agent Schwartz replied without hesitation. "Precious Jordan. She's different. Already had money from real estate and other legit ventures."

Hill narrowed his eyes. "What's her angle?"

"She opened two WIC stores under an LLC," Schwartz explained. "We got control buys—people cashing food stamps for cash."

Hill flipped through the files in silence. His voice was calm but deadly.

"They've stolen over ten million from the government. Freeze their accounts. Pick them up within seventy-two hours."

Yellow tape flapped in the wind deep in the woods. A female body lay under a white sheet. Forensics moved slowly around the scene. The lieutenant stood nearby, jaw clenched.

"Do we have a real name for Legs yet?" he asked.

"No, sir," Small replied.

The lieutenant didn't blink. "Two things could've happened—somebody cut ties, or Mike Mike's crew got to her. Either way, I don't like it. Let's get to the bottom of this."

That night at The Sweatbox, Brian and Jack sat in their usual corner. Champagne popped. Nerves settled.

"To the beginning of great things," Jack said, raising his glass. "Wealth, health, and trendsetting, my friend."

They toasted.

"These last hundred hours?" Brian muttered. "Wild. Mike Mike almost died. Lil B and Lil Eazy chasing millions in the dope game. Precious—into some shady shit I can't quite figure out. And she's with a guy who's been with my other son's mom... who just so happens to be his coach. Tara and her man are running a heavy operation. It's like the hood won't let me breathe."

Jack chuckled, then leaned back.

"I feel you. But enjoy the win. You stuck to your plan. Keep leading—they'll catch up."

The next morning, the smell of brunch floated through Brian's house. A private chef plated shrimp and grits as music thumped in the background. Kids danced and rapped along to "No Hands" by Waka Flocka, their joy unfiltered.

Pairs, Milan, and Boston tore through wrapping paper while Brian and Joyce hung new photos on the wall.

"How do you feel about Boston meeting everyone?" Joyce asked softly.

Brian smiled. "Excited. Nervous too. But I know he'll be welcomed. Are you good with Ashley stopping by?"

Joyce nodded. "He's your son. And yes, I mean it. It only makes sense that she meets everyone."

"One of your greatest gifts," Brian said, "is understanding."

The girls spun in unison, screaming lyrics and laughing. Brian watched, eyes misty with pride.

"Karaoke is coming up," he called out. "Don't start acting shy!"

"Dad," Pairs said, "Milan wants to be a singer and actress."

Brian beamed. "What's my motto?"

Together, Paris and Milan shouted: "Whatever you put your mind to, you can do it. And if your mind receives it, you can achieve it!"

He smiled, soaking in the moment.

His family. His empire. His future.

All under one roof, moving in harmony.

The storm had passed, but the air still held tension. In a world where money, blood, and betrayal exchanged hands daily, the real victory wasn't survival—it was clarity. Brian had built something real amidst the chaos. A foundation. A vision.

But as he knew too well, the game never ends... it just changes players.

And while some were ready to evolve, others were still chasing ghosts.

One thing remained true—peace has a price. And not everyone was ready to pay for it.

CHAPTER 54

Signs and Smoke

There's a moment in every storm when the wind holds still, and you think the worst is over. But that stillness—it's not peace. It's a warning. A pause before the next wave. And in the game these people play—where loyalty is thin and ambition's thick—those pauses don't last long. The real ones know: it's not what you see coming that gets you—it's what's moving in the dark, quietly positioning for the kill.

Inside the cold walls of the DEA office, LB sat stiff in a sterile interrogation room. His lawyer sat beside him, silent and focused. A small red light blinked on the recorder at the center of the table. Outside the one-way glass, Agents Miller, Moore, and Spencer spoke in hushed tones, the tension humming like static.

Spencer finally entered, her eyes sharp.

"This is your only chance," she said. "Get it right. If we catch you lying or hiding something, the deal's off the table. No immunity. Understand?"

LB nodded. "Yes."

Miller and Moore stepped in behind her as Spencer moved to a board covered in surveillance photos and mugshots.

"I point, you name. Then we go back for details," she said.

She tapped through the faces.

"Ms. Vickie—she runs a major operation. Hundreds of kilos," LB said. "Julio's one of her top players. He's got a warehouse full of product. Brian just got home, and now everybody's trying to get next to him. Al's connected straight to Santiago. He moves heavy weight mostly on the Westside —all the zones. Lil B, Brian's son, works with Al but also deals with Ms. Vickie's daughter, Felicia."

At Ms. Vickie's shop, the energy was low and tense. Behind a locked office door, her voice cut sharp and clean.

"Doctor told me to shut it all down," she said. "Something's not right. Everyone clears their debts and drops money in the stash. Quietly. No word to LB. He's the weak link."

Felicia looked skeptical. "Mom, you sure your root lady's right? Everything feels smooth."

"I've been on a thirty-year run with no major fumbles. Mary says shut down? I shut down."

Dominique leaned back. "Guess that vacation me and Clay talked about is right on time."

Slim exhaled. "So we cut LB loose?"

"He went behind my back," Ms. Vickie said coldly. "Now his connection's talking to the DEA—and he's missing. That's not a coincidence."

Felicia nodded slowly. "If Mary sees smoke, there's fire. What now?"

"I'm putting a plan together. Y'all just stay calm and play y'all part."

Brunch at Brian's house was chaos in the best way—music, laughter, cards flipping, plates clinking, kids shouting. The living room was full, alive.

"Nephew's so handsome and smart," Tasha said, eyeing Boston. "Looks like Lil B spit him out."

Tara raised her glass. "Ashley has always been cool. And she looked damn good today."

Later that afternoon, Brian stood at the front of the crowd, mic in hand. His kids and grandson stood proudly beside him.

"Pulled y'all out the cold to meet my son—Boston," he said. "He's eight. A beast on the football field. Straight A's and B's. That's his mama over there—Ashley. Some of y'all know her."

The crowd responded with love. People came up one by one, greeting Boston with handshakes and hugs.

"Alright now," Tasha called out. "Y'all ready for karaoke?"

"Told y'all it was coming!" Tara grinned. "Me and Al about to sing Keith Sweat—'Make It Last Forever.'"

Lil Eazy laughed. "Can't wait to see Al sweat."

"Boston, Paris, Malin—you up first," Brian said.

"Why are you putting us on the spot, Dad?" Pairs protested, smiling.

"We're ready," Malin said, elbowing her. "Right, Boston?"

"Yep."

The three kids took the mic and lit the room up. Singing, dancing, laughing. Black joy in its purest form. A rare calm.

Later that night, back in the DEA office, the questioning continued.

"You haven't spoken to Hosa since the night we nabbed you?" Miller asked.

"Correct," LB replied.

Spencer stood. "I like the detail. You can go. We'll be in touch."

Elsewhere, inside a dingy hotel room, paranoia and powder hung heavy in the air. Lines of cocaine blurred the table. Toni, Charlie Mo, and Amy huddled in silence, smoke curling into the shadows.

"I can't let this slide," Toni said. "They all gotta pay."

Charlie Mo kept his tone low. "We have to be smart. They expect us. We need info—who's in their circle, where they move."

Amy looked tired. "Y'all need to chill. They had Apple. Granny too. That's a long reach. And we still don't know who flipped."

The TV droned in the background. A news report flashed across the screen—an unidentified female body found in the woods. Legs. Asking for public tips.

"We're good at that, right?" Toni said.

"No way it leads back to us," Amy replied. "If anybody, it's Mike Mike."

At Brian's house, Cam was mid-performance during karaoke, belting out "Ms. Jackson" to a howling crowd. Mike Mike slipped over to Brian, quiet.

"Unk… thank you," he said. "I heard it was you who figured it out."

Brian nodded. "It's what I'm here for. But nephew—remember, this is your life. Pay attention. This could've gone really bad."

"I know," Mike Mike said, eyes serious. "I was ready for anything. But the one thing that broke me was thinking about my mom. I kept hearing her voice, over and over."

Across the room, Tara and Al grabbed the mic. The intro to

"Make It Last Forever" floated in the air.

Outside Ms. Vickie's building the next day, LB leaned against his car, posted up with Clay.

"We are heading to Punta Cana for a week," Clay said.

"A week? You crazy," LB replied. "We are just starting to work good again."

"Vickie's shutting it down after collecting. I got ten left to move. Then we gone."

"So you say."

Later that night at Lil Eazy's trap house, Felicia arrived with a heavy bag.

"It's in the trunk," she said. Lil B hugged her tightly.

"Thanks for the assist."

"Nah, you helping us," he said. "We lost almost two hundred K. You charging us twenty-five? Right on time."

"We'll take more if you got it," Lil Eazy added.

"I'll ask Mom. Gotta run. More stops tonight."

Cam walked in, gym bag in hand. No words needed.

Back at the DEA office, Spencer and Miller leaned over a spread of folders, phones, and maps.

"We have to be sharp," Spencer said. "Taking them down ripples across the whole city. We might have to use ghost dope, but LB's the key."

"Hosa's house was empty," Miller added. "Wife, kids—gone. Nothing at airports, buses, or trains. He vanished."

"Get more bodies on this. I'll see if we can tap Ms. Vickie's line and follow her girls. We're too close now to blink."

You can only hide for so long before the past pulls you out of the shadows. Brian's circle was getting tighter. The feds were closer than ever. And every move now felt like stepping across a chessboard made of glass—one wrong move, and everything would shatter.

But even with all that danger, one truth remained: in the world of hustlers and high-stakes plays, family, money, and survival never sleep.

And the storm?

It was only getting louder.

CHAPTER 55

Temptations and Trackers

The city doesn't sleep, and neither do the people hustling through its nights. Lust and loyalty, money and motives—all collide under neon lights and smoky rooms. And in this game, timing isn't just everything… it's survival. As the moves get bolder and the players more dangerous, it's clear: everybody wants a piece of something bigger—but nobody's willing to lose.

At The Sweat Box Sports Bar, the low amber lighting glinted off polished poker chips. Brian leaned over the table, cool and collected, reading the room with the eye of a veteran. Jack sat beside him, his gaze sweeping the players, recognizing tells without flinching.

The front door opened, laughter trailing behind as Precious stepped in with Roxy.

"Been telling Roxy about them crab cakes," Precious called out.

"Oh, crab cakes brought you in, huh?" Brian grinned.

"Yes, Brian—and to have a few drinks," she replied smoothly.

Roxy looked around, approving. "Brian, I like your spot. Nice."

"Appreciate it," he said. "Tia, take their order."

Across the room, cards shuffled and dice rolled. Half-smiles hid whole stories. The bar thrived under its usual blend of heat, hustle, and whispers.

At Ashley's condo, tension clung to the air like smoke. Cory sat on the couch with a drink in hand, that old gleam in his eyes. Ashley stood across from him, arms folded.

"Damn, I miss this," Cory said, scanning the space. "Where's Boston?"

"With his dad," she replied flatly.

"Damn. He moved in fast."

Ashley shot him a look. "No, he's just been a dad. Look—we don't need to go back and forth. This is just a booty call. I need some dick—point blank."

Cory blinked. Then smiled. "Damn… okay. I miss you too."

Words stopped. Intentions didn't.

Back at The Sweatbox, Precious and Roxy sipped from their glasses, leaned into the night, tipsy and glowing.

"These drinks have caught up with me," Precious murmured.

"Girl, we've had three or four," Roxy said, laughing.

Precious smirked. "I think I'm gonna give Brian some tonight— one time only. Get this lust outta me."

"You grown. I don't judge," Roxy replied with a shrug.

Across the room, Brian and Troup stood near the dice table, caught in a rhythm of side deals.

"I got a few ball players and rappers coming through Saturday night," Troup said. "They like to throw dice."

"That works," Brian nodded. "I've got a table for that. We'll make Saturday night dice night—call it Troup Night."

Troup smiled, handing over a rack of chips. "Cash me out. I'll be back later."

Brian nodded, eyes watching everything. "Looks like you've done well."

Inside Santiago's dimly lit warehouse, Al stood across from the man whose voice cut sharper than the knives some of his people carried.

"Think you can handle triple your load?" Santiago asked.

"Hell yeah—with more time. Need to line up a few new stash spots, but I can handle it."

"Good. Top of the year, we start moving differently. Ms. Vickie's shutting down for a while. I'm giving you most of her load."

"Sounds good to me," Al said, eyes steady. "Everything straight?"

"Yeah," Santiago replied. "Just some internal business she needs to flush out."

Deals made. Power shifted. The underworld had new hands on the wheel.

In a flickering parking lot, LB stood between two cars, low-talking with Jay and Nard under the orange hue of broken lights.

"Look here," LB said, pulling a phone from his pocket. "Tracking devices for all three of her daughters. I already hid 'em in their cars. Just figure out where the money's being kept, and we're rich as hell."

Jay grinned. "Man, just when I thought you were pussy-whipped by a cougar, you come through game six like MJ."

LB smirked. "My dad always told me—it's not what you do, but how you do it. And timing is everything."

"We are about to rock her world," Nard said, eyes wide.

"Y'all just don't mess it up," LB warned. "It'll never get sweeter than this."

They laughed—but the move was real. And deadly.

Ashley and Cory's tension exploded the way it always had—no words. Just need, memory, and regrets twisted in sheets.

Later that night, Precious sat in her car, engine idling under the moonlight. Brian walked up to the window, leaning down.

"You don't want to follow me?" she asked, eyes daring. "Make sure I make it home safe?"

"I thought you'd never ask."

Inside Precious' home, the front door barely shut before clothes hit the floor. They moved like old lovers who knew each other's flaws better than they knew their futures. Lust. Memory. Hunger. No questions. No hesitation.

Sometimes, it's not the big moves that change everything—it's the whispers. The glances. The shadows creeping where no one's watching.

LB just played a hand that could change the whole board. Santiago's shifting power, carving new lanes. Ms. Vickie smells the smoke and starts tightening her circle. And Brian—he's dancing with ghosts and women who still remember his name when the lights go off.

The streets are heating up again. Every smile hides suspicion. Every move carries weight.

And deep down, they all feel it in their bones...

Something's about to burn.

CHAPTER 56

Some Days Feel Like Chess

Some days feel like chess matches—quiet, methodical, dangerous. Others feel like dice games—fast, reckless, with everything on the line. But in this world, birthdays, blessings, and betrayals often show up at the same table.

The restaurant buzzed with life, energy, and the soft clink of silverware and glass. Cory's birthday dinner was in full swing—twenty deep, dressed sharp, bottles popping, laughter carrying across the polished space like jazz in motion. At the head of the table, Cory soaked it all in, his grin a mix of swagger and sentiment.

TA stood and raised his glass.

"To my brother, my best friend, and business partner—blessed to see another year. The big four-oh. We've come a long way from canned food and bologna sandwiches. Sometimes no food at all. Love you, brother. Happy birthday."

The table erupted in applause and raised glasses.

JP chimed in next, glass lifted high. "Toast to my brother, who showed me how to make my first million. Happy birthday, Cory. Love you, bro!"

The birthday chant took over, a warm haze of joy and music following. In the corner of the room, two uninvited observers sat quietly—Agent Schwartz and a female FBI agent. Their eyes scanned every laugh, every toast, like wolves in heels and tailored blazers.

"Let's send a bottle," the female agent murmured, smirking. "Might be their last one for a while."

She flagged down the waitress.

That night, inside Cory's dim bedroom, the energy was slower, heavier. Cory sat shirtless at the edge of the bed, sipping from a tumbler. Precious stood near the window, dressed in matching lingerie, her figure outlined in shadows and suspicion.

"How do you feel about Brian having an eight-year-old son?" Cory asked.

Precious exhaled. "I mean, me and Brian are in a good place. That was the past. It can't be undone. Plus, Boston's a nice kid—his sisters love him."

Cory turned, watching her. "Really? You've really taken the high road."

She narrowed her eyes. "Is there something you're trying to say? We've been divorced for over six years. What am I missing?"

"Nothing," he said, holding up his hand. "Sorry to ruffle your feathers. Now come give the birthday boy some love."

A grin spread across her lips as she straddled him. "The birthday boy trying to ruin the mood."

As they kissed, Cory's phone buzzed silently on the nightstand. The screen lit up: *"Happy Birthday, Ashley."*

Outside a house, Al's truck idled. He leaned out the driver's window, watching KK stand on the sidewalk, arms crossed playfully.

"Are you ready to move out of your mommy's house?" he teased.

"Daddy, you know I am. Me and you need all the space and time alone."

Al smiled, reaching across the seat to hand her a manila envelope. "Did you talk to your son's dad about moving in with him?"

KK nodded. "He agreed. Jabco's going at the end of the semester. It'll be just me and you, Daddy."

Al handed her the envelope. "Here's your down payment. The agent's waiting on your call."

KK squealed, hugging him tight. "Thank you, Daddy!"

At a local bar, Tara and Shan leaned against the counter, clinking their glasses beneath the low hum of the evening crowd.

"I'm so excited," Tara said, glowing. "I will close on my daycare next week. Had to call my BBF out to celebrate."

"I'm so happy for you," Shan beamed. "You deserve everything, sister."

They toasted again. Tara pulled two thick envelopes from her purse and slid them across the bar.

"I haven't forgotten what you asked last week. With Mike Mike, it's been crazy. Don't worry about paying me back until you're good."

Shan's eyes welled. "Thank you so much. This is going to help me out, girl. I've been stressing about my mommy losing her house."

Inside the station, Lt. stood with arms crossed as Small gave his report.

"Her name's Zora Higgs," Small said. "From New Orleans. She used to dance at Body Tap. She's twenty-four. Moved here five years ago."

Lt. frowned. "She has a family here? Friends? What are the streets saying?"

"She definitely had Mike Mike," Small answered. "Rolls with a crew of girls, but we don't have names yet. Something went wrong with that kidnapping."

Lt. nodded slowly. "We'll track Mike Mike down. It's time we get answers. Let's remind everyone who the real boss is."

At Al's work house, the room was quiet but focused. Al leaned against the table while Bo, Lil Eazy, and Lil B listened closely.

"Ms. Vickie's shutting down," Al began. "Santiago asked me to carry her load."

Lil B nodded. "I figured. Felicia mentioned something but wasn't clear. Said she'd explain later."

"I already manned up," Al said. "Y'all need to secure new stash houses—one for cash, one for product. Get low-key cars. Ride rentals. We're about to be targets. Play it smart."

"You sound like my dad now," Lil B said.

"Your pops had a great run," Al said. "Took a hit, went down, but still left the family straight. That's how you know you played the game right."

Bo leaned in. "I heard your pop took a million-dollar loss and kept smiling. That's what comes with being the brick man. We gotta stay a few steps ahead."

"Me and Lil B about to get new toys," Lil Eazy added. "Weekend cars only. When we not workin'."

"Cool," Al nodded. "Not telling you how to spend—just be smart. Your choices ripple through everybody."

In the hustle, some chase love, some chase paper, and some chase legacy. But only a few understand—when you play at the top, the weight gets heavier, the circles get tighter, and the snakes get quieter. In this game, being flashy ain't strategy.

Survival is.

And survival means playing every move like it's the one that decides the rest.

When the Bag Gets Heavy

When trust is thin, and the bag gets heavy, betrayal starts breathing down your neck. Every decision, every move, every silence—it all starts adding up. Fast.

June stepped out toward the mailbox, sunglasses on, hair tied up. Her mind was on the moment—until she heard the sharp click of two guns behind her. Nard and Jay closed in before she could scream.

"Inside. Now," Nard said coldly.

The barrel pressed into her back. The front door creaked open, and all three disappeared inside.

At Cowboy's house, a hard knock rattled the peace. He opened the door to find Agents Miller and Moore—suits pressed, expressions tight.

"Didn't think you'd see us again," Miller said.

"What's the problem?" Cowboy asked.

"We'll be straight with you. We've got you on tape talking with Julio. Now, how far that tape goes depends on you. When's the last time you talked to Julio?"

"The night y'all pulled me over."

"You know where he is? Or Hosa?"

"No. Like I just said, I haven't talked to or seen him."

Miller crossed his arms. "What's Brian into these days?"

"Nothing. Running a sports bar."

"How'd he get the money?"

"Maybe good credit," Cowboy snapped.

Miller's tone sharpened. "You need to help us. If not, you're going to jail. I think sixty-four is pretty old to do a bid."

Cowboy didn't flinch. "Y'all do what you have to do. I'm a man first, not a rat. Next time y'all come, have a warrant."

The door slammed in their faces.

Ms. Vickie pulled up in front of June's house with Slim riding shotgun. She rang the bell twice. No answer.

"Something's not right," she said, unlocking the door with a key.

They entered slowly, weapons drawn, moving through the quiet hall. She called out for June and Mo. Silence.

Downstairs, they found them—tied up, gagged, shaken to the core.

"Call your other two sisters," Ms. Vickie ordered. "Tell Bam and them to get here now."

That night, inside Nia's house, LB, Nard, and Jay sat on the floor, surrounded by duffle bags stuffed with cash. Their faces lit up like kids at Christmas.

"The money was heavy as hell," Jay said, laughing. "Glad we drove the truck. This gotta be a couple million."

"No might," LB said. "This is the jackpot. We gotta move quick. I'm hittin' the road tonight. Me and Nia."

In the other room, Nia sat quietly, eyes down, fingers flying across her phone screen.

Back in the basement, June was still trembling as Ms. Vickie, Felicia, and Slim hovered.

"I was just coming from the mailbox," June said softly, "when they walked up on me…"

Ms. Vickie's jaw tightened. "Damn, we slipped good. JB's behind this. I feel it in my gut. I underestimated him… but how the hell does he know about this spot?"

Felicia frowned. "That's the million-dollar question. I know nobody in here said anything."

"If it's not him," Ms. Vickie said, "then who? We are thinking inside the box—but the leak might be outside."

Slim looked around. "Can't think of nobody besides who's here right now."

"We have a serious problem," Ms. Vickie said. "Where's my phone? I must've left it in the car."

She turned to Bam. "Go get my phone. I need to make a call."

Later that night, LB sat with Nia on the couch, heart racing, eyes wide.

"Babe, we did it. We set for life. Don't pack anything—leave it all," he said, grinning. "In my Dave Chappelle voice: We rich, bitch!"

He pulled her close, kissing her hard.

In the corner, Nard leaned back, dazed.

"I don't even know what I'm buying first," he said. "It's like a dream—we hit the damn lottery."

"Ms. Vickie's smart," LB said, voice steady. "Y'all need to lay low. New money's loud. Trust—she'll be watching."

"You don't gotta tell me twice," Jay said. "I'm Texas-bound. Where everything's big."

At the trap house, the smoke was thick, and the table was cluttered with snacks and rolled blunts. Lil B, Lil Eazy, Mike Mike, and Cam were locked in deep conversation.

"I went over to Lenny and Pierre's," Lil Eazy said. "They were like seven, eight people on the computers. I asked what they did—they just smiled. Said each one makes two-fifty to three-fifty K a week."

"We in the wrong business," Lil B muttered. "Told y'all. They into fraud."

"We need to get into that," Cam added. "Heard some folks getting tax money who don't even work."

"I'm a firm believer—do what works for you," Lil Eazy said.

"True," Lil B nodded. "Wiz said we need to spend about two-fifty to break Cam's record."

Cam nodded. "I got fifty racks to throw in. I believe in myself. Wanna be like Jay-Z—own a piece of something, not just rap."

"That's heavy," Lil Eazy said. "But what Al just told us—we can make it work."

"He said we don't have to spend it all at once," Lil B replied. "Let's grind till April. Then go full speed."

"Hit the clubs, get DJs to spin the track, drop a mixtape in April. Get signed by September," Cam said.

Mike Mike flicked ash off his blunt. "I smoke to that. Got a couple coins to invest myself."

"Let's start a five-gallon jug," Lil Eazy said. "Only put hundreds in. Don't open it till we launch."

They all nodded in agreement. Silent plans stacked like poker chips.

In this life, some chases end in gold. Others in blood.

When the bag gets too big, it stops being a blessing—and starts becoming bait. The real ones know—it ain't about what you took. It's about what you can keep, and who's coming for it next.

Because once the scent of money hits the wind… everybody starts hunting.

CHAPTER 57

Some days feel like chess matches—quiet, methodical, dangerous. Others feel like dice games—fast, reckless, with everything on the line. But in this world, birthdays, blessings, and betrayals often show up at the same table.

Mo's House - Day

Bam returned to the living room and handed Ms. Vickie her phone. She looked at it, thumbed a message, and smiled.

"Looks like my ace in the hole has already reached out," she said. "Let's load up. We got business to handle. Bam, text your crew—tell them to meet us at this address."

Precious' House - Day

"I can't lie," Precious said, leaning on the kitchen counter. "All I've been thinking about is Brian. He just gets me. After all these years."

Roxy sipped her wine. "Girl, you better follow your heart. Brian's looking real good lately—he just got that swagger."

"I know," Precious sighed. "But me and Cory have these businesses. I just can't walk away. Cory's been good to me."

"One thing he can't say—he helped you get your first M. You were already straight. Can you just buy him out? Or sell it to him?"

"But Brian's with Joyce. He might not want to leave her."

Roxy leaned in. "Girl, his eyes still light up when he sees you. Cross that bridge when you get to it."

"I just don't know," Precious said quietly.

DEA Car - Day

"I've texted LB twice," Miller said, looking at his phone.

"Let's ride by Ms. Vickie's house," Moore replied.

"I have him until tomorrow. If I don't hear anything, we put out a warrant."

"What do you think about Cowboy?"

Miller shrugged. "We don't really have anything on him. We just gotta play a mind game with him—maybe he'll bend."

"Looks like this Ms. Vickie really has her stuff tight. She's been paying taxes for the last 20 years. She has her T's crossed and I's dotted."

"It's our first time this close," Miller muttered. "Her past boyfriends wouldn't bend one inch. Like she has a spell over them or something. Or blackmail. They took twenty."

Terri's Condo - Night

Terri, Blu, and Apple lounged on a velvet couch, hookah smoke curling into the air.

"We need to find a new gig," Apple said.

"I was thinking… go big on those rich tech white boys. Leave this city," Terri replied.

"Yeah, we've run our course here," Blu said. "We need a fresh start."

"I worry about my brother and cousin," Terri said.

"They can come," Apple shrugged. "If not, they're grown."

Outside Nia's House - Night

Ms. Vickie stood near two parked cars, Felicia and Bam flanking her.

"Look," she said, "she said three of them. They got guns."

"Are you sure we can trust her?" Felicia asked.

"She doesn't have a choice. I did my homework. Found out her and LB were creeping. So I had Bam pay her a visit—with pictures of her mom's house. Told her if LB crosses me, her mom's dead. If she doesn't cross him..."

"You a cold bitch," Felicia whispered.

"Always have been," Vickie said. "LB thought he was slick. Pretty boy. Had me on the ropes. Dick game strong, tongue stronger. But my money? That's my heartbeat."

"We're ready," Bam said. "The crew's in position."

"Handle business," Vickie nodded. "Don't kill him. I need to look him in the eyes before he leaves this earth."

Bar - Night

Cory, TA, and JP sipped brown liquor at the bar.

"Bringing the New Year in right," Cory said. "Buying 15 properties, getting more stores, and still got a million-plus in the bank."

"I love doing it with my sandbox boys," TA added. "We building for our kids' kids. Breaking the hold."

"We are putting money into parks, redoing fields, and building gyms. Paying for everything," Cory said proudly.

"Still gotta change gears eventually," JP said. "Government might get nosy. Can't ride the WIC train forever."

"That's why we're into real estate. Precious is scouting deals. And my uncle's into stocks."

"Let's toast," TA said. "To sandbox friendships, more millions, and brotherhood."

They raised glasses. Across the room, Cox took a picture with his phone.

Nia's House - Night

The door slammed open. Silence followed. Ms. Vickie, Felicia, and Slim stepped into the living room—guns drawn.

On the floor: Jay, Nard, Nia, and LB, zip-tied and face down.

"You know the only thing that beats a double cross?" Vickie said. "A triple cross."

She pointed at Nia. "Cut her loose. She's good."

Slim obeyed. Jay dropped his head.

"I told you, LB," he hissed. "Leave her out of this."

"Shut your mouth, little boy!"

Vickie knelt near LB.

"Tell me the truth. Your mom, your son, your sisters' lives depend on it. How deep are you in bed with the Feds?"

"Hosa set me up," LB stammered. "I didn't want to snitch on you. I was gonna leave the city…"

"How much have you told them?"

"Only that I went behind your back. They don't have anything on you. They asked me to set you up. Please, I can fix this."

"We're a long way from that," Vickie said coldly. "But I'll tell you this—I'm 50/50 on your family."

She stood. Footsteps faded.

Then came the screams.

Outside - Night

Ms. Vickie walked away under the moonlight.

"Hide the bodies well. Burn them if you have to. I don't want the Feds finding anything."

"No problem, boss," Bam said.

"What about the girl?" Felicia asked.

"She won't talk. She loves her family."

SweatBox - Night

Brian and Jack sat at a corner table. The bar buzzed.

"Grand opening in a few days," Brian said. "All this work? About to pay off."

"You came home and executed," Jack replied. "Even through bumps, you endured. Stayed out the streets."

"Mind is our greatest gift. Gotta trust the process. Streets don't love anybody."

"What time does the dice game start?"

"An hour. Troup said "rappers, ballplayers, and dope boys pulling up."

Later, the SweatBox thumped with energy. Dice rolled. Drinks poured.

Lil B, Lil Easy, Mike Mike, AL, Cam, and Bo arrived.

"Poppin' in here, Dad," Lil B said. "I see your vision."

"Just a soft opening. Grand coming soon."

"Mom told me about 8-Ball Jack and my dad's gambling house," Lil Easy added.

"Best legal money you can make," Jack grinned.

"I'm getting in the crab game," Lil B said.

"See that lady? Give her money. Get chips. Be careful—real hitters over there."

"I see Big Will, Troup, Cheeseburger, Al, 21, Thug—my kind of party," Lil Easy said.

"Unk, can I get the DJ to play my track?" Cam asked.

"You'd be a damn fool if you don't," Brian smirked.

DEA Office - Day

Miller slumped in his chair. Moore leaned in.

"We have a serious problem. No sign of LB. Two star witnesses are gone."

"We gotta tell Spencer."

"She won't like this. Case is slipping."

"Even his mom hasn't seen him. Dead or just MIA?"

"Don't know. How would Vickie even know he was in trouble? Doubt he told her."

"What about the woman he was messing with? We need to find her. Fast."

"You're right. Let's move."

AL's Work Spot - Day

Money and guns on the table

"Brian's onto something," AL said. "That sportsbook? Players everywhere. Even if he gets 10%, that's 100K easy."

"When we get our next load in, we go hard," Bo said. "Tara's closing on two properties."

"I told KK to get something started. No reason she should be just sitting around."

"What about that other fine one you met?"

"She's cool. But Tara wants to go to church for New Year's."

Every plan has a price. Every cross leaves a scar. When the dust settles, what matters is what you kept—and who's still breathing beside you. Business is shifting. Blood's been spilled. The streets are watching. The year's not over yet.

But the war's already begun.

CHAPTER 58

The last night of the year draped the city in a strange silence, as if it, too, needed a moment to catch its breath. Fireworks hadn't yet started, but the spark was in the air—on lips, in champagne bubbles, in half-spoken resolutions, and raw conversations soaked in alcohol and truth. Some people welcomed the new year with hope. Others, like the ones moving in shadows, braced for what would follow once midnight passed.

INT. HOTEL ROOM – NIGHT

Mike Mike and Sonya sat close on the couch, the low light catching the gold trim on the champagne bottle beside them.

"Are you ready for the new year?" Mike Mike asked.

Sonya nodded. "Yes. This year's been crazy. We lost a lot of people."

"True," Mike Mike said. "Too many."

The silence between them carried memories, regrets, and unspoken feelings. Mike Mike leaned in, brushing a lock of hair from her face. They kissed—slow, needing. The kiss deepened, turning into something urgent and intimate. They made love, bodies intertwining as the clock ticked closer to midnight.

INT. LIL EAZY'S HOTEL ROOM – NIGHT

Lil Eazy and Leah sat on the edge of their bed. Their energy was different—grounded, vulnerable.

"Leah, you're really changing the way I look at things," he said. "In a good way. I love you."

Leah looked down, then met his eyes. "I won't lie, Russell. You're the first street guy I've ever dated, and I must say, I'm head over heels for you. There's something else I need to tell you."

Lil Eazy leaned in. "I'm all ears."

"I'm pregnant... and I'm confused, knowing you already have a baby on the way," she said. "I always planned to be married before I had a child."

"Wow. I'm happy," he said. "Is that why you stopped drinking and smoking? I promise I'll be a good father. Don't be confused—I want to be with you."

"What about Hannah and her child?" Leah asked. "She's about to have your baby. It's just not fair or right."

"Sometimes things happen that we don't understand," he said. "But in the end, it all works out. Look at Swizz Beatz and Alicia Keys—it worked out perfectly."

INT. ANOTHER HOTEL ROOM – NIGHT

Felicia and Lil B were tangled up on the couch, high and relaxed. Champagne bottles and smoke filled the air.

"After the New Year comes in, I've got two freaks coming up to join us," Felicia said. "I wanted to bring the New Year with me and you first."

Lil B grinned. "My type of party. So, how have you been?"

"So much has been going on," Felicia said. "My mom put most things back in order, but we still have to lay low for a while—be on the safe side. We're going to Mexico—maybe for a month. Stay a week at each spot, move around, then maybe LA and San Diego for another month."

"It's like that?"

"Yeah. My mom's boyfriend caught a case. We don't know what he said or how long he's been talking."

Lil B raised an eyebrow. "Damn. LB turned snitch?"

"Pretty much," Felicia said. "But when we come back, be ready. I'm going to be your lady, so do whatever you have to do with Aaliyah."

INT. STUDIO – NIGHT

Wiz, Cam, Kiara, and a few others passed weed and laughed. A chilled champagne bottle sat unopened in the corner.

"Cam, you sure you don't want to go out, bring the New Year while playing your song, having a good time?" Kiara asked.

"No, babe. I'm where I want to be," Cam said. "If I'm not making money, I want to be here."

"I feel that," Kiara nodded. "I read a book that said do what you love, and it'll pay you later."

"I'm gonna be a top ten rapper out of the South. Just watch. I'm not gonna let anything get in my way."

"I believe you, baby."

They clinked red cups. Cam pulled from the blunt and looked over to Wiz.

"Wiz, I think I'm gonna redo that verse. I can sound better—it feels rushed."

INT. TASHA'S HOUSE – NIGHT

At Tasha's house, Bre, Black Rick, Tasha, and Vanessa passed around drinks and laughs. Cigarette smoke blended with the smell of weed. Black Rick was fiddling with his gun.

"Girl, I think I'm done with the bars," Vanessa said.

"Why do you say that?" Tasha asked.

"That guy from the other night? Showed up at the guy's house I left with, banging on the door, begging me to come out," Vanessa said. "The guy got off me, mid-stroke, went outside, beat his drunk-ass friend down, came back in like nothing happened—and climbed back on top. I'm about to be 50. I need a man, not a mess."

"Damn. You better be careful—you might end up with a real stalker," Tasha said. Then she turned to Black Rick. "Rick, why are you playing with that gun in my damn house?"

"After listening to Vanessa, we might need it," Black Rick said. "I'm getting ready to shoot for New Year's."

"I told you I don't like that. Innocent people get shot every New Year's."

"Don't worry. I got it under control. Been doing it for years."

"Mom, I'm about to head to the club. I'll see you later," Bre said.

"Okay. Be safe. Please don't drink too much."

INT. CORY'S HOUSE – NIGHT

Cory, Precious, TA, Tammy, and a few others gathered around a large table. Cigar smoke hovered in the air, and hookah pipes bubbled on the side.

"JP and Imani just plan to go to Miami for New Year's without telling anyone," Cory said.

"Maybe they just want some 'them' time," Tammy offered.

"Nah, babe," TA said. "For the past few years, we've brought in the New Year together—praying, planning, executing. They are not right. Gotta call a spade a spade."

"Well, did y'all reach out, call him?" Precious asked.

"He was not answering," Cory said. "It's all good. We are together. What's next on the list to take over?"

"I think strip malls. High passive income. That's the next power move," Precious said.

"I toast to that," TA replied.

"How much do you think?" Tammy asked.

"Depends on the location, but the market's down—it's a win-win. I'll run the numbers and text y'all," Precious said.

"I've been thinking about 18-wheelers," Cory said.

"Yep, that's a money printer," TA nodded. "I'd like to consider a used car lot too."

"Oh, we are cooking now. Put our minds together—we can conquer the world," Cory said.

INT. BRIAN'S HOUSE – NIGHT

At Brian's home, vision boards covered the table. Scissors, glue, and magazine cutouts were everywhere.

"Remember—anything you like, want to be, or do, Boston—cut it out and put it on your board," Brian said.

"The subconscious mind attracts what we tell it over and over."

"Daddy, what's the subconscious mind?" Boston asked.

"It's your spirit mind. It works day and night, no limits, making what you want real."

"In plain English," Malin added, "whatever your mind receives, you can achieve."

"And don't forget—your attitude will be your latitude," Pairs said.

"Brian out here raising a young genius," Joyce smiled.

"Nothing better than mastering the mind and controlling emotions," Brian said.

TWO WEEKS LATER

Brian stood by the window, phone pressed to his ear, grinning.

"Man, you were right! That Apple stock went through the roof—$250,000 profit off $27,000. Insane compound interest! Option trading is really the way."

"Yep, compound interest," Jeff said on the phone. "And more to come. We wait for the dip and go back in. Right now, I'm looking at Ford, Amazon, Netflix—charts look good. Just need the right entrance."

"Man, let me get ready for this Grand Opening."

"I'll see you there. I'm proud of you. Thanks for believing in me. Your investment changed everything."

"Nah, bro. Your knowledge changed my whole life. I didn't understand 'make money in your sleep' until I met you."

A new year doesn't fix the past. It doesn't erase the pain or promise a perfect path forward. But it does offer something rare—permission to begin again. From luxury hotel rooms to studio smoke sessions, from family tables to underground plans, each character wrestled with what to carry into the new year... and what to leave behind. Some would rise. Others would fall. But one thing was for certain—nobody would remain the same.

CHAPTER 59

The Water Is Over My Head

The new year loomed like an edge no one was ready for. Change had been stirring in the air—quietly, violently, urgently. And as daylight fell across the city, across neighborhoods built on hustle and heartbreak, the players of this story were stepping into position. One move away from everything crashing... or crowning.

EXT. TASHA'S HOUSE – DAY

A sharp knock echoed across the porch. Tasha opened the door to find Lt. and Detective Small standing tall, their expressions grave.

"May I help y'all?" she asked, crossing her arms.

Lt. nodded. "We're looking for Michael Jordan. Goes by Mike Mike."

"He's not here. What now? Is my son in some kind of trouble?"

"Not officially. But we really do need to speak with him. From our understanding, he was kidnapped—but no report was ever filed."

Tasha's throat tightened. The name "Legs" lingered in her chest like smoke she couldn't cough out.

INT. FBI HEADQUARTERS – DAY

Agents buzzed through the hallway like bees around a busted hive. Hill skimmed over a stack of notes, eyes sharp.

"All the banks and cards are frozen," an agent reported.

"Good," Hill replied coldly. "This should cause them to panic."

"Our goal is to pull them in one by one. Break them down. Get them to point fingers."

"Then make it happen," Hill said. "Let's see what bubbles up when their money dries out."

EXT. CAR LOT – DAY

Lil B and Lil Eazy strolled across the lot like royalty—chains gleaming, laughter easy, money loud.

"Man," Lil Eazy grinned, "we are about to run the city."

"AL said Santiago's giving him the keys," Lil B replied. "Let's grab those AMGs. That's a statement."

They each opened a car door like it was a throne. The dealership clerk smiled so wide it looked painful.

INT. TARA'S HOUSE – DAY

AL lay back in bed, sheets tangled around his legs. Tara stood in the bathroom doorway, towel wrapped tight.

"Let me hop in the shower, then we gotta get ready for my brother's grand opening," she said.

"I'm coming with you. He really made this happen."

"My brother has been pulling rabbits out of the hat since we were kids," she said, disappearing into the steam.

INT. TASHA'S HOUSE – NIGHT

Tasha stood in the hallway, phone pressed to her ear, hand trembling.

"Michael?" she said.

"Yeah, Mom?" Mike Mike answered on the other end.

"You need to meet me at your uncle's spot. The police just left here looking for you."

"What'd they want?"

"They know about the kidnapping. And I think something happened to that girl... Legs."

"It wasn't me—"

"Boy, shut your damn mouth and meet me there," she snapped.

EXT. BANK – DAY

Cory and TA stepped out of the car with confidence.

"Crazy how far we've come," TA said. "Two $100K cashier's checks. We are really about to shake this market."

They entered like kings. But they were met with a storm.

"Sir," the teller said, "your account has been frozen by the federal government."

Their faces drained.

"We might be f***ed and broke," Cory muttered. "I had 3.2 M's in there."

"I'm right behind you," TA said. "Calling my lawyer now."

INT. JEWELRY STORE – DAY

"Mommy, look!" The Pair smiled. "We like these matching rings!"

Tammy laughed. Precious pulled out her card.

"Sorry," the cashier said. "Your card's been declined."

"Run it again," Tammy said, suddenly tense.

"Same result," the cashier replied. "I'm sorry."

Precious's phone buzzed.

TEXT FROM TA: "The Feds froze everything. We gotta talk. Now."

INT. FBI HEADQUARTERS – DAY

"Two weeks ago, Mrs. Jordan wired $500,000 to Brian Jordan," the agent reported. "He just got out on drug charges."

"What's their relationship?" Hill asked.

"They used to be married."

"Pull his file," Hill ordered. "Let's dig."

EXT. RED ROBBINS LOUNGE – DAY

Brian pulled up, the crowd buzzing with anticipation. Tasha rushed him.

"The police came by. Looking for Mike Mike. Homicide," she said.

"Where is he now?"

"He's on the way."

INT. CORY'S HOUSE – SAME TIME

"The FBI is investigating us," Cory snapped. "Charges could drop any moment."

Precious stared at her phone, hollow. "I didn't even know what we were doing was fraud…"

Brian's voice echoed in her mind—*"Don't let money cost you more than it's worth."*

EXT. LOUNGE – DAY

Lil Eazy and Lil B pulled up. Diamonds danced across their necks.

Brian saw them and flashbacked—two kids in the yard, chasing dreams.

Mike Mike stepped out.

"They killed Legs," he said.

Brian's phone buzzed.

TEXT FROM PRECIOUS:

"Sorry I can't make it. I need to talk to you in person. The water is over my head."

Brian closed his eyes.

Then Diamond tapped his shoulder.

"The media's here. We're ready to cut the ribbon."

He walked through applause like a ghost.

He raised the scissors.

He cut the ribbon.

Balloons exploded upward.

Behind flashing cameras, Spencer and two agents posed like fans. Across the street, a black SUV idled. Inside sat Terri, Apple, Toni, and Charlie Mo—guns resting on their laps. Eyes locked.

Waiting. Watching. Plotting.

Sometimes you survive just long enough to throw your own party... right before the storm hits.

TO BE CONTINUED IN PART TWO...

OTHER BOOKS BY TIERRE FORD

TIERRE
PRESENTS
All
FOR TEN MINUTES
of
Fame

DARRIN DEWITT HENSON
ROBIN GIVENS
TOBIAS TRUVILLION
AND KEITH ROBINSON
BASED ON THE NOVEL BY TIERRE FORD
THE PRODUCTS OF THE AMERICAN GHETTO
DIRECTED BY HENDERSON MADDOX
A DIFFERENT KIND OF AMERICAN DREAM